W9-AAD-944

BLOOD GROOVE

BLOOD
GROOVE

Alex Bledsoe

TOR®

A TOM DOHERTY ASSOCIATES BOOK

NEW YORK

BLOOD GROOVE

Book design by Ellen Cipriano

A Tor Book
Published by Tom Doherty Associates, LLC
175 Fifth Avenue
New York, NY 10010

www.tor-forge.com

Tor® is a registered trademark of Tom Doherty Associates, LLC.

Library of Congress Cataloging-in-Publication Data

Bledsoe, Alex.
    Blood groove / Alex Bledsoe.—1st ed.
        p. cm.
    "A Tom Doherty Associates book."
    ISBN-13: 978-0-7653-2196-1 (hardcover)
    ISBN-10: 0-7653-2196-3 (hardcover)
    ISBN-13: 978-0-7653-2308-8 (trade paperback)
    ISBN-10: 0-7653-2308-7 (trade paperback)
    1. Vampires—Fiction.   I. Title.
    PS3602.L456B55 2009
    813'.6—dc22

                                        2008046456

First Edition: May 2009

Printed in the United States of America

0 9 8 7 6 5 4 3 2 1

To the memory of
Duncan Browne (1947–1993).
His album Streets of Fire *(1979) was the*
sound track to the writing of this novel.

SPECIAL THANKS

Valette, Jake, and Charlie

Grace West

Marlene Stringer and Barbara Bova

Tom Doherty and Paul Stevens

Theresa R. Simpson, for help in re-creating 1975 Memphis

Don Breithaupt and Jeff Breithaupt, whose books *Precious and Few: Pop Music in the Early '70s* and *Night Moves: Pop Music in the Late '70s* were invaluable references in recalling what songs came out when

And Lin Browne

NOTE

The first poem quoted in chapter six is "Blake, Chapter 74" by Martin R. Delany (1812–1855).

The second poem is "The Misanthropist" by James Monroe Whitfield (1822–1871).

You can't know what's going on if you're asleep, I bet ya.

—"I Bet You," Funkadelic

BLOOD GROOVE

CHAPTER 1

Memphis, Tennessee, 1975

"SHIT," SAID PATRICIA. It was an understatement.

"Yes, ma'am," her assistant Joe agreed, and scowled at the musty odor, strong despite the morgue's chill.

The body inside the enormous coffin had the unmistakable look of someone buried alive. The limbs twisted in the folds of dry, brittle clothing; the jaw hung open in an eternal cry of despair. But the knife driven through his heart, still gleaming after more than half a century, was what held their attention.

It was solid gold.

Joe moved around the casket taking photographs. The hum of the flash recharger echoed in the silent room. Patricia took a magnifying glass from the table and leaned into the coffin to examine the knife.

"Careful," Joe said. "One wrong move, we've got nothing but a big ol' pile of dust."

"Not after only sixty-some-odd years," she said good-naturedly, but he had a point, and she forced herself to be extra cautious.

At first she thought the knife was some ceremonial dagger, but a closer look showed it to be a crucifix, with an inscribed three-inch crosspiece and, visible between the ribs, a base sharpened to a point and flattened into a blade. The artwork was exquisite, with tiny Aramaic characters strongly suggesting a Middle Eastern origin. It was out of her area—she taught pathology—but she still knew impressive workmanship when she saw it.

"Christ on a stick," Joe said, and wrinkled his nose as he took the film from his camera. "So that's really a"—he made an exaggerated frightened face—"vampire?"

"No, it's a crime victim," Patricia said. "See the knife? He was murdered, allegedly by Sir Francis Colby, sixty years ago."

Joe put the camera aside. "And they want an autopsy done on him *now*? Is that Colby guy still alive or something?"

"No, he died quite some time ago. I'm not sure why the museum wants it, but it should be interesting as a technical exercise. You don't see many corpses like this."

"You mean ones that might rise from their coffins?"

Patricia scowled at him. "Did you read anything past the first paragraph of my memo?"

Joe rolled his eyes. "Yes. This is the corpse of Baron Zginski, the only man to have ever been legally proved to be a vampire. His trial was one of the first live broadcasts ever in Europe, but no recordings exist, and the various transcripts don't agree on details."

"You *can* read, then."

"But *why* are we cutting into him now, after all this time?"

She shrugged. "Professional courtesy. Someone at the museum wants to know the cause of death, and since we're part of the state system, they don't have to pay us extra. And you don't get experience with a body in this condition very often, so if you're serious about your education, you'd do best to shut up and pay attention."

She ran her hand along the coffin's firm, expensive wood overlay. The casket looked like a bulky version of a standard coffin, but they'd had to use a forklift to move it from the Colby Archives warehouse into the medical school's morgue room to examine it. Under the paneling the coffin was solid metal, probably lead.

"He looks . . . dried out," Joe observed. "Not decayed. Mummified."

"Until the rubber dry-rotted, there was an airtight seal on this thing. The fluids drained out of the body while it was sealed, and when the rubber started to go, they evaporated."

"He does look like he has fangs," Joe pointed out.

"Just slightly enlarged canines," Patricia countered. "My grandmother had teeth just like that and she wasn't a vampire, either."

Her eye kept drifting back to the cross. If it was real . . .

She forced her attention back to the moment. "Okay, we're pathologists, time to pathologize. Let's cook some tissue samples and see what really made everyone think this Baron Zginski was a vampire: porphyria, anemia, or just plain psychosis."

"There's no chemical test for psychosis."

"Your point?"

"It's nearly six o'clock."

"You have a date?"

He looked down. "No," he said pathetically.

"Well, you do now. With a Bunsen burner."

"I'm your T.A., not your slave," he said.

Patricia's eyes widened in mock outrage. She was the only black on the school's faculty, and one of only three women. But she'd worked with Joe long enough to know he had no idea how appallingly insensitive his remark, intended as a joke, might be. Maybe someday this would change, but now, in 1975, she decided to simply treat it as intended.

"All right, all right, I'm going," Joe said, and went to gather the test tubes.

Two hours later, while Joe prepared the tissue samples in

the lab, Patricia went into the empty teacher's lounge, poured the last of the god-awful coffee, and settled onto the green vinyl couch. The museum curator had been kind enough to send along Sir Francis Colby's original documentation on the Zginski case, in which Colby had been prosecutor (*and* executioner, as it turned out). She opened the folder and read the first yellowed, handwritten page.

16 June 1915

Passelwaithe nestled amongst the Welsh hills, almost cut off from any sign of civilisation. Were you to stand in the centre of the town square and look in any direction, only green hills and grey sky would greet you. The people were equally isolated, aware of the modern world but preferring to exist in the superstitious nether regions of their ancestors. Magic still existed in Passelwaithe, or at least the *belief* in magic persisted.

I journeyed to Passelwaithe in response to a cryptic summons from one Arthur Jermin, the local physician. He'd been referred to me by Professor Alistair, and his letter described a problem so unusual I was unable to resist. I arrived just before sundown, as requested. It was a relief to be away from London, after the zeppelin air raids at the first of the month. Here in Wales, no trace of the ghastly war could be found.

The town seemed to be deserted as I climbed from my motorcar. Usually the sight of the great rumbling beast, technology's dire imitation of the horse, drew entire populations. I lit a cigar and waited to be noticed, one foot rakishly on the running board; that is, as rakish as a man my age could be.

In a few moments another man, as middle-aged and portly as I, literally skulked towards me, checking frequently behind him. Finally he stood erect and made an effort to reclaim his dignity. 'Sir Francis?' he asked.

'Indeed,' I said. 'And you are Dr. Jermin?'

'Quite. Come, let's get inside, in case—' He caught himself before giving away too much, and I followed him into the nearest building.

A typically Welsh choice, it turned out to be the local pub, and the entire male population of Passelwaithe filled it. Dark, muscular men with faces like battered gargoyles, they gazed upon me with an expectancy almost religious in its intensity. Dr. Jermin stepped forward.

'We have only a few minutes of safety left to us, lads,' Dr. Jermin announced. 'This is Sir Francis Colby, the eminent spiritualist. He's here to rid us of our problem. Is that not correct?'

'I must know this problem first,' I demurred.

'It's that devil, the Baron!' one man cried.

'Aye, Baron Zginski!' echoed another.

'And who is Baron Zginski?' I demanded.

'A vampire,' a man in a cleric's collar stated. 'An unholy being who survives on the blood of the living. And he'll be the ruin of us all if he's not stopped.'

Having been briefed somewhat by Professor Alistair, I was not entirely surprised. The grip of superstition was still firm in Passelwaithe. Indeed, they knew me only as a spiritualist, not understanding that my primary mission was to expose fraud and misinterpretation.

'True vampires,' I said carefully, 'are not native to this land. They exist only in isolated central European districts, or in books by Irish theatre managers. How is it one may be found here?'

'He came to us as a rich immigrant,' Dr. Jermin explained, 'claiming to have been disenfranchised by the war, and to have barely escaped with his life and fortune.

That was six months ago. Since then, our wives and daughters have begun exhibiting strange behaviour. Our young men are disheartened and morose. And all due to this . . . this *foreigner!*'

A grumble of assent rose from the gathered menfolk.

I understood all too well the dynamic at work here. 'Tell me, is this Baron Zginski a young man?'

The priest nodded. 'He appears young, yes. And handsome as the very devil. Yet rumours say he is centuries old.'

I considered my words carefully. This young, rich Continental European was clearly such a threat to the stolid males of Passelwaithe that they'd inferred supernatural origins to his attractiveness. Inwardly I was amused, but to all appearances remained deadly serious.

'Gentlemen,' I said, 'if this Baron is all you say, we must proceed with caution. Vampires are the devil's own tricksters, and—'

'Very little gets past them,' a new voice said.

A dashing, debonair young man stood in the doorway. Of medium height, slender, with raven-black hair and moustache, he dominated the room with his blazing eyes. The royal blood of Europe clearly flowed in his veins, and he stood for our inspection as if he were used to such scrutiny. His clothing was more appropriate for a Parisian salon than a Welsh pub, but he wore it with ease and flair.

'Sir Francis Colby, I believe?' he said in a light Eastern European accent.

I stepped forward. 'Indeed. Baron Zginski?'

'Baron Rudolfo Vladimir Zginski,' he said with a bow. 'At your service. I understand my neighbours have some rather unusual ideas about me.' Each man at whom he gazed directly immediately turned away.

'Some concerns, I believe,' I said in as conciliatory a tone as I could muster. 'I'm certain at the root it's mere misunderstanding.'

'No doubt,' Zginski said. He had none of the pomp of royalty, but rather an unassuming quality that was most endearing. 'When I heard you were to visit, I thought between the two of us we might clear this whole thing up. Your reputation for discovering the truth in such matters is spotless.'

'Devil,' someone muttered.

'Incubus,' came another voice.

Zginski smiled. His teeth were quite white, quite even. He said, 'I am open to any suggestion you make, Sir Francis. I wish only to live in peace with my neighbours, in my adopted country.'

'Very well. I suggest, then, that at this time tomorrow evening we meet here as a judicial body. We shall, Baron Zginski, put you on trial for the crime of being a vampire. Because of my experience in such matters, I shall act as prosecutor.'

Zginski clearly understood my meaning. 'And I shall defend myself, Sir Francis,' he said with a slight smile, 'with the mere truth.'

'Is there a magistrate?' I asked Dr. Jermin.

A white-haired gentleman announced, 'I am the magistrate. Alun Toomley.'

'Very well. I shall return at this time tomorrow evening, at which time we shall meet here to settle this. Oh, and incidentally—while I shall abide by any ruling you make, sir, I shall take steps to insure no prior prejudice will be allowed to operate. Baron Zginski will be judged on the facts alone.'

Baron Zginski nodded his assent and departed. Conversation resumed around us, low and bitter and menacing. I motioned Dr. Jermin to join me at a table.

'This is not an example of Christian charity,' I said quietly. 'That young man is rich, handsome, and, I assume, unmarried. *That* is why your village menfolk feel threatened.'

'I thought so at first, too, Sir Francis. Yet why would a rich, handsome bachelor pick such a tiny, out-of-the-way village? Why not London, or Glasgow?'

'Perhaps he has different priorities,' I said.

Jermin considered carefully before he spoke. 'Or perhaps he was aware that, in all of the United Kingdom, no village has as large a population of women. I've lived here for forty years, and attended births for nearly that long. In that time, daughters have outnumbered sons almost three to one, and the isolation we face here has kept most of them unmarried. If I were a young, handsome rich man, this would be an ideal location. And if I were also a *vampire* . . .'

I finished my pint of bitters. 'Your fingers clutch at the proverbial straws, Dr. Jermin. Vampirism is a superstition, nothing more. Tomorrow night, we shall prove it.'

'I thought you were to be the prosecutor.'

'And I shall be. I shall submit Baron Zginski to every test of vampirism I know. And when he passes them all, we shall have settled this nonsense. Agreed?'

'Agreed,' Jermin said reluctantly.

As I drove from Passelwaithe, two things impinged on my consciousness. One was Dr. Jermin's description of the male-to-female ratio in the village; it was, indeed, an ideal situation for a male creature that fed on living blood.

The other was a moonlit glimpse, nothing more, of two figures on a hill, clutched in an embrace. One was a slender, dark-clad man, as Baron Zginski was. The other was smaller, paler, and unmistakably feminine.

The second figure seemed to have swooned in the arms of the first.

At the time, I convinced myself they were merely lovers meeting for a tryst. Subsequent events would prove otherwise.

Joe tapped on the lounge door and opened it. "You decent?"

"Much as I ever am," Patricia said.

"Everything's running right now, so we should have basic toxicology screens pretty soon. I'm going to get something to eat, if that's cool. You want anything?"

She stood and stretched. "No. I'll probably be down in the morgue when you get back."

"Hanging out with the guest of honor?"

"Sometimes you spot new things if you keep looking. Have fun, but be back in an hour."

"Yes, massah," Joe said. Patricia merely sighed.

For reasons she couldn't really pinpoint, Patricia wanted to read the rest of this story in the room with what was left of poor Baron Zginski. Sure, it was morbid, but she was a pathologist, and she'd done her thesis on historical murders. Besides, being a black professional woman in Memphis, she knew just how strong provincial resentment could be; she felt like she and Zginski had something in common. Had anything really changed between 1915 and 1975? Different was still different, and still feared and hated.

She closed the door, buttoned her lab coat against the cold, and dragged a chair next to the coffin.

As promised, I returned to Passelwaithe the following evening with two security measures. One was quite obvious—I brought along an army signalman and his broadcasting apparatus. Passelwaithe was too wrapped up in itself, and this connection with the outside world would prevent any hysterical mob violence. The experiment served two masters: it provided the scrutiny needed to insure justice was done, and it allowed the military to test aspects of their latest equipment with a broadcast of such absurdity that no spy could take it seriously.

The other measure was insurance against a possibility so outlandish I chose to keep it my secret.

By prior arrangement, Dr. Jermin would escort Baron Zginski into town, and the tavern would be set up for our purposes. When Signalman Reynolds and I arrived, quite a crowd had already gathered outside the low building, trying to peer through the closed blinds and locked doors.

At the sight of the gathered masses, Signalman Reynolds immediately perked up, straightened his uniform, and put on his best winning smile. The image of Mercury on his cap badge accented his jaunty air. The group clustered outside the tavern was exclusively female, and all frowned with desperate concern. The women and girls of Passelwaithe had gathered there to learn what fate their bitter, jealous men had in store for the handsome stranger who had brought excitement into their isolated and dreary lives.

The women parted ranks to let us through. I noted another curious detail: a full third of the women wore neck kerchiefs or scarves, an unlikely fashion and certainly not due to inclement weather in this warm Welsh summer. The bescarved women all looked pale and drawn, as if recovering from some wasting illness.

Reynolds lugged his portable wireless unit into the tavern, where the unruly menfolk clustered in little grumbling knots. Baron Zginski sat in the corner, in a large isolated chair, as if either a prisoner or some sort of exhibit. He seemed unmoved by the open hostility around him, and perhaps even a bit amused. Dr. Jermin stood nearby, and I nodded to him as we entered.

Signalman Reynolds established communication with his unit and confirmed the broadcast connection. Magistrate Toomley called the assembly to order, and I stood before them to make my opening pronouncement.

'Gentlemen of Passelwaithe, tonight we shall enter the modern age together. This is Signalman Reynolds of His Majesty's armed forces. He shall supervise the broadcast of this proceeding, so the entire outside world will be aware of what goes on here. And I shall aid you in dispelling this superstitious nonsense once and for all.' A few dissident grumbles were heard, but most said nothing.

Toomley banged a judicial gavel on the bar counter. 'I hereby open this meeting of the Passelwaithe Town Council. Our first item of business is the charge against Baron Rudolfo Zginski of being a vampire. Sir Francis?'

Dr. Jermin had provided me with a list of the most vitriolic accusers. 'I call Arvel Walker as my first witness,' I said.

I will refrain from boring the reader with a detailed account of the witnesses against Zginski. Enough to say that, to a man, they presented evidence not of supernatural evil, but of very mortal jealousy and resentment. My irrational misgivings of the previous night faded with each man who spoke.

After the testimony, I established that Dr. Jermin had that very day, and on numerous other occasions, seen Baron Zginski moving about during the hours before sunset (the very reason I'd arranged for the good doctor to be Zginski's escort). Although the tradition varied a bit, most authorities agreed that vampires stayed motionless and inert whilst the sun hung in the sky, and that a glimpse of its cleansing light would be enough to destroy them.

I reminded the assembly that several witnesses had testified that the Baron easily crossed streams and rivers. In folklore, running water formed an impenetrable barrier to vampires.

Finally it was my turn to question the Baron himself. First I asked him to eat some garlic, which he did. Then I held a mirror up to him, which clearly cast his reflection. I sprinkled holy water on him; it caused no damage. The Baron was calm, confident, perhaps even amused by these bits of folklore, as any normal man would be. Still, something in his demeanor struck an odd chord.

Nonetheless, I went ahead with my most theatrical test. A virgin white mare was brought into the room. If Zginski had been a traditional vampire, the horse would have become quite violently agitated. She merely looked around the room and waited patiently to be led away.

The crowd was silent. They were forced to confront the real root of their resentment, Zginski's wealth and handsomeness, and this did not sit well. As Toomley asked meekly if anyone had any other evidence to present, I surreptitiously studied Zginski, attempting to identify what about him disturbed me so.

Suddenly I isolated it. The man was *not breathing*.

Impulsively I took his wrist and felt for a pulse. By the time he yanked his arm away, I'd learned the truth.

'Great guns!' I ejaculated. 'He *is* a vampire!'

The room collectively gasped. Zginski regarded me with a look of superior disdain. 'Whatever,' he said calmly, 'are you on about?'

Dr. Jermin leapt to his feet. 'Heavens above, Colby, are you certain?'

I met Zginski's cold, lifeless gaze. 'Beyond any reason,' I said, and before he could respond, withdrew my revolver and fired point-blank into his chest.

The report rang out, silencing all in the room. Zginski remained in the chair, eyes wide, then looked down at the smoking hole in his expensive waistcoat. Before he could react, I turned to the assembled roomful of gaping Welsh mouths and said, 'As you can see, he has been shot point-blank and yet does not bleed, nor has he registered any pain.' Facing Zginski, I concluded, 'Your concealment was almost perfect. But now you have been exposed.'

Zginski smiled weakly and started to speak. Then, with no warning, he leapt to his feet, his face twisted into a mask of fury and animal intensity. He grasped me by the throat in a grip of iron, his eyes blazing with demonic power, and pushed me against the nearest wall.

'Fool!' he hissed. 'No one need have died this night, if not for you! Now I shall slaughter them all, and you shall be the first!'

His arrogant confidence proved his undoing. While he flaunted his immense physical strength, he failed to note the second security measure as I produced it from within my waistcoat. He did notice, however, when I plunged it into his heart above the still-smoking bullet hole.

Instantly he stumbled back, clawing at his chest. It took mere moments for him to collapse and, at last, expire on the floor, his body frozen in twisted agony.

I glanced at Signalman Reynolds. He was as pale as Baron Zginski's now-lifeless corpse.

I knelt by the fallen vampire. Protruding from his chest was a golden cross, a crucifix found by Richard the Lionheart on his first crusade to the Holy Land, blessed both in Jerusalem and later in Rome. A metalsmith monk in a distant cloister had reshaped it into a thin-bladed dagger for me, and it had proven too sharp indeed for the luckless continental nosferatu.

Patricia put the manuscript aside and pulled on surgical gloves. She leaned over the coffin and examined the spot where the cross entered the withered tissue. The damage was so slight it was barely visible: just a tiny, thin slit where the blade parted the flesh. She took the handle in two fingers and gently pulled the cross from the corpse. It slid away easily, although she felt a little tingle when it finally pulled free, like a tiny arc of electricity just strong enough to pierce the rubber gloves. When she looked back, the injury had vanished into the folds of the wrinkled, dry flesh.

The cross rested in her hand, solid and heavy, the sharpened end stained black with sixty-year-old blood. She held it under the illuminated magnifier, studying the wealth of detail carved into the soft metal. This was a genuine piece of art, and would make a magnificent display in the university museum. She placed it carefully in a plastic bag, sealed it, and put it on the nearest examination table. It looked even more unreal and majestic against the cold, flat stainless steel. She removed her gloves and turned to the final page of the manuscript.

I was charged with murder at the official inquest, but had two factors in my favour. One was, of course, a roomful of witnesses who supported my claim of self-defence. The other was the report of the official examination by Dr. Jermin, establishing that the rate of decomposition in Zginski's body was consistent with a body that had actually died at least thirty years earlier. No one could explain that, of course, but neither could anyone dispute it.

How could Zginski have been a vampire, and yet

passed all the classic tests? I can only assume that vampires, like other creatures, are capable of evolving and adapting.

Baron Rudolfo Zginski was understandably refused Christian burial in the local cemetery. As there was no identifiable next of kin, I claimed the body and stored it in my cellar. I sealed it in an iron coffin, grounded through a lightning rod. I considered burning the body, which is the only way to be thoroughly certain a vampire cannot return. Yet Baron Zginski was such a singular character, I could not bring myself to do so. He had learned to mimic human behaviour to an astounding degree, and forced me to rethink many things about which I was previously certain. I knew that as long as the cross remained imbedded in his heart, the world was safe.

Patricia's heart raced with excitement. This could be her academic ticket out of this backwater college if she could identify some rational, physiological explanation for the events Colby described, something that showed the face of prejudice in 1915 Wales as clearly as she knew it in 1975 Tennessee. After all, vampires didn't exist, so it simply couldn't be that.

She looked up with a start. An overpowering odor suddenly filled the room. It was no chemical she could identify, or any organic process she recognized. She jumped to her feet and peered into the morgue's darker corners, looking for a spilled bottle or leaking container. Then she gingerly approached the air-conditioning vent. The smell did not grow stronger near it, which was a relief. The danger in any educational environment was that some careless or stoned student might accidentally mix two harmless substances into something lethal, and if those fumes got into the ventilation system it could hurt a lot of people.

The odor was, in fact, the scent of *recomposition*. Its unique tang was reminiscent of ripening fruit, meat being warmed over a slow fire, and blood pulsing from an open wound. It was the olfactory by-product of a process so rare that only a handful of people in all human history had ever witnessed it, although none had survived to document it. The fumes themselves were harmless; it was what they heralded that uniformly proved lethal.

The smell began to fade almost at once. Patricia sighed with relief; whatever it was, it was neither extensive nor, apparently, dangerous. Probably the residue of some cleaning chemicals mixed by accident in the garbage elsewhere in the building. She turned her attention back to Colby's manuscript.

She smiled as she straightened the pages. She could only use excerpts from Sir Francis's narrative in her professional paper. Whatever his other skills, one thing was painfully obvious.

Sir Francis Colby couldn't write worth a da—

CHAPTER 2

FAUVETTE WATCHED THE moon watch her.

Despite the summer heat, the night wind blew cool and damp off the Mississippi River, ferreting pathways through the crumbling remains of the old cotton warehouse. When it finally reached her and traced its chill across her skin, she felt it the same way the river felt rain.

She stood only partially in the shaft of moonlight, and the beam seemed to vertically bisect her. She studied her reflection in the window's intact panes. Vampires didn't cast reflections in the movies, but in real life—she almost laughed at that—they did. Nothing had changed; like the face of the moon, nothing about her *ever* changed. Her shoulders were still soft, her breasts still small with dark nipples, her belly still just a bit plump where the baby fat had never gone away. And her face, big brown eyes and dark straight hair, was still that of the fourteen-year-old virgin she'd been when she'd died forty-five years earlier, just after the start of the Great Depression.

She pushed her hair from her eyes, disturbing something small and crawly that had taken up residence in the strands; she ignored its panicky flight down her back. She hadn't bathed in maybe a year, and her hair was slimy with accumulated grease, dirt, and pollen. Dust and soil coated her skin, and she idly brushed a string of ants from the curve of one breast. She spent most of her time naked—dressing a walking corpse seemed ridiculous—and lately she seldom left the dry-rotted confines of her coffin. Only when the hunger grew too loud, too insistent, did she venture forth.

Was it the hunger this night, she wondered, or the uncharacteristic chill in the air that woke her? She was awash in memories of her death, of the autumn night she'd been killed in the Kentucky hill country. She'd worn her best Sunday dress to the revival meeting, hoping to catch the eye of handsome Junior Caldwell. It had not worked; Junior had been seized by the spirit and carried off by his brothers as he filled the air with God-given gibberish. He never even knew Fauvette was there.

Heartbroken as only a teenage girl could be, she took the shortcut home through the woods, usually a safe path between the church and her family's farm. The vampire had been old, and looked feeble, but his hand at her throat had been like steel, and her struggles for her life did no more than annoy him. He took her quickly, efficiently, and thoroughly, draining her blood in less than five burning minutes and tossing her aside like an empty soda can. Her last living memory was of his wet, satisfied belch.

But the worst thing was afterward, when her body—still warm and supple, even though her soul was gone—had been found and violated by the kind of backwoods thugs who would rape a dead girl. Hovering invisibly above the scene, she'd watched them rip away the beautiful dress made by her mother and aunts, and attack her body in ways she could barely comprehend at the time. The full moon had watched her that night as well.

Fauvette felt suddenly conspicuous under the moon's gaze,

and slid out of the light. The undead, the damned, did not deserve to be seen, only feared and whispered of around hearths guarded by garlic, crosses, and the sanctity of belief. They dwelled in shadow; the light frightened them, like supernatural cockroaches. The bravest of vampires could prowl the streets in a semblance of life, but if anyone looked too closely, they could not maintain the illusion. Fauvette was not a brave vampire.

As with any building left untenanted and untended, the warehouse was a disaster. Glass, metal shards, nails, wire, and pipes littered the big open floor. Rats, birds, and snakes lived in the available crevices. Fauvette never considered cleaning the place; it was dead, she was dead. At least the building had the luxury of falling apart with time.

The warehouse had been abandoned for a decade, forgotten as the city grew north away from the river, around the new bridge that led to Arkansas. The land ownership was tied up in court, and the location wasn't very valuable anyway, so no one came around much except for local kids who liked to get high on the crumbling shipping dock out back. Fauvette found the place already hidden by weeds and trees in 1970, moved her coffin into the basement boiler room, and then allowed the others to occupy it as well. Actually, "allowed" wasn't the right word; she didn't care one way or the other. She'd *apathied* them in.

Her eyes scanned the enormous empty room. Vampire vision saw everything despite the darkness, saw the debris, the roaches, the rats, the dead bum decomposing in the corner. She felt silverfish scurry down her legs from their temporary home inside her, and it sent a little tickle through her. She almost smiled; she was still ticklish.

She walked over to the hobo's body, ignoring the sharp-edged detritus that punctured her bare feet; she didn't feel them, and after a good day's slumber in her coffin, any damage would be gone. Toddy had put a stolen fiddle in the corpse's hands as a joke—"he's de-composing, y'all, geddit?" Toddy was always doing things like that.

She stared down at the body, observing the changes since the last time she'd examined it. She wondered what it felt like to rot, to decay, to feel your body dissolve into its components. If she were to die now—if she strayed into the sun, or was caught and burned in her coffin, or staked through the heart—it would be sudden, the effect of half a century in an instant. No slow dissolution, no dignified breaking down of complex chemicals into simpler ones. None of the slack, empty peace she saw in the bum's receding features. She was forever kept from this peacefulness, by no choice of her own.

The junkie's eyeballs were long gone, his skull a home to thousands of larval insects, but his empty sockets seemed to regard her with pity. Emotions she'd tried valiantly to kill stirred in her chest, in her cold unbeating heart.

"Ah, damn," she breathed.

"Thinkin' them Joni Mitchell thoughts again?" Toddy said.

Fauvette shook her head, long strands of matted hair slapping her bare shoulders. "No," she replied, her voice dry and raspy, the tissue desperate for blood. He hadn't surprised her; nothing moved within thirty yards that she didn't sense. But the last thing she wanted was Toddy's half-assed amateur psychotherapy.

Toddy moved out of the darkness, his tread so light glass did not crunch under his feet. He wore an open dark green trench coat and nothing else; his body gleamed white and clean, like new ivory. "Beginning to think you weren't never coming outta your box again," he drawled.

She turned and smiled, letting her inner vampiric power reach out to Toddy. She understood the survival necessity for vampires to sexually excite their victims—why else would someone come willingly into the embrace of a walking corpse?—but she was surprised at how easily it worked on some other vampires. Not all, of course, but definitely Toddy. She almost laughed out loud at the pop-the-weasel suddenness of his erection.

"Sweetie pie, you're raising my crankshaft," he said, his voice husky. Toddy was a baby even by vampire standards, with only ten years since his death at age seventeen; a white country boy who came looking for sex with sophisticated city girls and instead met doom in Fauvette's embrace down the alleys behind Beale Street. He had a crew cut, soulful eyes, and full lips that covered his fangs unless he laughed.

"I know, Toddy," Fauvette said wearily. She had not created him on purpose that night; she'd simply forgotten to take her usual precautions. And she felt nothing much about him one way or the other now, but she knew he'd keep pestering her, so at least this way he'd shut up. "Come on."

He took her on the floor in front of the corpse, his trench coat forming a dark tent over them. She spread her thighs and he plunged into her without preliminaries, ignoring her initial cry of pain. His weight drove shards of glass and nails into her soft buttocks, and when she arched her back to get off a particularly annoying piece of rusted metal, he moaned as if he'd drawn the motion as a response. She almost laughed.

After the first few moments, once the sharp jolt of agony faded into the standard vampire numbness, she felt nothing. When he finally climaxed, ejaculating the cold jellied substance that passed for vampire semen into her, she shoved him off contemptuously and rolled onto her side, thighs clamped against the loss of blood.

"Wow," she heard him gasp, "that was *intense*. It's always great with you, hon, you know that?"

She gritted her teeth against the pain, and her eyes against the tears. As he had every time before, as every man would until the end of time, he'd taken her virginity. Since she'd died a virgin, been raped in death and reborn as a vampire, her maidenhead (her mother's quaint, blush-inducing term for it) reappeared intact the next night after it was taken. Most vampires who were virgins at the time of their creation were immune to any sexual arousal, and thus never felt it; but she was denied that. She felt lust as much as any of them, only in her case, giving into it was agony.

She wondered why only that wound hurt, only that wound *bled*; once, out of boredom, she'd sliced open her own stomach and studied her entrails without either pain or bleeding.

"Wow," Toddy repeated. Then he noticed her whimpering in pain. "Hey, Fauvette, y'all all right?"

"Go away," Fauvette said.

"No, wait, I wanna ask you something." He knelt beside her and touched her shoulder. "You planning to go out and hunt tonight?"

Dark, sticky liquid oozed out as she shifted her legs. "Reckon I have to now." Which, she realized, was why she'd turned him on, because without this immediate need she might not have hunted, and wasted away even more. Apparently even the sub-dead had a subconscious.

"Well, wait, before you go, I, uh . . . got something for you."

"*No*, Toddy, not again. Not right now."

"No, no, not that. Something that'll make you feel *good*."

She looked up in surprise, for a moment astounded that he'd gained some genuine insight into what she felt. But instead he held up a small plastic bag filled with gray powder.

"What is that?" she asked.

"Takes away the hunger," he said with a slight smile.

She sat up straighter. "What hunger?'

"*The* hunger."

She got to her knees and studied the bag in his hands. "What is it?" she repeated.

He opened the bag, licked his finger, stuck it into the

powder, then extended it toward her. "Here, baby doll, take a lick for yourself. See if ol' Toddy ain't telling you true."

Her lips closed around his fingertip. Somewhere in the building a telephone rang.

CHAPTER 3

RUDOLFO ZGINSKI, CLAD in the loose-fitting green garments and white coat he assumed delineated a physician, peered from the morgue doorway into the empty hall. He had been animate for less than twenty minutes, but he had already killed once and knew he had to get far away as quickly as possible.

Since the moment Francis Colby drove the crucifix into his heart, he'd been trapped in a timeless, blank limbo. When the woman removed it, physical agony greater than anything he'd ever known consumed him. He *felt* his dry, brittle flesh crack and split, his muscles snap free from their tendons and great chunks fall away as he tried to move. Each sensation roared through his newly roused consciousness with the ferocity of a dull saw scraping living bone. If his lungs had worked he would've screamed.

Then he sensed blood.

With no idea where he was or whose blood called to him, he lunged toward it with every bit of pitiful energy his corpse form possessed. He felt soft skin and tight, curly hair, and buried his fangs deep in the heated jugular. The victim's choked scream rattled in what was left of his ears. The human struggled, but even in this skeletal body he possessed vampiric strength. Blood gushed forth into him with each heartbeat, reconstituting him like water poured on powdered milk. The victim's struggles gradually faded as his body absorbed her life.

As his other senses returned and the pain subsided, he realized he held a Negro woman in his arms. Already her body was almost thoroughly drained, and by the time he gained the strength to stand upright she was dead. He let her drop, and fell awkwardly from his coffin. He dislodged a tray of surgical instruments, and the horrible clanging sound terrified him.

Naked, he twitched and convulsed on the cold tile floor while his body soaked up the woman's entire blood supply. After what felt like an eternity (and he was qualified to make that analogy), he was able to control his limbs enough to move around, although at first all he did was hug his knees and weep. But like his physical self, his emotions gradually fell under his control. He had no idea where he was, or how long he'd been "dead," but he would learn nothing crying like a huntsman's lost child. And waiting here beside the dead woman was a very stupid thing to do.

He stood, luxuriating in the movement of his limbs. He ran his hands over his body and found everything where it needed to be; he even had an erection. He started for the door, then stopped and smiled at his own obliviousness; however long it had been, he doubted that people paraded around the streets naked.

Zginski's original clothing had long since crumbled to dust and rags. He sized up his victim, who appeared to be of African descent, about thirty-five, heavyset, and tall. Her name tag identified her as "Dr. Patricia Johnson." He scowled at this; a woman, let along a Negro woman, should never be allowed to practice something as complex as medicine. Catch one in the wrong mood, and she'd be as deadly as any nosferatu. As always, things had changed for the worse.

Her clothing appeared androgynous. At the very least, the trousers would suit a man as well as a woman. He stripped her down to her shamelessly scanty undergarments and placed her body in his own coffin. He took a knife from the fallen instrument tray and sliced into her breast over her heart; naturally no blood came forth. He proceeded to efficiently remove her heart and place it beside her in the coffin. He'd never created another vampire, and didn't intend to start by conferring immortality on this total stranger. Following Serbian custom, he then cut off her toes and looked around for a nail to drive through her neck. Among the surgical tools he found something long and thin, like an ice pick, and pushed it crossways from jugular to jugular. Since he did this before her resurrection, she would never return as a vampire, even if someone removed the pick and restored all the missing parts. Wherever her soul had gone at death, it would be grateful.

The woman outweighed him by at least fifty pounds. Her clothes were baggy on his slender form, but the drawstring cinched tightly at his waist and held them in place. He put on the white coat, astounded that, in his desperation, he hadn't marred it with a single drop of the woman's blood. The shoes were more difficult, until he figured out the elaborate strings that held the canvas tops closed. He wondered what the word "Converse" stitched on the side signified; were there shoes that were "inverse"?

As he dressed, he examined his surroundings in more detail. The tables and general cleanliness spoke of a medical atmosphere consistent with the dead woman's title. On the ceiling, long metal tubes glowed with an uncomfortable intensity and scalded his weakened eyes. The room had no windows, and evidently only a single metal door with a large handle. He opened some of the square hatches in the wall, and behind each found a dead body on a sliding metal tray. All appeared to have been cut open again and sewn shut as if by a vivisectionist. He examined the cabinets, with their drawers of carefully arranged surgical instruments.

Then he opened the refrigerator. A dozen bottles of distinctive reddish liquid rested there, behind a small box marked "pizza." He took one out, fiddled with the lid until it opened, then inhaled the aroma of something he'd never experienced before — *chilled blood*.

He dipped his finger into it and touched it to his tongue. He scowled; the liquid tasted odd, *wrong* at this temperature. He could wait for the real thing. But it gave him an idea. He took the bottle and poured its contents into the coffin, around the woman's body. A bloodless victim would arouse suspicion, and perhaps this way whoever found the body would believe she had been attacked and subsequently bled to death.

He regarded the empty bottle in his hand. If the authorities found it, his ruse would be immediately discovered. He looked around for a place to discard it, and noticed a garbage can with a newspaper crumpled in it. He picked up the paper and sought the date on the masthead.

Zginski stared. 1975. *Sixty years* had passed.

He vividly remembered the fearful look on Sir Francis Colby's face as if he'd seen it no more than a few minutes ago. In the space of a blink, he'd missed half a century. What would the world be like?

He flipped past the news to the advertisements; what people bought would tell him more than any political information. He recognized clothes and food, and vehicles that clearly descended from the horseless carriages he'd known. But what were these other strange devices? 8-track, hi-fi, C.B. . . . what was a "mo-ped" and why was the family in the ad so happy to have one?

Finally he turned back to the front page. He was in America, in Memphis, a Southern city he'd read of in the works of Mark Twain. How had that happened? And why had his sixty-year-old supposed corpse been in a hospital? Conventional medicine certainly could not help someone dead as long as he'd been. Had resurrection become commonplace in the last half century?

He skimmed stories that mentioned public cruelty that both excited and repulsed him, then stopped. At the bottom of the front page ran a story about a "teen racial slaying." A bloody body lay on a stretcher similar to the ones stacked against the wall beside him now. Men in uniforms held back the crowd, mostly young Negroes. But there, at the front of the crowd, behind the barricade, was a vampire.

The girl, also a Negro, dressed no differently than the others, but Zginski could instantly tell. There was an indefinable weariness, a way of standing that conveyed maturity that far outreached the physical appearance of youth. The eyes, cold and lifeless, reflected light like polished tin. And if this colored *child* was a vampire, here in the American South, then there had to be others. He'd need shelter until he acclimated to this new world, and they would know where to find it, even given their inferior race.

He tossed the paper aside. He'd committed a murder, so the first thing was to distance himself from the scene of the crime, along with any evidence that might implicate him. He put the empty bottle into one of the jacket's voluminous pockets and started for the door. Light glinted off the crucifix dagger that had held him in demonic limbo for sixty years, where it rested on the main examining table. He pocketed it as well.

He was about to turn away when he noticed the faded manuscript pages. He skimmed through them, and when he realized what they were he smiled for the first time. *This* would make interesting leisure reading; how much credit had the old man given himself for his cleverness? Did he acknowledge that it was Zginski's own overconfidence that ultimately did him in, or had he shaded events to make himself out to be the hero? He added the sheets to the bulging pocket.

And then Baron Rudolfo Vladimir Zginski stepped out of the morgue and into the polyester era.

CHAPTER 4

THE BELL OVER the door jingled and Mark Luminesca
looked up from the small black-and-white TV behind the
counter. Mr. Wiggly's, the only all-night bait and tackle store
in Memphis, seldom got customers in the dead time between
1:00 and 3:00 A.M., and those that did wander in usually
wanted alchohol or cigarettes, which the store didn't sell.

The man who entered was black, with an enormous Afro
and a large black pick comb stuck in the back of it. He wore
burgundy pants flared at the bottom, a wide white belt, and
a yellow shirt with the collar unbuttoned halfway down. His
eyes were red from drinking or smoking dope, and he weaved
a little when he tried to stand still. He looked around the
small store with the kind of dangerous, intimidating swagger
Mark had seen on punks of all races. "Y'all need some help?"
Mark called.

"Naw, man," he said, conveying both superior cool and
insecurity. He strolled slowly down the short aisles, examining the fishing lures and rolls of line with exaggerated care.
His dance-club getup didn't automatically mean foul play;
perhaps he intended to greet the sunrise by reeling in a channel cat from the river.

Mark settled back behind the counter. If the guy became trouble, he'd worry about it then. Another car pulled up outside and parked beside the black guy's Cadillac.

At last the man approached the counter with a pack of hooks. "Gimme a box of crickets, too," he mumbled. To fetch the bait Mark would have to leave the cash register, and suspected the other man knew it, too. He stepped around the counter to the big wooden box. Through the screen-covered hole in the top, he heard the soft chirping of the crickets. He scooped up a handful into one of the cardboard containers. It was more than he was supposed to give, but he had no desire to spend time winnowing it down. He closed the box and went back behind the counter.

The man had his right hand in his pocket. The pants were far too tight to hide a gun, but he might be going for a knife. Mark waited patiently.

Instead, he brought out a wad of bills and peeled a couple off. "How much?"

Mark told him. If he was a robber, maybe he wanted to see the cash register open, to gauge if it was worth the effort. He took the man's money, punched the heavy keys, and pulled the handle to open the drawer.

As he reached for the change, the door burst open and a tall white teenager with torn jeans, shaggy hair, and a sad beard burst in, handgun already pointed. "Gimme all your money, motherfucker!" he shouted, his voice high.

The black man casually raised his hands. "Whoa, just be cool, dude," he said. His red-rimmed eyes tried to open in astonishment, but lacked the juice.

"Yeah, y'all be cool," Mark said. "Here, check this out."

When he knew he had the robber's full attention, he picked up a stray cricket and, slowly and deliberately, stuck it in his mouth.

The gunman stared. Mark grinned, which ordinarily gave an unobstructed view of his fangs. But in this case, all the gunman saw was the live cricket squirming between his teeth. When he was certain the man was riveted, Mark bit down, squirting the insect's juice out of his mouth. "Yowsah, yowsah, yowsah," he said and swallowed it.

The gunman turned even paler, muttered, "Oh, fuck this!" and ran out of the store. In a moment tires squealed out of the parking lot. With his vampire vision Mark had no trouble seeing the license plate through the front glass, but of course he would never call the police.

He heard a thump. The big black man had passed out cold. Mark wondered if it was from fear of the gun or the sight of him eating a live cricket. He wiped his chin and lips with a Kleenex. Either way, the unconscious man had just won the lottery, in the Shirley Jackson sense.

Mark locked the door and flipped the CLOSED sign over. Chances were slim anyone would come by, see the sign, and complain to his boss. Then he effortlessly tossed the unconscious man over his shoulder and carried him out back into the alley. The bait store was next to an auto repair shop, and Mark had no trouble jumping the security fence and forcing open the door of one of the broken-down cars. He placed the man in the backseat, then searched his pockets. Sure enough, there was a butterfly knife tucked in beside his wallet.

Mark twirled the knife open and efficiently made three slashes down the length of the man's nearest wrist. Blood flowed at once, and Mark forced himself to let the first few pulses splatter on the car seat. Then, when he was sure there was enough to convince people the man had bled to death, he pulled the sliced arm to his mouth and began to feed.

It did not take long to drain the body, and he spit the last mouthful on the ground outside the car door for good luck. Since he had not actually bitten the man, there was no danger he would come back as a vampire. He dropped the knife beneath the other limp hand, easily jumped the fence, and returned to the bait store. The whole procedure had taken only ten minutes. He flipped the sign to OPEN, unlocked the door, and settled back behind the counter. On TV, the Channel 3 late movie was over, and the late-late one was beginning.

He picked up the phone and dialed the warehouse number. On his own, he'd installed a phone in the boiler room where everyone rested during the day, tapping into the wires that ran along the seldom-used nearby road. He'd worked for the phone company for three years and knew how to set it up so no one would ever know. He wanted to alert the rest to the fact that he'd already fed in this area, and they should choose another part of town for their own excursions. Too many bloodless bodies in the same part of town, even minority thugs disguised as suicides, would draw unwanted attention.

After sixty years, forty of those with his immortality reasonably certain, Mark assumed he'd develop some sort of calm center; but despite all that time, people who weren't where they were supposed to be still made him crazy. Of the five vampires who used the warehouse, he was the only one who made any effort to pass in the real world. He held a job and paid his taxes. He had a checking account. And he tried to teach the others how to blend in, not stand out. It wasn't altruism; he remembered the death Praline had suffered at the hands of that Oklahoma mob, and knew that if any vampire drew attention, *all* vampires would be in danger.

So he got a phone, and at first it worked. Leonardo, Olive, and even Toddy picked up faithfully. But lately, no one answered. He knew Fauvette was there—she hadn't hunted in months, and the strain was starting to show on her, but that was her business. He just wished she'd answer the phone.

Toddy was the one that worried him, though. The little bozo would go out in public clad in nothing but that stupid trench coat, and would actually give people his real name when he met them. He was known among the street people and the really dangerous downtown gangs as a psycho because he'd demonstrated his strength by lifting the front end of a car one-handed. He also once tried to have a mortal girlfriend, but it only lasted a week; the police investigation lasted much longer, until most of the body parts were found.

Mark sighed, ran hands through his short brown hair, and closed his eyes. After a half century, he was really tired of his existence, not because it was hard, but because it was complicated. He never asked to be den father, especially to loonies like Toddy or Quaalude cases like Fauvette; he just wanted to quietly exist at the fringe of the mortal world, exploring and taking as he needed. But he was the one the others looked to for guidance, for leadership, and it wore him down. Sometimes he wished he'd just crumble to dust and blow away, embraced by the death he consciously abandoned at the height of the Dust Bowl. He almost felt the wind blow through him, carrying him away, spreading him thin . . .

He opened his eyes and, by coincidence, saw himself in the curved shoplifting mirror.

He was transparent.

It was only for an instant, but he knew he had seen it, the floor and the wall behind him visible through his *Happy Days* Fonzie T-shirt, as if for just a moment the wind *had* blown part of him away. Then he blinked, and everything appeared normal again.

What the hell—

"Hey, Mark-o Polo," Gwinny called as she came through the door. "How's business?"

"It's Friday night in a dang bait shop," he said easily; luckily he had a knack for appearing nonchalant. "How much business do you think we're getting?"

"Hey, where's that tall hunk of man who belongs to that Cadillac out front? He looked good in those pants, I tell you what." Gwinny was a big-breasted black woman with two children, and so full of life that at times she felt to Mark like a giant blood-filled carrot dangled before him. But she also worked in the fast-food drive-through across the road from Mr. Wiggly's, and had been seen talking to him many times. So he kept himself under tight control around her, and tried to seem like just another down-and-out white boy with a crummy job in a bad part of town.

And now he felt particularly dumb, since he'd completely blanked on the dead man's car. Maybe he deserved a stake through the heart for stupidity. "Don't know, he just looked around and then left."

"Oh, well, his loss. Might've missed out on a trip to Gwinnytown." She winked and tossed him a paperback book. "And thanks, by the way. Great book, even if he does call us 'niggers.'"

"I warned you about that."

"Yeah. And I didn't get the ending."

This was the other reason Mark never turned Gwinny into dinner. "What about it?"

"Well, why did Marlowe tell the chick that Kurtz said her name when he died?"

"I guess—and this is my own opinion, you know—that maybe, thanks to Kurtz, Marlowe had looked into his own heart of darkness, saw it for what it was, and was able to lie knowing he was doing the right thing."

"You mean, like, total honesty might do more damage than a lie that made people happy?"

He grinned. "Kind of, yeah."

"Well, *I* figured he just didn't want to, like, dishonor the memory of what ol' Mistah Kurtz had shown him."

Mark blinked in surprise. "Hell, Gwinny, I never thought of that."

"Got a lotta time to think standin' over the deep fryer. Well, it's about time for the bus. See you later, Polo."

Mark was so surprised by Gwinny's literary insight that he forgot about the car outside, the phone, and the moment he thought he saw through himself.

CHAPTER 5

SKITCH MUELLER, THE newest forensics resident at the Shelby County Coroner's Office, sauntered into the staff break room. His hair feathered over his ears and hung outside his collar in the back. "Hey, Danielle, you hear about Patricia yet?"

Assistant Head Coroner Danielle Roseberry looked up from the *Commercial Appeal* newspaper. She let smoke trail out her nostrils as she spoke. "Patricia who?"

"Patricia Johnson over at the college. Black doctor, remember? Taught medical forensics? Somebody killed her last night."

Danielle blinked in surprise. "Seriously?"

"Yeah, right in the morgue. Their morgue. Cut out her heart, stuck a probe through her neck, and sliced off her freakin' toes. Made a huge mess; blood everywhere."

"Cut off her *toes*?" Danielle repeated. She wasn't close friends with Patricia Johnson, but the Memphis forensics community was pretty small, and Patricia had been its only black member. Danielle had even spoken to her classes a few times. "Shit," she said in disbelief. "Do they know who did it?"

"Yep. Satanists."

" 'Satanists'?"

"Yeah. They also stole some exhumed body she was examining for the museum. Cops figure she caught 'em at it and they went a little nuts." He mimed taking a long hit off a joint. "Know what I mean?"

Skitch poured himself some coffee, then held the carafe out to Danielle; she shook her head. "They're talking to all the leftover hippies and Jesus freaks in town," he said.

"Wow," Danielle said. "I mean . . ." She let the words trail off. She'd been offered Patricia Johnson's job once, three years ago, and turned it down. If she'd taken it, would she now be a heartless, toeless corpse? "Wow."

Skitch took a long, loud slurp of his coffee. "Oh, by the way, the cop that told me all this also brought *us* a new package."

Danielle nodded, ground out her cigarette, and stood. She was a slender, tiny woman, a little over five feet tall, with short dark hair and a face that hadn't aged appreciably since she was sixteen. As a result bartenders always, *always* carded her. But her professional reputation made sure she got the respect at work that her baby-faced demeanor denied her everywhere else.

Later, in fresh scrubs, Danielle and Skitch approached the sheet-covered form on the metal table. "So how'd the testifying go this morning?" Skitch asked.

"The same way it always goes," Danielle said with a sigh. "Before anybody takes me seriously, I have to prove I'm not somebody's little girl just playing at being a coroner."

"What happened?"

"I gave my description of how the guy died, along with all the evidence for it. I used small words so the jurors would understand. So what's the first thing the defense attorney asks me? 'How old are you, Dr. Roseberry?' "

"You do look young."

"I know that, believe me. So after I establish that I am a

legal adult, and that I did, in fact, go to medical school, you know what he asks me then? 'Do dead bodies give you nightmares?'"

"Boy, he doesn't know you at all, does he?"

"Luckily even the judge got offended by that. But I couldn't just let it go, you know?"

"What did you say?"

"I said no, I don't get nightmares, because I have my defense attorney Ken doll to keep me company. And he's anatomically correct . . . for a lawyer, that is."

Skitch howled and had to sit down as Danielle started the Dictaphone recorder. She stated the date and time, then said, "Okay, hyena boy, what've we got here?"

Skitch wiped his eyes with his forearms, stood, and whipped the sheet back with a flourish. "Today's *mort de jour* is one teenage boy, fourteen to seventeen years of age, found dead in a downtown alley wearing a long green trench coat and nothing else."

"Kids these days," Danielle muttered, then bent close and examined the inside of the nearest elbow for needle tracks. "You're not supposed to be a flasher until you're too old to be a rapist. Is he baked or fried?"

"Neither. No obvious signs of foul play or drug use. No trauma. No clear cause of death. That's all we know now, and thank you for dining with morgue central." He offered her a clipboard with the official police report attached.

Expertly, searching only for key words, Danielle verified the summary. She trusted Skitch, but she'd learned not to accept anything at face value. "Not hit by a car, huh?" she said as she gave him back the clipboard.

"Nope," he confirmed. "Unless it was a little bitty one."

"Name?"

"Albert, but everyone calls me Skitch."

She smiled a little. The only reprimand in her file was for making "nonprofessional" comments on these official recordings, but she simply couldn't maintain the stoic, vaguely sepulchral tone her superiors preferred. She understood why this bothered them, of course: she was the only doctor on staff who truly, genuinely *enjoyed* doing autopsies, and she simply couldn't hide that. So she accepted the reprimand and changed nothing about her procedure, even if the tapes occasionally made for odd passages in the transcriptions. "No, *his* name."

"No identification on the body. Waiting to hear from the fingerprints and dental records."

"Little Johnny Doe, back with us again, huh?" A full third of the bodies that came through the city morgue were unidentified, at least at first. She pursed her lips thoughtfully and leaned over the body, examining the face. In the bright fluorescent light, the John Doe body looked as if it were made of gray crepe paper stretched over a skeleton. His cheekbones and ribs were plain, and there was a sickly pallor that had nothing to do with death about him. His musculature was prominent but undeveloped, the result of too little body fat instead of too much exercise.

Her eyes traveled up and down the naked body. The kid was thin, but his abdomen wasn't distended like true starvation. And indeed, as Skitch had reported, there were no apparent marks indicating drug use or violent death. Actually, she realized, there were no bruises or contusions of any kind. That was really odd, since fragile, malnourished skin like this should have marked at the slightest bump.

She looked closely at the features. They were lean and angular, almost aristocratic; sharp nose, strong jaw, and lips that even in death held a slight puffiness, almost a sensuality. Even his crew cut, years out of style, did not diminish his appeal. In life, this boy was probably the one parents warned their teenage daughters about to no avail.

"Pretty boy, isn't he?" Danielle murmured.

"Yeah," Skitch agreed. "I used to hate those guys in school."

"Jealous?"

"Hell, yeah."

Danielle smiled. She may not have known this John Doe's real name, but she knew him; she'd seen kids like this all over downtown, lurking in shadows and doorways, standing in huddled groups, walking aimlessly down the streets. They never did anything, though; they just stood there, watching life pass by with their dead shark eyes, like people watch fish in an aquarium. Many still sported flower power fashions in style during the late sixties, the typical fashion lag between Memphis and the rest of the world. They were dangerous, but it was such a vague danger it was hard to take them seriously. They all looked so weak, so fragile, that it seemed impossible they could actually do any damage. *Until*, she thought wryly, *they start cutting off your toes*.

And this one, lying naked in front of her, flat and flaccid, didn't even look remotely dangerous now. Just sad, in a disgusting sort of way. The only menace he held was the negligible chance he might be able to hide his own cause of death from Danielle. She wasn't worried, though. Far smarter corpses had tried that and failed.

"Well, we won't learn anything just sitting here rehashing the obvious. Let's go take a look." She nodded at Skitch. "Show me your stuff. Start the blood work."

"I would have," Skitch said, "except . . . well . . ."

"What?"

"Well . . . and I swear I haven't been watching those monster movies on Channel 3, but . . . there's no blood."

"Cause of death is blood loss?" homicide detective Lyman Newlin repeated.

"Severe blood loss," Danielle said into her office phone. She sat with her shoes off, stocking feet propped on her overturned wastebasket. She was not looking forward to this conversation. "There's a difference."

A little whine of disbelief tinged Newlin's voice. "I looked him over myself, you know. There wasn't a mark on him."

"Yep, we noticed that, too."

"And no blood anywhere around him. So how exactly did he bleed to death?"

"Well, that's the jive part of it. There are no injuries, no internal damage, nothing. The only breaks in the skin are the ones we made after we got him here, and even as overworked as we are lately, I'm pretty sure we didn't just misplace all that blood."

"Jeez, how much did he lose?"

Danielle paused before answering. Up until now it was an odd case, but not an exceptional one. Her answer to Newlin's question would seriously up the ante, and Newlin and everyone else would expect *her* to solve the mystery. Once you got the reputation as a wonder woman, it never went away. She closed her eyes and said, "All of it."

" 'All'?"

"Yep. Not a drop left in him."

She heard Newlin slap one broad hand down on the surface of his desk. "Okay, Danielle, you're the expert. What can do that?"

"I don't know at this point. No injury, that's for sure. Even a cut into a major artery couldn't drain him this dry."

"Must be some kinda new disease, then."

"You the coroner now, Lyman?"

"Sure, I'll be the coroner. How hard is it to go, 'I dunno'?"

"Oh, kiss my ass, Lyman, I'm being serious."

"Don't get your blood-spattered apron in a wad. And I'm being serious, too. *Could* it be some kinda new disease?"

"Well, sure, it could be, if it's one I've never heard of, and if this kid happens to be its very first recorded victim. And I've already checked with the CDC in Atlanta, by the way; they've got nothing like this."

Newlin whistled. "This is weird."

"Yeah." She lit a fresh cigarette from the stub of her old one. "That's the word of the day, all right."

Newlin called her office the next day. "My turn to freak *you* out. We ID'd that kid."

"Yeah?" Danielle said.

"Yeah. Name's Todd Jonathan Crealey. Disappeared August 19, 1965, from Tupelo. Considered a runaway."

"God, he must've been just a baby. Was he kidnapped?"

"Well . . . not exactly. Are you sitting down?"

"No, but I'm firmly leaned against a load-bearing wall, will that do?"

"We'll see. According to the missing-persons report filed at the time, he was seventeen when he disappeared. He'd be in his mid-twenties now."

"Then it's the wrong kid," Danielle said with certainty.

"Nope, checked and double-checked. One hundred percent certainty. ID'd by fingerprints, dental records, photo ID by family. It's him."

"Oh, come on, Lyman, this kid's not much more than sixteen or seventeen *now*. Believe me, I know what it's like to look young for your age, but not *that* young."

"I know. But it's him. I spoke to the parents myself. They showed me a picture of him. He'd lost some weight, but otherwise he looks just like he did when he vanished. Even has the same haircut. Damnedest thing I ever saw." He paused. "Are you sure the body was . . . fresh?"

" 'Fresh'?"

"Yeah, you know. Maybe he'd been stuck in somebody's meat freezer all this time and just now thawed out?"

"He was fresh, Lyman," she said in annoyance. "Look, there is *no way* that is the body of a twenty-seven-year-old man."

"I believe you. I saw him myself. But there's the truth."

"Christ, Lyman." She rubbed her temples with her free hand. "All right, I'll go back and check—"

"Can't. Parents are here to claim the body."

"Don't *they* think it's weird? Don't they want to know what happened to their son?"

"They think the Lord taketh away and the Lord giveth back, blessed is the name of the Lord, and don't try to figure out His ways."

"Oh, God," Danielle said with disgust. "Baptists?"

"You know it."

"Can't you find some reason to hold the body?" She felt like a child trying to change a parent's mind. "We have to be missing something important here."

"Sorry. Dropping dead on the street ain't a crime. I'd love to know, too, but we got to consider the family here. They've been waiting a long time to find out what happened to their boy."

"Shit." She hung up, shut her office door, then snapped every pencil on her desk in frustration.

Lyman Newlin opened the double door and led the couple down the tiled hall. The rooms, once painted a vivid lime green for some reason, were now faded and stained so that the passage gave a vague sense of nausea to outsiders. The antiseptic odor and cold air didn't help. The summer sweat on his neck felt like it was freezing to his skin.

Newlin knew this corridor far too well. A fifteen-year veteran of the Memphis police force, he'd suffered through the awful events surrounding the death of Dr. King, where for a few hours it seemed as if the race war many whites feared was about to erupt. He knew that the truth had not come out in the Ray trial, and probably never would: too many reputations at stake, and too many appalling lapses of judgment and decency. But compared to that hellish period, a regular investigation, even one as quirky as this one, was a cakewalk. After all, once the body was identified and claimed, this case was closed.

Newlin frowned as they approached the door to the autopsy room. Danielle stood outside it, arms crossed. She was dressed impeccably, her short hair styled and makeup neatly applied. It made her look a little like a small girl imitating her mother, but the glare in her eyes was all adult, and all aimed at Newlin. She managed a sincere-looking smile for the parents.

"Detective Newlin," she said as he approached. She turned to the others. "And you must be Mr. and Mrs. Crealey. I'm so sorry for your loss."

They were certainly of a piece, Danielle thought. Mr. Crealey looked a lot like his son, down to the old-fashioned crew cut. His skin was tanned, with a red flush along his neck and the tops of his unprotected ears. The tan ended, she bet, just above his elbows and just below his collar. The rest of his skin would be pasty white, never seen in the light of day except in the privacy of his bedroom. The slight bulge in one side of his lip showed where his tobacco chaw usually nested, and the network of reddish veins on the end of his nose betrayed his drinking habits.

Mrs. Crealey had a beehive hairdo that made her almost as tall as her husband. She was round in every direction, and wore a flower-patterned dress with white lace at the too-tight collar. She carried a small purse daintily in both hands, from which she withdrew a crumpled tissue to wipe her eyes. She'd eschewed mascara, which was good. If only she'd done the same for her eye shadow. There was enough blue paint under her eyebrows to redo the dented fender on Danielle's old Malibu.

"I'm Dr. Roseberry, assistant head coroner," Danielle said politely. "I wanted to be here to answer any questions you might have."

"That's mighty kind of you," Mrs. Crealey said between sniffles. Mr. Crealey nodded.

"Isn't it, though?" Newlin said, glaring at Danielle. He knew exactly why she was here; normally this kind of duty was delegated to someone like Skitch, since it could become uncomfortably emotional. "Well, *Doctor* Roseberry, would you please get on with it?"

She led them into the morgue, where their son's body lay on a gurney, covered by a sheet. Mrs. Crealey moved close to her husband, who put one arm across her shoulders. His face was impassive.

"I should warn you," Newlin said, "that the body's condition might surprise you."

"Is he all tore up?" the father asked. It was the first time he'd spoken, and his voice was raw.

"The exact opposite," Danielle said, and pulled back the sheet.

Even though she expected it and was braced for it, the caterwauling wail that burst from Mrs. Crealey made Danielle jump. The woman's knees buckled, and her husband had to grab her under the arms to keep her from falling to the floor. "That's my baby!" she wailed. "My baby!"

Newlin again glared at Danielle. The woman's pain was so genuine it should make them both feel like intruders, but Newlin suspected that, deep down, Danielle felt little or no real sympathy. She merely waited for the right moment to ask her questions, to solve this abstract puzzle. It was a contradictory aspect of her personality usually masked by her prim, proper surface. Even though he often felt paternal toward her, and occasionally lustful, at the moment Newlin considered Danielle just as thoroughly creepy as any other coroner he'd known.

"Why?" the mother wailed. *"Why?"*

"Is that your son, Mr. Crealey?" Newlin asked sympathetically. The man nodded. Newlin pulled the sheet back over the body. "Well, then, we can go."

"Excuse me," Danielle said, sliding smoothly in front of Newlin. "Mr. and Mrs. Crealey, did your son have any unusual medical conditions?"

Mrs. Crealey shook her head. "No, ma'am, he was as healthy as a horse all his life. All his life . . ." She let out another wail and clung to her husband.

Newlin physically shoved Danielle aside. "That's all we have time for, Dr. Roseberry. Thank you for joining us." When she started to speak again, he glared at her with all his considerable authority. She bit back her comments and, fuming with frustration, watched him escort the parents out.

Then she was alone again with Todd Crealey. Echoes of his mother's wails continued for several moments.

She drew back the sheet and stared at him. His handsome face seemed to mock her with its inscrutable peace. "You pissant bastard son of a bitch," she said. "You will *not* outsmart me, no matter what." He neither reacted nor responded.

CHAPTER 6

THE BELL OVER the bait-shop door rang as Gwinny entered. "Hey, Mark-o Polo, you around?"

Mark looked up from behind the counter, where he'd just finished cutting fresh apple slices for the cricket box. It was 2:00 A.M. "Hey, Gwinny. What's up?"

"Nothing's up for me, white boy. I'm going home to a cold bed," she said as she wiped her forehead. "Three more weeks and I'm supposed to go to first shift. 'Bout damn time."

"I'll sure miss you," Mark said genuinely.

"Aw, I think you mean it," she teased as she leaned meaty forearms on the counter.

"I do," he said. With his hands clutched over his heart he said in mock seriousness, "You make the night shift bright as day."

She laughed, big and hearty. "Brought you today's paper," she said, and used it to swat a fly on the counter; it made a loud smack. "So how you making it with that poem book I gave you?"

Mark smiled. Tonight Gwinny smelled like pastries, not fried chicken, which meant she'd changed duties again. He preferred this one; the aura of fried anything reminded him too much of the smell of burning flesh, and that made him think of Praline. "It's pretty good. I dig that one poem, 'How Long.' Lot of righteousness in it."

"Damn straight." She patted the paper. "Every time I read in the news about some more kids getting wasted out of their lives, I ask myself that question." She mimicked his pose, hands over her heart. "'How long, O gracious God, how long / Shall power lord it over right?' It takes on a whole new meaning when you got your own to look after."

Mark nodded. "And I keep thinking of the line from 'The Misanthropist,' where he says, 'From earliest youth my path has been / Cast in life's darkest, deepest shade.'"

She looked at him skeptically. "Now what's so hard about *your* life, Polo? You a nice-looking, polite white boy. You could always go to college and then get a job where you don't have to spend all night tending to worms and bugs. You just here because you either want to be, or you think you don't deserve any better. Every time I see you, I try to figure which it is."

"Now, Gwinny, you know I work here just for the chance to discuss literature with you, don't you?" He winked. She'd never know how true that really was.

She narrowed her eyes. "Polo, how come you always changing the subject whenever I ask how you ended up here?"

"Because half of romance is mystery, you know."

"Romance," she snorted. "One time I'm gonna come over that counter and show you romance. Then maybe I'll get some straight answers."

"You betcha," he said, imitating her accent and head bob. "Hard and straight."

She laughed, a loud bark of surprise and amusement. "You too full of it, Polo. See you later."

Mark checked the security mirrors to verify that the store was currently empty, and placed the newspaper neatly on the counter, front page first. He read every word of every story methodically, and so it was thirty minutes before he reached the second page of section B, Local News, and found the story of Toddy's body discovered downtown three days previously and claimed by his parents yesterday.

Danielle sat on her couch and drank her third Michelob as the TV droned on in the background. It was Friday night, she was a little drunk, a lot perplexed, and wished there were more than three TV stations in Memphis to choose from. PBS didn't count; all frilly collars and snooty accents.

In the time since Todd Crealey's parents picked up his body, she'd autopsied seven victims of violent or untimely ends, whether they needed her expert attention or not. In each case she'd pinpointed the cause of death precisely, to the point of being able to make an accurate educated guess about either the caliber or dosage involved before the lab results came back. To all outward appearances her whiz-kid reputation was secure, and her coworkers went to great lengths to let her know they considered the Crealey thing a fluke. Hell, sooner or later everyone ran up on something they couldn't explain, right? The Grand Unification Theory eluded Einstein, and nobody thought any less of him. And nobody would think any less of Danielle Roseberry because of one fluky case.

Right.

She reached under her shirt and unsnapped her bra. With a deep sigh, she slipped off her shoes and knee-high stockings and stretched out on the couch. She'd been a practicing coroner for six years now, but she still felt the same rush when she took her first look at a new body, a delicious puzzle waiting to be solved. She liked dealing with the dead, morbid though it was, because of that beautiful consistency.

Corpses weren't like living people: they died from one cause, and that didn't change by the next day. Sick people were always changing, and too many of them changed beyond anyone's ability to help.

She'd embarrassed many of her elder colleagues on her way up the department ladder, but their resentment and attempts to sabotage her career couldn't overcome the fact that she was just a whole lot better than they were. Even Dr. Francisco, the head medical examiner, had to grit his teeth and smile when she diplomatically pointed out errors in some of his work. As the cops who worked directly with her rose within the police force, they assisted her rise to assistant head coroner. Prosecutors loved putting her on the stand, and she secretly enjoyed the attention.

She had no desire to move up any higher, because the top spot was mainly an administrative one, and Francisco filled it admirably, always ready to answer the media's insistent questions. She lacked the patience for such nonsense, something she and everyone else in the department knew full well. She liked it in the trenches, liked being the expert, liked the way people came to her to solve the enigmas when everyone else had failed, and *really* liked the way respect lit up in their eyes when she did it.

And now this damn twenty-seven-year-old-who-looked-seventeen crew-cut *bozo* was going to destroy all that.

It'd be a subtle change, she knew. The admiring looks wouldn't be as intense, and no matter how many times she got it right after this, she'd always be less than perfect. Eventually, some new hotshot would come along, blithely solve the old case (probably known by then as "Roseberry's Folly"), and replace her as the department golden child. It would probably be a man, able to navigate the good-ole-boys network and advance far more rapidly than she'd done. God, what would she do then?

She took another drink. It was the weekend, she was

alone thinking of dead people, and it felt perfectly normal. On TV, part-mechanical Lee Majors applied his bionic charms to a California lovely; was Danielle's life missing something? She hadn't had sex in a year and half, but she hadn't really missed it, either. She'd never had what she would call "good" sex, the kind she'd read about where you writhe and scream and sweat. She was no women's-libber interested in one-night stands for the fun of it to prove her equality with men. And she was so settled now, she couldn't see rearranging her whole life just so some guy could spend fifteen minutes on pointless copulation.

No, as weird as it would sound to anyone else, she knew the truth. Her work was her life, the autopsy was her sex, and the moment when she pinpointed the cause of death was her climax. If it was a simple matter, like a bullet wound to the head, it was a quick and insignificant one; if it was more complicated, then there was the exquisite buildup, the total submergence in the act to the exclusion of all else, and then the gorgeous release when it all became clear. It was odd, but it was her.

And suddenly she sat up straight. She knew, in a flash of scary personal insight, why Todd Crealey's death gnawed at her. She was *horny* for it. This was the ultimate fuck for her, the one with a buildup so prolonged, so sweetly torturous that it was as much agony as pleasure. And, waiting at the end along with Todd Crealey's cause of death, was the sweetest professional orgasm ever. It was, as Skitch would say, motherfucking *necrophilia*, plain and simple.

She fell back against the cushions and laughed. God Almighty, what would her coworkers think of that? She knew they considered her quiet, virginal, the spinster librarian of the M.E. world; could they imagine her dripping with lust, sweaty and trembling with desire? Did any of them harbor desires as dark as her own, needs they could barely fathom and never articulate?

The beer spread its wooziness through her. *Fine,* she thought. She'd find out what had killed the little bastard, all right. And then she'd lay back, smoke a cigarette, and mutter to the corpse, "Was it good for you, too?"

CHAPTER 7

TWO HOURS BEFORE dawn, Mark twisted the padlock off the warehouse door. The protesting metal echoed his own simmering fury. Then he shoved the door aside so hard it flew off the end of the sliding track, balanced for a moment, then hit the floor. Birds in the rafters, startled awake, chirped and fluttered about to new roosts. Rats and other vermin scurried in fright.

"Goddam, boy, what's the matter with you?" Leonardo called from the darkness.

Mark lifted the door and slammed it back into place, bending the track so that it was jammed shut; he'd fix it later. "Where's Fauvette?"

Leonardo dropped from the shadows near the ceiling, stroking a rat held in his fist. He wore an orange Tennessee Volunteers jersey and blue jeans, and might've been any athletic black boy from any Memphis neighborhood. He was the oldest of the warehouse vampires, born around 1900, but he'd never been more specific and it was against Mark's nature to pry. At least Leonardo took care of himself and made a serious effort to pass when he went onto the streets. "You make a lot of noise."

"Where . . . is . . . Fauvette?" Mark said through his teeth.

"Whoa, honky bro. The walking ant farm is down in her box, far as I know." He grinned. "Damn if that don't rhyme."

Mark pulled the clipping about Toddy from his pocket and pressed it into Leonardo's free hand, then went toward the door marked BOILER ROOM—CAUTION. He slammed the door behind him just as he heard Leonardo exclaim, "Aw, man, no *way!*"

Debris, including some old office furniture they'd found in the weeds out back, filled the stairwell to the boiler room where Fauvette, Toddy, and Leonardo kept their coffins. Passage would be monumentally difficult without a vampire's natural grace and strength, and stealth would be impossible. The drawback, and the reason neither Mark nor Olive slept down there, was the lack of any rear exit. Mark's reasoning was practical: he didn't want to be pinned in, like Praline had been. Olive had never shared her reason.

The boiler room was a large, dark cavern of broken pipes, wiring, and concrete. Mark's vampire eyes saw it clearly, though, and again he was astounded at just how immature creatures could be that had existed for half a century. Leonardo's coffin was shiny and black, lined with red silk. A Tennessee Vols sticker decorated one end, and a poster of Donna Summer, with vampire fangs added, hung to greet him upon awakening. Two dozen sports-related T-shirts lay neatly arranged on a horizontal pipe, and his sports card collection filled three narrow white boxes. Given how long he'd been collecting them, they probably *were* pretty valuable.

Still, his little nest was a model of maturity next to Toddy's. The sides of his simple pine box were painted with the Confederate battle flag. Clothes stolen from Laundromats were piled on the floor, and three sets of army boots waited for feet that would never return. Worst was the severed lower leg of his former girlfriend, hung by the ankle above the coffin and currently home to half the Southeast's maggot population. The toenails were still painted sky blue.

Fauvette had found the warehouse, so she had the best spot, inside the shell of the old boiler. Her coffin was simple brown mahogany that was once very expensive, but had dried and mildewed over years of neglect. The metal strips peeled away at the corners, and the lid was no longer attached. It lay askew, covering Fauvette's face but exposing her legs from knees to toes. Around the coffin, shoved into the holes where pipes once carried steam from the boiler, were the shreds of her clothing.

Fauvette had once been a beauty, and when Mark first moved into the warehouse she enjoyed parading as a princess of the night, enticing only the most beautiful boys (never any girls, to Mark's knowledge) to their doom. But sometime during the last two years she had lost the drive, the desire to feed, and lately had become, as Leonardo said, "a walking ant farm." That is, when she bothered to walk at all.

Mark tried valiantly to control his fury, but he knocked the lid from Fauvette's rickety coffin out the door and halfway across the boiler room. She lay on her back, naked, her skin drawn so tight that her ribs and hip bones were plain. Her closed eyes were sunk deep into their sockets, and her lips were drawn back from her teeth as if the skin had shrunk away. For a moment he actually thought she was really dead. Then she turned her head slightly, a roach scurried from her ear, and she opened her eyes a slit. "What?" she rasped.

Annoyed that he'd been concerned even momentarily, Mark kicked the coffin. "Get up," he snarled.

"Go away," she said diffidently, and closed her eyes again. He wondered how long it had been since she'd fed. Blackish dried blood stained her thighs; she'd recently had sex, which usually meant she *had* to hunt. How could she resist the hunger for fresh blood once she'd lost some of her own?

"Don't play possum with me, Fauvette. Toddy's dead."

Slowly, Fauvette's eyes opened again. She blinked, trying to comprehend. "What?"

Mark grabbed her by her slimy hair and yanked her from the coffin; the beetles that nested under her skittered away. The box fell over with a crash, and scurrying creatures of all sizes ran from the tattered lining. Mark held her by the shoulders and shook her with all his considerable fury. "You heard me. He's *dead*, really-not-coming-back dead. I know he had a crush on you and would've bragged about anything that he'd gotten into. So tell me."

She feebly struggled in his grip, and couldn't meet his eyes. "Mark, please, I don't—"

He grabbed her by the throat, and had to squeeze extra hard to grip her greasy skin. "Fauvette, I am one one-thousandth of a second from locking you up on the roof so the sun can just finish what you're trying to do the slow way. I *know* you saw Toddy a few nights ago." He glanced down at her bloody legs. "And I have a pretty good idea of what the two of you did. Now what did he tell you?"

She grabbed his wrist helplessly with both hands. She weighed nothing, as insubstantial as misery. "We fucked, and he left," she wheezed. "That's all, Mark, I swear." Her feet kicked feebly against his legs.

"Uh-huh." He dropped her, and she fell in a heap, unable to stand. Her legs sprawled out awkwardly, and she pulled them slowly up to her chin. She still wouldn't look at him.

He couldn't stay angry at this pathetic stick girl. He sighed, kicked the coffin again, and turned away. "They identified his body, you know that? I'm sure somebody somewhere is wondering why a seventeen-year-old kid hasn't aged in ten years; personally, I'm wondering why those ten years didn't catch up with him like they should have. Would you have any ideas about that?"

"No," she said in a small voice.

Mark stuffed his hands in his jeans pockets. His anger, slow to start, was conversely quick to fade. Now he was just weary and sad. "All right. If you say so."

"I'm sorry," she whimpered, so softly no one but another vampire would've heard her.

He sighed. Child care, that's what it was. Unending, eternal child care. "Get up, Fauvette. You've moped around here long enough, you need to eat."

Fauvette sighed. "I'm not hungry."

"I don't care. You need to hunt."

She brushed her hair back, trying to regain a little dignity. "I said I'm not hungry, Mark. I'll hunt when I'm ready."

"All right," he sighed. She sat immobile, hands around her knees, covered in dried blood and slime and filth. "Fauvette," he said quietly, "aren't you tired of this?"

"Yes," she agreed, a sigh barely heard. "I'm very tired . . ."

"Then maybe this'll get your skinny ass in gear." Just as she'd done to Toddy, he reached out with his vampiric power.

She looked up sharply as her loins suddenly pulsed, her nipples tightened, and she felt the rush of carnal heat through her ice-cold body. Mark had never done this to her before, and she stared, unable to speak, trying to marshal some defense. But he was well fed and strong, and she had no reserves to draw on.

"Go hunt, Fauvette," Mark said. "Or I'll fuck you."

She stared. Mark knew what losing her virginity again would mean, and certainly so did she. But at the moment she wanted more than anything to feel his weight on her, his cold prick entering her, pushing through her eternal barrier, and finally filling her with his chilled seed. "You know how much that hurts me," she raggedly gasped. One hand sought her breasts, squeezing in oblivious response. If she'd had the strength, she would've crawled to him and clawed him down to the floor with her.

"I don't care, Fauvette. I'm not taking a chance on you dropping dead in public, too, and maybe leading people to the rest of us. Now will you hunt?"

She was too weak to fight it, too malnourished and blood-starved to resist. "All right, yes, I promise. Just . . . either fuck me now or stop doing this."

As quickly as she felt it, the arousal went away. She sobbed, her body still responding even though the source of the desire was gone. She took a moment to gather her strength, then stood. She held her back straight, shoulders squared, and glared at him defiantly. "Don't you ever do that to me again, Mark. I mean it."

Mark was not intimidated. "Then don't ever let yourself get in such crappy shape again."

She grabbed a ratty T-shirt from the pile of rubble behind her and pulled it over her head, then found a pair of threadbare denim cutoffs. Once they'd highlighted her curves; now the ragged cuffs billowed around her bone-thin thighs.

"It's nearly dawn," he said. "Just so you know."

"I'll be all right," she said, running her fingers unsuccessfully through her matted hair.

"Are you gonna clean up first?" he suggested.

She sighed. "I'm a creature of the shadows, Mark. Whoever I take won't need to see me. And I'll be careful."

He nodded, started to leave again, and again paused. "Fauvette," he began, then stopped.

"What?"

He sighed; now he was committed. "I was thinking . . . after tonight, maybe we could all go hunt together. You, me, Leonardo, Olive. Be a gang again. Like we used to."

"Without Toddy?"

"We quit *because* of Toddy, remember?"

"Oh, yeah." Then she smiled, the first smile he'd seen from her in months, and in it was the glimmer of the old princess of the night. "We'll see. Maybe that'd be nice." She walked past him into the stairwell.

He stood in the boiler room for a long time, thinking of that day on the prairie so long ago.

Juvenile Crimes detective Leslie McCammon yawned and picked at her salad. She'd been on duty since 5:30 A.M.; it was now fifteen hours and counting since she'd gotten any sleep. She accepted Danielle's invitation that morning without realizing she'd be so tired by dinnertime. She tried to be good company, but she was fading fast.

Leslie was younger than Danielle, although she looked older; hell, *everyone* looked older than Danielle. Physically she was a tall black girl with slender hips, sizable Afro, and an attitude to match. Since she worked with the children of poverty, neglect, and violence, she needed confidence to spare. She was proud that in five years on the force she'd never had to draw her weapon in the line of duty.

They sat in a booth in the back of the restaurant, where the light from the wall-sized aquarium was almost bright enough for them to see the food on their plates. A barge drifted by outside the wide window that overlooked the river, its running lights flashing slow and even. Danielle had wolfed down her club sandwich almost immediately, and now flipped through the stack of files Leslie had brought, pausing only for swallows of coffee. They were typical cases for Leslie, stories of runaways, gangs, drugs, prostitution, suicide, and homicide, all committed by individuals the legal system considered "juveniles." Leslie watched her friend's face go from astonishment to horror to almost sick amusement as she turned the pages.

"Christ, Leslie, this is incredible," Danielle said at last. "I mean, I had no idea these things were this widespread in Memphis. New York, Chicago, yeah, but here? No way."

"Way," Leslie said flatly.

Danielle closed the last file and lit a cigarette. "How many of these kids live to be eighteen?"

Leslie tossed a strand of wavy hair from her face with the same hand that held her fork. "We beat the national average."

"Where do they *come* from?"

Leslie stopped in mid-bite. "You're kidding, right?"

"No."

Leslie looked at her in disbelief. "You cut up dead people all day, and yet maintain your naiveté. Someone should do a study of you."

Danielle sighed smoke from her nostrils. "Humor me."

Leslie sighed. "All right. Most of the colored kids come from right here in Memphis. Minority poverty breeds delinquents like stagnant water does skeeters. The white kids come from all over, especially the little podunk towns, usually to escape abuse, sometimes just for a change of scenery. There's still that hippie ethos at work, and the whole decadent big-city thing." She chewed and swallowed her bite of salad. "They may be under eighteen, but more of them know exactly what they're doing than you might think."

Leslie paused and studied Danielle. "You look tired, you know that?"

"So do you."

"Yeah, but a good night's sleep will fix *me* right up. I know you, Danielle. You don't think like most people do anyway, and I bet you've been lying awake at night worrying about that Crealey kid, thinking about what it'll do to that precious reputation of yours." When Danielle started to reply, Leslie cut her off with, "And I've studied psychology, so don't mess with me."

Danielle took another drag on her cigarette and scowled. "Okay, smart gal. What is it you want to tell me?"

She leaned across the table and spoke quietly. "I know

you've got some sort of plan worked up, so you might as well let me in on it."

Danielle looked out at the river, the lights of the bridge into Arkansas twinkling in the distance. "What do you know about the Crealey case?"

"He was found dead downtown. You said he bled to death, but you couldn't figure out how. No evidence of foul play."

She nodded, wincing inside at all the implications of her inadequacy. She gestured with her cigarette as she spoke. "That's about it. And I've been going over it and over it, and I'm convinced I looked for every possible cause. And *that* means the cause is something I didn't know to look for, which means it's new."

"New," Leslie repeated flatly. Then her eyes opened wider. "A new disease?" she whispered.

Danielle shook her head. "Maybe. If I could've held on to the body longer, I might've found out. But the boy didn't *look* sick, except for the fact that he was dead. The more I go over it, the more I think it's a new drug."

"Drug," Leslie repeated.

Danielle nodded. "I don't know if it's an upper, downer, hallucinogen, or what, but I think one of the side effects may be the complete and total breakdown of blood, and its absorption into the surrounding tissue."

"That's pretty weird."

"Of course it is. The whole idea of taking drugs is weird, if you ask me."

Leslie scowled at Danielle as she blew out a puff of smoke. "Uh-huh," she said ironically.

Danielle laughed. "Come on, you know what I mean."

"I know I sympathize with these kids' desire to get away from the world. Watergate, the energy crisis, the situation in the Middle East, the Russians, black versus white . . . it's a terrible time to be young. You see no hope for the future, so why not have a good time now?"

"That's a cop-out," Danielle snapped. She actually knew very little of what was happening in the outside world; current events only interested her when people died from them. "And immaterial to this. Have you busted any kids with any new drugs, or run across rumors about something you haven't heard of before?"

She shook her head. "No, and believe me, I'd have heard of it if anyone else in the department had. Juvie is a gossipy bunch, and sometimes they still forget I'm on staff and not one of the cleaning crew, so they'll talk about anything around me."

"Then maybe we're lucky. Maybe this is the first one, and we can catch it before it spreads."

" 'We.' "

Danielle scowled, annoyed. "This is your problem as much as mine."

"What do you plan to do?"

"First I want to talk to some of the kids. On the street, as they say. I was hoping you could help me with that."

Leslie snorted. "There's no such place as 'the street,' you've been watching too many cop shows. And if we go down to any of the regular hangouts, we won't find anyone who'll talk to us about drugs. They all know me."

"And none of them trust you?"

"The ones that *do* trust me aren't down there anymore, they're in schools or halfway houses or jobs."

Danielle twirled her lighter absently. "Well . . . what if I go alone?"

Leslie stared at her. "Then you'll get raped, and killed. Probably in that order, but I wouldn't swear to it."

Danielle stubbed out her cigarette in the ashtray. "I have to do it, Les. I have to *know*. If I can confirm my suspicion on this, maybe even get a sample, then we can get the word out before it gets out of hand."

"The 'word'?" Leslie repeated. "Danny, you sound so earnest, you're like a public service ad. Do you even remember what it was like to be a kid? 'The word' comes from 'the Man,' and he's over thirty, white, still thinks we should be in Viet Nam and that black people shouldn't be allowed to vote. They won't listen to 'the word.'"

Danielle sighed, defeated, and shook her head. "Then we may be scraping dozens of them off the street."

"Yeah, well, we should've thought of that before we criminalized marijuana and bombed Cambodia. I'm sorry, but I can't condone sending my best friend off to buy illegal drugs. Promise me you won't go. Please."

Danielle nodded, keeping the crushed expression. But it was an act. Leslie's political leanings were coloring her professional opinion; Danielle doubted more than a fraction of the kids Leslie dealt with could even tell you who was president, let alone how he got that way. They were kids being kids, in an unsupervised and potentially deadly environment.

Besides, she already had her plan. She'd spotted the same street names over and over in Leslie's reports, and now knew where to find her answers. The risk to her safety was a distant second to the damage her pride might suffer if she *didn't* go. They finished dinner in peace, giggling over Leslie's active dating life and forgetting all about kids on the street.

CHAPTER 8

FAUVETTE FOUND HER victim easily, less than five miles from the warehouse: a small-town boy passed out in the bed of his pickup behind a redneck bar at the city limits. Set back from the road in a line of auto dealers, pawnshops, and diners, the place was dangerous enough to be popular and safe enough to be crowded, even near dawn, with enough drunken good ole boys that no one would miss this one. Traffic on the road was light, and none of the other businesses that lined the highway showed any sign of life.

She climbed over the tailgate so stealthily the worn suspension made no sound. The boy lay on his back, mouth open, snoring. His pants were around his knees, although she couldn't tell if it was for sex or urination. She didn't care. Normally she would have taken only a little blood, but now that she acknowledged it, her need overwhelmed her. This boy would die.

She crawled beside him and stretched out, draping one leg over his. She felt his erection flutter and then jut up against the fabric of his white jockey shorts. Still unconscious, he moaned and tossed his head, his drunken dreams now filled with ultra-vivid sexual fantasies.

She brushed the hair back from his face. He had a wispy mustache and pimples on his neck. His lips were full, almost girlish. He moaned again, and she traced one ragged fingernail around his mouth.

She latched on to his wrist first, taking the blood from his pulsing artery, and chewed the wound to obliterate any sign of her teeth marks. As the warm salty liquid flowed into her, she felt queasy, like a starving man given a chocolate sundae. Then her system adjusted as she drank, absorbing the blood where it was most needed. The thump from the bar's jukebox mirrored the boy's heartbeats at first, as if the music felt his life pulsing into her.

"Oh, baby," she sighed, and got to her knees. He was already bone pale in the security light. Her arms went under him and lifted him in a mock lovers' embrace, and she shifted her bite to his jugular. She let the blood pool in her mouth, the liquid forming a seal between her lips and his neck. Then she drank voraciously.

At the last moment his eyes fluttered open. He was too weak to speak or scream, but he managed to raise one hand to her face. His dying fingers caressed her cheek, touched the place where her lips met his flesh, then fell limp. His heart gave out three beats later.

Fauvette lowered him gently to the truck bed, then dug her fingers into his neck and ripped out the chunk of flesh with incriminating teeth marks. She tossed it into the weeds, where the raccoons and possums waited. Then she drove her index finger straight through his sternum into his heart, puncturing the organ as surely as any wooden stake. Without an intact heart to revive, the boy would never rise to prowl the night.

She leaned back against the fender, gasping with satiation. Her head cleared as well and she realized how near the brink of real, true death she'd been. The gray powder Toddy gave her had completely deadened the desire for blood, even after she'd lost some of her own, which usually triggered gargantuan bloodlust. Where the hell had he gotten it? And what was it? She still had the bag stashed at the warehouse, but hadn't touched it since that night. It numbed even the desire to consume more of the powder itself. But that was okay: one dose had almost killed her. Apparently it *had* killed Toddy.

She looked down at the white-faced corpse. Mosquitoes hovered over it, their instincts confused by the smell of blood coming from the rapidly cooling body. Inside the bar some-one let out a tremendous "Yeeeeee-HAH!" The boy was probably not old enough to legally drink alcohol, and this might have been his first night out in the big city. Marriage, career, children, all those dreams were gone. His parents would never applaud with pride as he graduated, never hold grandchildren on their laps. She took that from them, took their joy, their hope.

The blood in her stomach churned at this realization. She had not asked to become this dark monster, but neither had she made any effort to end it, and her one real attempt—the gray powder—had, once its numbing effect faded, left her so ravenous that she'd had to kill this boy instead of merely feeding on him. She felt guilt, and shame, and remorse.

Then she vomited most of the fresh blood back onto the corpse.

Her insides wrenched in agony; part of her tried to hang on to the precious fluid, while the rest worked to get rid of it. *I'm a monster, I'm a maggot, I'm a disease,* her conscience screamed. But somewhere in the back of this cacophony, her true voice protested: *These are not your thoughts, you are what you are, you do not pity yourself.* And then the two voices merged into a miasma she could not filter. She leaned over the side and sobbed.

Finally the immediate anguish passed, leaving her weaker and more depressed than before. With great effort she climbed awkwardly out of the truck and stumbled into the weeds, headed toward the warehouse. Dawn was less than an hour away.

From the roof of the bar where he sat on one of the humming air-conditioning units, Rudolfo Zginski watched Fauvette stagger off. He tracked her until he was certain she lived at the big, abandoned warehouse in the distance. He'd be waiting when she emerged the next night, and follow her until he caught her alone. He sent out a call to the local "children of the night," and immediately four lean, rather decrepit coyotes and a feral German shepherd emerged from the field behind the bar. They silently scrambled into the truck bed, claws loud against the metal, and began devouring the softer parts of Fauvette's victim. What they would leave would give no hint of a vampire.

He leaped from the roof to the bed of another pickup, his step so light the vehicle barely moved, then bounded over four more cars to hit the ground in a pool of shadow beneath a broken streetlamp. He moved onto the sidewalk and drifted down the road, unseen, unheard, no more than a darker whisper of shadow in the night. He'd accomplished one of the things he set out to do: find another vampire. Now it was time for the second thing.

Upon leaving the morgue after his resurrection, Zginski found himself in a maze of corridors all reeking of blood, flesh, and antiseptic. He met another man dressed in identical scrubs and jacket, and mimicked his professional nod as they passed. When he reached the main lobby, he saw that the building belonged to a university, and found himself suddenly among a crowd of young people all rushing about to reach their next class. Someone bumped into him and said, " 'Scuse me, Doc."

He ducked into a public lavatory, marked simply with the word "MEN." A half-dozen young men entered the room after him, milling about and discussing obscure things like "Pink Floyd" and "cheerleaders." He retreated into a stall and waited for the crowd to thin out. He heard the word "disco," and the term "fall of Saigon," and even discussion of large metal dirigibles. A student entered the stall beside him and lit a crudely rolled cigarette. Zginski smelled something sweet and pungent.

A bell rang somewhere in the building, and immediately everyone departed except the man in the stall. Carefully Zginski stood on the toilet and peered over the divider wall. The man was young, with long sideburns and bangs that fell into his eyes. He wore an orange T-shirt with "55" on it in large white numbers. He drew another lungful of smoke from the cigarette, then let it out in a contented sigh. Zginski recognized it as a narcotic, although he was certain it was neither opium nor heroin.

The young man looked up and saw Zginski spying on him. His eyes were red-rimmed and glazed. For a moment neither moved nor spoke, then the man held up the cigarette. "Want a toke?" he said, his voice oddly tight in his throat.

"No, thank you," Zginski said.

The young man looked puzzled at his accent. Then his eyes lit up. "Hey, you're a Russkie, ain't ya?"

Unsure of the term, Zginski nodded.

"Well, how-de-do. I never met a real Red before. I hear they make you hate us for being all capitalistic and stuff. Do you hate me?"

"You confuse me," Zginski said honestly.

The man snapped his fingers as if an idea just occurred to him. "I know—you defected, dincha? Y'all got a little taste of a free market, and boom! Here you are." The thought seemed to amuse him.

"There are many things about your society that interest me."

"Well, you just ask away. In case you ain't heard, here in the South, we're always glad to help someone who's strayed from the path get back onto the straight and narrow. Ask me anything."

Zginski pointed at the floor. "What is that?"

When the man looked down, Zginski leaned over the wall and struck him once on the back of the skull. The blow would likely give him a concussion, but it would not kill him. It *would* confuse his memory, if the pungent cigarette had not already done so. Zginski jumped the divider and wormed into the stall with the unconscious man, quickly if gracelessly swapping clothes with him.

Clad in bell-bottom jeans, an orange Tennessee Vols jersey, and battered tennis shoes, Zginski emerged from the stall. He stopped in front of the mirrors and looked at himself. His hair, dark and wavy, hung to his shoulders. A neat mustache and goatee encircled his wide lips. As always, he appeared about thirty years old, and pale as if recovering from an illness.

He couldn't believe the clothes he now wore were considered acceptable for an academic institution. The number on the shirt was cracked, faded, and peeling away in places, while the denim trousers were ragged at the cuffs. He pulled the wallet from the back pocket and found paper money, an official-looking card with the man's picture in one corner, and several photographs of what must have been his family. He took the money, the photo of one attractive young woman, and tossed the rest back into the stall with the man.

He turned toward the door just as a campus security officer entered the bathroom. The paunchy, middle-aged man stopped when he saw Zginski. He sniffed the air and smiled knowingly. "Well, reckon somebody's been smoking cannabis in the can, haven't they?"

Zginski said nothing. He had no idea what the man was talking about.

The guard looked him over. "You go to school here?" he asked dubiously.

"Yep," he said, trying to mimic the drawl everyone seemed to possess.

The guard frowned. "Saying 'Yes, sir' might be in your best interest, boy."

Zginski noticed the man had no visible weapon. "Yes, sir," he said.

"That's better. Now why don't you hand over the dope and we'll forget about this whole thing?"

"I have no . . . dope," Zginski said. He tried to maintain the accent, but failed.

The guard suddenly looked suspicious. "What's your name, boy?"

Zginski made a distasteful survival decision. He could easily incapacitate the man, even kill him, but there was already one body waiting to be found. He would love to slap this arrogant peasant hard enough to shatter his jaw, but again it would not be efficacious. So, repugnant as he found it, he reached out with his vampiric powers.

The look on the guard's face was comically confused as the big man's body suddenly responded sexually to Zginski. There was an unmistakable bulge below his belt buckle, and his cheeks flushed red.

Zginski smiled despite the fact that the sensation was almost vile to him; he had never enjoyed arousing another man. "Are you all right, Officer?" he purred.

"Y'all get outta here," the guard said, and waved toward the exit as he quickly went into one of the empty stalls and slammed the door behind him. Zginski did as ordered.

He emerged from the building into the bright sunlight,

wincing as it seared his eyes. He ducked under a tree and waited for his vision to adjust. It took longer than it would for a normal human, but was apparently the trade-off for having such exceptional eyesight at night. When he could see well enough to navigate, he set out to find the one thing all universities possessed: a library.

CHAPTER 9

THE GIRL FROM the wallet photo sat across from Zginski, twirling a straw in her drink. Her wavy, dark blond hair was tied back and she wore a low-cut shirt with lace at the sleeve cuffs and neckline. Without makeup her freckles were very prominent, and he found he liked them immensely. She asked, "So, Mr. Mysterious Stranger, what's your name?"

Zginski squinted into the afternoon sunlight that streamed through the big glass window. The *third* thing he needed to do was acquire some of the spectacles with darkened lenses that he'd seen on various people. The second thing, after insuring no one connected him to the death of the Negro doctor in the morgue, was to arrange a steady source of blood. This time he would keep it simple and traditional, one victim for as long as she lasted. In Wales he had been indiscriminate, and that had not turned out well at all. Here he would choose a single woman and seduce her slowly until she was so desperate for him she gave herself willingly. Such blood was always the sweetest.

This wasn't the first victim fate had dropped in his hand, and he learned through experience that you ignored such gifts at your own peril. He'd found the girl's name written on the back of the photograph from the stolen wallet, and deduced correctly that she was the sister of the man whose clothes he'd stolen. In the photo she was smiling but not grinning, and the straight line of her shoulders set off the delicious curve of her neck, bare above a black drape.

Tracking her down was simple once he grasped the new telephone technology. Bell would have been astounded at how ubiquitous his invention had become. Zginski had the girl's name, as well as her brother's name and address printed on what he later learned was a driver's license. With this information he'd found the correct phone number in a large book of them at the library, and when he called was told by someone, probably her father, that she was at work down at Harman's Grill. The man had not even asked how Zginski knew his daughter. With the use of another thick book filled with business phone numbers and advertisements printed on yellow paper, he'd found the restaurant's location. A taxi brought him here, and he spotted her at once: soft, feminine, in very short and tight pants that showed vast amounts of bare leg. It was a societal trend Zginski had noticed during his brief time on the campus, but he was at best ambivalent about it; without mystery, where would romance be? Still, when the legs on display were this exquisite, he was willing to forgo his prudish nature.

It had been short work to use his vampiric powers to draw the girl's eye to him as she passed his booth serving others. Now she was on break, seated opposite him and smiling shyly. He had her.

"Rudy," he now replied to her question. A quick look through names in the phone book convinced him that his full name would attract too much attention. He still hadn't mastered the local dialect, but his own accent was less prominent.

"I'm Lee Ann," she said. "Lee Ann Felton."

He nodded at her name tag. "I know."

She blushed and ducked her head. "Sorry." She took a

long drink from the straw. Zginski had only barely touched her with his power, enough to attract her attention without overwhelming her. He was still relatively weak after his ordeal. He could tell by the way her feet twisted on the floor beneath the table that she was aroused, but saw no need to force things. They would happen in their own time, and if he needed to, he would feed on strangers until she was ready.

"I told Celie Jo I thought you were cute the minute you walked in here," she said. Her eyes flashed up at him. "She said you're too old for me. I don't think that matters, though, do you? I mean, yeah, I just graduated from high school, but I *am* over eighteen. In case you were wondering."

"In my country, women your age are considered at their most desirable."

She grinned again, and blushed pink beneath her freckles. "Well, people here might look at us funny. They might think you're my daddy or something." Again she looked down. "I mean, if we were to go out or anything."

"Then we will be discreet," he assured her.

Her eyes flashed up at him almost in wonder. In a soft voice she said, "So you do want to take me out?"

He smiled, careful not to display his fangs. "I would love to show you the night," he said carefully and sincerely.

She shook her head, as if unable to believe her luck. "You know, Rudy, I keep thinking I should take this slow, learn more about you, maybe have you meet my folks and stuff. But I have to tell you, part of me really wants to just go somewhere with you right now and . . ." She looked down and hunched her shoulders shyly. "Jump your bones."

"What does that expression mean?" Zginski asked innocently, though of course the context made it plain.

She leaned over the table toward him. "It means I want to have sex with you," she whispered, the words sounding awkward in her voice.

He smiled and feigned embarrassment. "Lee Ann, I do

not think that's a good idea. As you say, you are very young. You may not be ready."

She reached over and took his hand. "Rudy, if I get any readier I might melt right here." Her eyes opened wide. "Wow, your hand is *cold*."

"Then you should warm it," he said.

She pressed it between her hands and then, after glancing around the diner to make sure no one was watching, pressed his palm to her breast. The shudder that went through her made her gasp.

Zginski gently disengaged his hand. "I should go. You have your job, and I have mine." Then he withdrew all of his influence except the barest hint, enough to keep her fixated to distraction until that night. "What time do you finish your shaft?"

"Shift," she corrected with a smile. "At eleven. I'm working a split this week."

He had no idea what she meant, but assumed it didn't matter. "Then I will be waiting for you at that time."

She watched him as he stood, paid at the register, and left. He'd used money stolen from her brother to purchase new trousers and a more dignified shirt, but still wore the tattered tennis shoes. He worried that she might recognize them, but her mind was far away from such details. Like many of his past conquests, she was a simple peasant girl, unsophisticated and trusting; he would teach her many things in return for the blood he needed to live. Now, though, he was weary and sun-drained, and needed to find a dark place to rest before the night. The vampire from the warehouse had looked weak and wasted, but he'd been fooled before. He needed to be strong enough to defend himself, if necessary, when he located her.

Danielle looked at herself in the mirror and sighed. She felt ridiculous.

She'd washed her hair and let it dry naturally, with no

blow-drying or hair spray. The limp ends of the bangs hung annoyingly in her eyes. She wore no makeup, and without it the creases around her eyes and mouth made her look like a tired high school girl instead of a mature woman. It figured that not even normal crow's-feet and smile lines made her look her age.

She wore ragged denim jeans low on her hips, with a wide leather belt. The flared cuffs had a stitched checkerboard pattern at the bottom, and her shoes, toeless and with inch-thick cork soles, were the tackiest she could find. She debated between a more demure T-shirt or her final choice, and decided the bright red halter top would imply confidence that she didn't really feel. It was a bit too small, so it also gave her cleavage and made her boobs look respectable even though she felt hugely self-conscious. Luckily it would be dark where she was going, and no one from work should be anywhere around.

She had a knife taped to her right calf, like Leslie had once shown her, and a small Mace sprayer in her pocket. Fifty dollars in cash was distributed between two pockets. If she couldn't cut, blind, or buy her way out of a tight spot, then she had no one to blame but herself. If someone did attack her, she hoped that she'd have the presence of mind to remember what was where, and not die because she tried to spray the knife at somebody.

And that was it; her disguise was complete. She left a note on her kitchen table outlining her plan and where she intended to start. If the worst happened, then this would give the police somewhere to start looking for her body. She knew one of her own morgue slabs might be waiting for her at the end of the night, but she almost quivered with exhilaration at the danger of it. Would Lyman feel the need to personally avenge her? Would Skitch actually get her job? Would Dr. Francisco speak at her funeral?

She climbed into her car and headed downtown.

· · ·

Fronting on Dudley Street, Elmwood Cemetery was the oldest graveyard in Memphis. Its residents went back to 1852 and included victims of the *Sultana*, a riverboat that sank in 1865 and killed an unbelievable seventeen hundred people. Danielle had supervised two exhumations there, so she recognized the address immediately in Leslie's files. It didn't surprise her that it was also a place where teenagers might go to do things adults wouldn't condone. The place had isolation, the spook factor, and acres of dark grassland suitable for all sorts of illicit activities. But she doubted that single white girls just wandered into it looking for a good time. She'd need to find some other people, tag along with them, hope they wanted to get high on the new stuff, and procure a sample. Simple as death.

She parked in a paid lot and locked her car. She carried only the door and ignition keys; everything else, keys to her apartment and office, were hidden beneath the felt-covered cardboard bottom of the locked glove compartment. If she got rolled, they might take her car, but they'd never find those other keys.

It was a warm and scaldingly humid night, and for that reason alone she was glad she'd chosen the skimpier top. Sweat beaded on her shoulders and lower back. She fought the urge to suck in her bare stomach. Her breasts bounced with each step; she recalled watching Suzanne Somers jiggle her way through *Battle of the Network Stars*, and for the first time really felt sorry for her. As she took in the dark, gritty neighborhood, she kept hearing the refrain of a Three Dog Night song: *Mama told me not to come . . .*

She walked with her head down along the empty sidewalk until she turned onto Decatur Avenue, a three-lane street lined with bars, porn peep shows, and businesses closed behind barred windows. The light, noise, and traffic were a total change. Not only were cars cruising, windows down and music blaring, but little knots of teenagers, the very creatures she sought, milled about or prowled the sidewalks. Most were white boys, and she knew that once she caught their eye, they'd be all over her. It was not vanity, but psychology: she'd dressed to be provocative, after all. How bright, she suddenly realized, was *that*?

She recalled other really stupid things she'd done, like driving drunk two hundred miles to a concert in college, or having condomless — and very fast — sex with her high school prom date. Most vividly, she remembered the time when she was twelve, immersed in books on reptiles, and developed a burning desire to see a real rattlesnake. Armed with only her field guide and a stick, she'd gone poking into areas that the book called "likely habitats." Sure enough, she found one, and sure enough, it bit her right on the foot. But its fangs missed by the barest fraction, instead imbedding in the rubber sole of her tennis shoe. She'd run screaming all the way home, the hapless snake trailing from her foot.

And here she was twenty years later, poking into another likely habitat. Would she be as lucky this time?

The four boys accosted her outside a convenience store. They huddled around the pay phone attached to the wall beneath a bright strip of fluorescent lighting, catcalling and whistling as she passed. She hunched her shoulders and walked faster, but sensed them peeling away from the wall and slouch-rushing to catch up. "Hey, baby, whatchu afraid of?" one of them called.

She kept her head down and sped up. This was a really bad idea, just as Leslie warned, and her courage completely failed her. She wanted to get back to her car and get the hell out of there, but with the boys behind her she'd have to loop the whole eighty-acre cemetery to do that. They drew closer, and she heard one plainly drawl, "Ain't nothing to be afraid of *here*, baby." The others laughed, and she didn't have to see the gesture to know what he meant by "here."

It took all her resolve not to run screaming down the street. The boys were close now. They'd drag her into an alley and have her bent over a garbage can, or on her back on the filthy concrete. It would only be rape, if she was lucky and didn't put up a fight. Then again, maybe they wouldn't want to leave her alive as a witness. Fight or flight, she tried to decide.

Then suddenly one of them fell into step beside her. She suppressed a startled yelp. "Sorry 'bout what we said back there," he said, and his regret sounded genuine. "We thought you were somebody we knew."

She glanced at him but did not slow down. He was cute, maybe sixteen, and clearly a little drunk or stoned. He stared brazenly at her jiggling boobs. "She must be a lucky girl," she said.

"Hey, I ain't trying to cause any trouble with you. You just looked kinda lost and"—he stammered awkwardly—"p-pretty, and I thought you might need some help."

"My hero," she said wryly. The other three followed at a discreet distance, giggling and nudging each other. Had this one won the bet to talk to her, or lost? She slowed to a normal walk. "Do you always swoop down on girls you don't know?"

He grinned, both shy and bold. "I don't know about 'swooping,' but I always talk to a foxy chick anytime I can."

She stopped outside a brightly lit Laundromat. He seemed harmless, and if he was the leader of this "gang," she felt no danger from them now. If anything, she should be able to keep herself safe by judicious application of feminine wiles. The flood of relief left her giddy. She faced him, hands on her hips. "So talk," she said.

"My name's Billy Blankenship. What's yours?"

"Danny," she said, and instantly wanted to kick herself.

She had a whole alternate secret identity as a Nashville college girl named Jessica ready to go, and now she'd blown it.

"Well, hey there, Danny, good to meet you." He leaned closer and said softly, "Me and my boys are meeting some other girls in the cemetery, to get high and stuff. Want to come?"

She peered past him at his friends. They stifled their laughter and looked away. "I don't see any other girls," she said suspiciously.

"Like I said, they're meeting us there. You'll like 'em."

"Uh-huh."

"No, I swear, Scout's honor."

"What about Boo Radley's honor?" she deadpanned.

"Huh? Look, nothing bad'll happen. Hell, sometimes when he's in town, Elvis even sends his guys around to take us to Libertyland for free, so it could be extra-cool."

She made no effort to hide her doubts on that one. "Oh, come on, that's bullshit."

"No, serious. He rents the whole place out in the middle of the night for his daughter. He wants Lisa Marie to see other people around having a good time, so we get in free to ride all we want, as long as we look happy whenever she runs into us." He giggled. "And that ain't so hard to do with a good nickel bag like we got."

Danielle knew Elvis *did* rent out the amusement park, but the rest of the story sounded awfully thin. She examined Billy with exaggerated skepticism. "You better not be telling me all this just to try to get in my pants. I'm not like these citified girls; if I don't like you, you'll draw back a nub."

The other boys laughed, whether at Billy's discomfort or her defiance she couldn't tell. Billy laughed as well. "Danny, I swear. We smoke a little, hang out, that's all. You're welcome to come."

Well, she thought, *this is exactly what I hoped would happen. Can't ignore an answered prayer.* She tapped his chest with her finger, trying to pretend she wasn't twice his age. "Okay, hot stuff. But you better behave."

"Cool," he said with a big grin. Then he took her hand and led her down the street. The others rushed to catch up.

They were a typical ad hoc group of friends, drawn together by ennui and geography more than any shared interests. Billy appeared to be the leader, but only by default; she could imagine none of them getting too worked up about anything. His T-shirt proclaimed *KISS Tour '74* and featured the band members dressed like aliens, or so Danielle thought. He was slender but soft, the result of indolence overcoming natural leanness.

Tom was the tallest, and by far the handsomest. He had that smooth attitude that told her he was used to girls finding him irresistible. He wore a clean polo shirt and neat jeans, and his tennis shoes were new. When she made eye contact with him he smiled and winked, letting her know it was okay to check him out. She wanted to slug him on behalf of all his future girlfriends.

Mike looked to be the youngest, probably not even old enough to drive. He wore a faded Confederate flag T-shirt with the sleeves ripped off, and cutoff jeans that hung to his knees. He had the typical teenage insecurities about girls writ large on his face, and would not meet her eyes. She pitied him.

Finally there was Ling, with his four-hair excuse for a mustache. He wore a floppy camouflage seaman's hat and a tank top, and when he spoke had the same accent as the rest. Fully Americanized. She guessed his background was Taiwanese.

The five of them ducked down an alley between a bar and an insurance office. A man sang to himself as he urinated on the wall, so drunk he never noticed them. The chain-link fence around Elmwood Cemetery ran behind all the buildings on the street, and here one section hidden behind a ragged shrub showed evidence of having been lifted up and bent back several times.

Tom held it so Danielle could slip under after Billy. She froze again: it was insane, running down an alley with a bunch of strange boys. But Tom seemed so earnest, so harmless, that she felt no danger from him. He looked up at her with wide, guileless eyes. "You coming?" he said softly. "It'll be okay, I promise."

Danielle smiled. This felt like the kind of group acceptance she'd never actually had in high school; now the cool kids *liked* her, and wanted to hang out with her. "I'm holding you to it," she said with a warning wag of her finger.

"You can hold me any way you like," Tom said with a grin. Danielle laughed as she crawled under the fence.

The boys knew their way around, and Billy pulled Danielle along at a faster pace than she liked. She stumbled over footstones and plot markers, until they finally reached a small gazebo deep in the cemetery grounds. There were no lights except the glow from the city reflected on the intermittent clouds overhead.

"Welcome to our little party crypt," Billy said. The gazebo had seen better days, and Danielle was glad her tetanus boosters were up-to-date.

The four boys took positions around the small structure with the male certainty of previously established territories. Danielle stayed with Billy, who sat on the steps. Tom went inside and leaned one leg nonchalantly on the rail, while Ling plopped in the octagon's darkest corner. Mike unfolded a wad of aluminum foil to reveal a plastic bag filled with marijuana. Ling handed him rolling papers and a plastic cigarette machine. He picked a sheltered corner out of the night wind and began rolling a joint.

Billy clearly had other things on his mind with Danielle, and ran a finger lightly down her bare arm. "So how old are you, nineteen or twenty?" he asked, trying for casual and sophisticated. He fell far short.

"Legal in Mississippi." She did not pull away, but she wasn't about to encourage him. "Are you?"

"I ain't too worried about the law," he said with a smile. "Just a certain pair of lips."

He leaned close, and because she was fighting not to burst out laughing, Danielle let him kiss her. It was almost comical in its chastity: closemouthed, no tongues, just a soft pressing of lips. As he drew back, he smiled as if he'd just convinced her of something she doubted.

Don't laugh, she told herself, biting the insides of her cheeks. If you laugh at him, he'll never tell you anything.

"Ready for launch," Mike announced, holding up the finished joint.

"Let's get high and see what happens," Billy said to Danielle, aiming for Barry White sexiness. He never even reached Manilow. She nodded, afraid that if she spoke, giggles would overcome her.

Soon the joint had been passed around three times, and although Danielle faked drawing the smoke into her lungs, she began to feel an undeniable lethargic euphoria from the contact high. She hadn't smoked dope since graduating from medical school, and it had the same effect now as it did then; she began to yawn and her thoughts grew sluggish and wandering.

During one yawn she felt a hand slip around her waist, and she was pulled close to Billy. He pressed his lips to hers more insistently this time, and his tongue sought its way into her mouth. She felt so disconnected from the actual sensations that she opened her mouth to him, and when his other hand clumsily kneaded her breast through the halter, she thought nothing of it. She lifted one leg and draped it over his lap, going with the movement until she was straddling him, still kissing him, his hands now beneath the halter.

Well, this *isn't very smart,* she thought remotely. *Sixteen can still get you twenty, even if the jail bait's a boy.*

She broke the kiss and shook her head to clear it. "Whoa, shotgun," she murmured, and pulled his unresisting hands away. "Slow down a little."

"Hey, sure, whatever," he said, feigning nonchalance. At least he wasn't the kind of guy who took resistance personally. She climbed off his lap and sat on the steps, although she did allow herself to lean against him. She adjusted the halter and decided she'd better stay on topic before she became a child molester. The joint came her way again, so after the next fake toke she asked, "This is the best stuff you got? This is okay if you're killing time before a concert, but what do you do for a *real* party?"

Ling snorted. "We don't do no smack or nothing like that. That stuff'll kill you. Killed my cousin out in San Francisco."

"Well, I hear there's something new going around," she insisted. Her skin still tingled where Billy had touched her, and it was hard to concentrate. "Something that'll knock your socks off."

Billy nudged her with his shoulder. "Hey, you ain't a narc, are you?"

"She's a *narc*?" Ling almost shrieked.

Oh, shit, Danielle thought. Leslie had told her many stories about the undercover cops who ended up dead in a variety of creative ways after blowing their covers. Now she had to get these boys back on her side before they pursued that line of thought any further.

"Jeez, do I *look* like a narc?" she said dismissively, and then added with faux sophistication, "I'm just *bored* with this. I can get weed anywhere, I thought you big-city guys would have the latest shit."

Billy's slack face fell at the idea she thought him uncool. She felt a twinge of guilt for hurting the poor sap's feelings, but Billy's broken heart would heal a lot faster than her slit throat.

Luckily, thanks to the provincial weed, the moment passed as if Danielle had not spoken. Mike and Tom returned to their rambling dissertation on the merits of the Electric Light Orchestra. "Like I was saying, the point is, they bring the whole orchestra into the rock scene, and use it to illuminate their songs," Mike said. "That's why they picked the name. They *are* the electric light, showing everyone how the orchestra can be as rock and roll as anything else."

Danielle looked at Billy. He ignored the argument and stared down at the ground, his shoulders slumped. He looked almost ready to cry. She took his hand. "Hey," she said softly, "I'm sorry. I didn't mean anything personal by it."

"That's horse shit," Tom snapped to Mike. "They're just copying Zeppelin. Jimmy Page was using strings and shit way before Jeff Lynne."

"And Page, he just copied all the old nigra blues players," Ling added, desperate to be included.

Then a new voice said, "You keep talking like that and we just might go find some new friends."

CHAPTER 10

"HEY, LEO, I was stickin' up for you black folks," Ling said. "You didn't think I meant anything bad by calling you nigras, did you?" He held out his hand for a soul shake, which involved many back-and-forth slaps and grips with the new arrival.

The black boy looked a little older than the others, and wore a Dallas Cowboys sports jersey. He had a big Afro with a pick comb on the side and eyes that seemed to catch the light even when there wasn't any. "Hell, no," he said, grinning. "Just like I can call you a chink."

"Damn straight," Ling agreed, a little too emphatically; he clearly relished being able to use the word "nigra" with impunity.

Another new arrival appeared beside the first. She was also black, younger and heavier, yet with that indefinable sexiness some big girls possessed. Leslie had it, and so did this girl, in spades; Danielle giggled in her head at the mental pun.

The girl turned sharply and looked at Danielle as if she'd heard her laughter. Christ, had she done it out loud? Danielle was too stoned to remember. She pinched her thigh through her jeans, hoping the pain might clear her head.

"Hey, Olive," Billy said to the new girl. The other boys also turned immediately to her, big goofy smiles on their faces, as if this pudgy black teen was as attractive as Farrah Fawcett-Majors.

Olive showed no surprise at her reception. She wore a tube top and polyester pants, like Cleopatra Jones in the movies. Yet the blatant sexiness seemed incongruous, because she didn't look even old enough to drive.

She stopped before Billy and ran her fingers through his hair. If she noticed Danielle holding his hand, she paid it no mind. "Hey, there, Billy boy," she practically purred. "How's my vanilla shake tonight?"

"Doing better with some chocolate syrup," he said in his "sexy" voice. Danielle practically sucked her lips into her lungs trying not to laugh.

The boy Leo sat down on the steps and took a hit from the offered joint. Danielle noticed that he, like her, only faked inhaling it. "Well, hi," he said to her. "Ain't you a fine little thing. This your new girl, Billy?"

"No, she's just a friend. She thinks we're a bunch of hicks."

"Hey, I never said—" Danielle started to protest.

Olive knelt behind Billy and put her arms around him. Danielle had not even seen her go up the steps. Was she really that stoned? "I'll be your friend, Billy," Olive said. "We'll be an ice cream sandwich."

Billy turned his head and Olive kissed him, openmouthed and sloppy. The blatant sexuality blanketed them all, and suddenly Danielle felt very alone, and very scared. Only the dampening effects of the marijuana kept her from bolting.

"Hey," Tom suddenly blurted. "Where's Fauvette? You said last time you'd bring her along."

"She'll be here in a bit," Leo said.

Olive broke the kiss long enough to say, "I thought she left before we did?"

Leo shrugged. "You know Fauvette. Things to see, people to do."

Olive nodded, then whispered something into Billy's ear. He giggled, then followed her off into the dark graveyard. "Me and Billy are going to go look for the moon," she said over her shoulder.

"The *dark* of the moon," Ling said. Everyone laughed except Danielle.

Leo turned his odd, almost metallic-looking eyes to Danielle. He touched her shoulder, and his fingertips were ice-cold. "So where you from?" he asked.

"Nashville," she managed, falling back on her story.

"Here for the summer?" His voice had all the sensuality that had eluded poor Billy.

"Going to school in the fall," she said, glad now for the dope's relaxing effect. "Premed."

"Oh. Smart girl, eh?"

Not at the moment, she thought, but instead just smiled. His attention, so overwhelming and out of the blue, was shifting the balance between dope-addled lethargy and blind panic. The boys, who had seemed so harmless before, now looked at her with blatant suspicion and desire. She was not racist, but it seemed like the arrival of the two blacks had completely changed everything. Her heart pounded madly and she was sweating.

Suddenly she was on her feet. She pressed her hand against her leg, feeling the dubious comfort of the Mace sprayer. "I have to go," she blurted. "Thanks for the smokes."

"You don't liked hanging out with the coloreds?" Leo asked almost mockingly.

"Hey, now, Leo's our pal," Tom said defensively. "Don't be a Klan Fran."

"A 'Klan Fran'?" Ling said. "Did you just make that up?"

"Sure."

Danielle started to reply, but without a conscious decision suddenly dashed off toward the fence, hoping she could find the exit in her still-dotty state. The boys laughed, especially Leo, whose derision almost seemed to follow her. Tears of fright struggled to burst from her eyes, but she held them in check. Time enough for that on the drive home, assuming she lived to reach her car.

The graveyard became a maze in the dark, and she painfully fell over three tombstones hidden by the shadows. Limping and thoroughly disoriented, she turned a corner around a mausoleum and shrieked in surprise.

Billy and Olive were locked in a clinch against the wall. Olive looked up, startled. Billy, his back against the stone, didn't move. His pants were unzipped, and Olive's right hand curled around his erection.

At that moment a breeze rustled the trees shadowing them, and the pinkish illumination from above shone full on the black girl's face. To Danielle's trained eye, there was no mistaking the gleam of fresh blood on her lips. Then she glanced at Billy. The girl had *bitten* him in the neck, and two thin trickles bled down onto his shirt and bracketed the "I" in the KISS logo. His eyes were open and glassy, and his mouth worked in soundless gasps.

Olive chuckled, a wet sound as if it came through fluid still in her throat. Billy ejaculated onto her hand.

Danielle was about to scream when a strong, ice-cold palm slapped over her mouth and she was yanked back against a tall male body.

CHAPTER 11

AT THE SAME moment Danielle locked her car and began her amateur undercover work, Zginski sat in Lee Ann's vehicle and stared at the illuminated radio dial. The noise it emitted was second only to Lee Ann's response to it for utterly inexplicable behavior, and for the first time he feared he might not be able to acclimate to this new world of the future. He had tried every rational explanation and found none applied, so at last he turned to her. "May I ask you a question?"

She stopped tossing her head to the music and answered breathlessly, "Sure."

"What is 'the funk'? And why do those singing tribal people want it?"

"Singing tribal—oh, you mean the nigras. Yeah, they're black, and I guess 'the funk' is sort of what they call doing the deed."

"The deed," he repeated blankly.

"You know, *the deed*," she said, trying to sound worldly.

"Ah." *That* at least he understood.

As she parked her battered '69 Chevy Malibu outside their destination, Lee Ann wondered for the first time if pursuing this sudden crush might not be a good idea. "You mean *this* is where you're staying?"

"It suits my purposes for the moment," Zginski replied, his voice soft, deep, and smooth. He understood her initial response: even to his eyes, the Graceland Motel was clearly on the low, common end of the spectrum. However, the cash he'd taken from her brother was running out, and this was the only place he could afford. All this would change as he grew more acclimated to this new time and secured funding for the appropriate lifestyle.

She looked over at Zginski, his eyes hidden in the gloom. Red light from the motel's flashing neon sign illuminated his lips and chin. The image sent a shiver through her, and all her mother's warnings about strangers, foreigners, and men in general sprang fresh to her mind. But then she remembered how she felt when he looked at her, and everything faded except that. If he wanted her in a ratty motel room, then he could have her there, in any way he desired.

He stepped around to the driver's side and opened the door for her. For the first time he noticed the "G" was unlit in the motel sign. A glowering black man emerged from one of the nearby rooms, spent a moment staring at the two whites, then climbed into a Dodge Charger and squealed tires out of the lot, fishtailing as he entered the traffic to many disgruntled honks.

The car gave Zginski a rush of visceral excitement unlike any he'd experienced in over two centuries. Mastering the skill of driving looked complicated, but if someone like Lee Ann, a mere woman, could master it, he should be able to do the same. These terrific machines, capable of such bursts of speed and power yet filled with amenities like cool-air generators and small wireless devices that produced music, were the first genuine improvement he'd encountered in this new time. He couldn't wait to learn the techniques needed to operate one.

Lee Ann took his arm and they entered room 12, down-stairs by the pool. Zginski was desperate to feed on the girl, but he knew the benefits of taking his time. First he closed the drapes so she would not notice his unusual pallor. He'd left the air conditioner off so the room would be warm, and thus his skin not quite so cold and repulsive to her touch. When he looked at her again she stood in the middle of the room enveloped in his full influence, trembling so that her legs could barely support her. He held out his hand, and she put her fingers carefully in it. At the moment of contact she made a little gasp, and he knew she'd experienced female fulfillment. Her face flushed with blood, and he found him-self trembling as well.

"Come to me, Lee Ann," he said in a low, deep purr.

"I'm scared, Rudy," she whispered. "I've never felt like this."

"Is it your first time with a man?" he asked with a know-ing smile.

"What? No, don't be ridiculous. It's just . . . I never *wanted* it like this. This much. It hurts, almost. Like you've put a spell on me." She managed a smile at her own silliness. "Or maybe a curse. I can't imagine saying 'no' to you."

He slid a hand around her waist and pulled her against him. Because of her platform sandals he had to look up into her eyes. She was breathing heavily, and her whole body shivered. He could possess her now in any way he chose.

"On your knees, Lee Ann," he said softly.

With no resistance or comment, she slid to her knees, sat back on her heels, and looked up at him. Her hands rested demurely in her lap.

"If I told you I was a demon, with the fires of hell in my heart, would you run away?"

"No," she said raggedly. She wrapped her arms around herself, but continued to stare into his eyes.

"If I told you I intended to take the life from you slowly,

and that as you grew weaker I would grow stronger, would you flee my presence?"

"No," she repeated. Her eyes shone with tears now.

He brushed a strand of hair from her face. "Lee Ann, by your own word I have taken possession of you this night. I will summon you at a moment's notice, and the pain of not responding will be more than you can bear. I may debase and demean you, and use you in any way I choose. There is nothing you can do to resist me, because I have claimed part of your soul. Do you understand this?"

"Yes," she replied promptly, in a child's voice. The tears spilled forth down her face as she continued gazing up at him.

He touched her cheek with his fingertips, and again she gasped. His first estimate of her had been correct: beneath the sophisticated trappings of her modern world she was a simple peasant girl, lacking the intelligence and will for even a token resistance. He smiled, now making no secret of his elongated canines.

"Are y'all really gonna kill me?" she asked softly.

"Not tonight," he said. "Now rise, and disrobe." He wanted to feed before setting out to find the other vampire from the warehouse.

Lee Ann stood and pulled her loose paisley blouse over her head. She let it fall to the floor, followed by her bra. Zginski sat on the foot of the bed and watched with detached interest, comparing her to the dozens of other women he'd put through similar rituals. It struck him that despite the amazing technical advances society had made while he was in limbo, a naked woman remained the same treasure to be uncovered. At least no corsets were now involved, nor those voluminous layers and hoop skirts that required teams of servant women to remove. Nor was that horrendous makeup apparently in favor anymore; the girl's eyelids and lips were painted, but little else. He found he preferred that simpler look. And he'd always hated wigs.

Finally Lee Ann stood naked before him, sniffling with barely suppressed tears. She kept her hands flat against her thighs, shoulders hunched and head down. The red glow from the sign outside shone through a gap in the curtains and cast a line of crimson light across her throat. He smiled at that. Somewhere another car squealed tires, and voices raised in disagreement momentarily rang out. Lee Ann jumped at the sounds, but otherwise did not move.

"Stand up straight," he said.

She put back her shoulders and raised her chin.

"Come here," Zginski said softly.

As if her feet weighed a ton, she moved to stand in front of him, her navel at his eye level. He put his hands on her waist, and she gasped. He looked up into her face, framed by her falling hair.

"Do you know what I am, Lee Ann?"

She shook her head; the ends of her hair brushed her nipples.

"I am a vampire. Do you know what that is?"

She nodded. "I seen movies about 'em on TV."

He was unsure what she meant by the terms "movies" and "TV," but clearly she knew what he was. "I have lived for centuries, Lee Ann, and will exist for centuries more." He brushed her hair back behind her shoulders, displaying her pale breasts. "Tonight I will drink your blood. Not all of it, but enough to replenish my strength. It will not take long. It will weaken you, but not kill you. Do you understand all that?"

She nodded.

"I can make you endure it, or enjoy it. The choice is yours."

She had to swallow hard before speaking. "I don't know what 'endure' means."

He smiled. His hands traveled up her back. "Then I will make certain you enjoy it," he said, and pulled her down onto the bed.

As he'd promised, the tryst was brief, and he sent her away with a look of anguish on her young face; he had taken more than mere blood from her, and he knew she would ache for him until he deigned to summon her again.

Once she'd gone, he quickly hurried through the night to intercept the girl vampire from the warehouse. He was freshly fed and at the height of his powers; she dared not oppose him. And she would serve a purpose very different from Lee Ann's.

CHAPTER 12

THE ARM AROUND Danielle might have been a metal band, for all that her frantic struggles did to move it. The palm clamped over her mouth was cold to the touch, like the touch of the boy Leo, but whoever held her now was considerably taller. Reflexively she tried to scream, and the hand clenched until it felt as if it would crush her jawbone. She froze, all buzz from the dope gone.

 "What the *hell*, Olive?" Mark demanded, effortlessly holding the struggling woman. He shouldn't be surprised; if the air depended on Olive's good sense, they'd all suffocate in five minutes. "I can't leave you alone long enough to park the fucking truck?"

She shrugged and nodded at Billy. The boy's mouth worked silently, and his erect penis bounced up and down on its own, pumping out white fluid. "He's out of it, don't worry."

"Yeah, what about this one?" Mark nodded at Danielle. "Are you just totally blind? She *saw* you, and if I hadn't been here she would've screamed her head off by now."

Olive shrugged. "I was gonna have her join us, if you

hadn't come along." She wiped the semen from her hand with the tail of Billy's T-shirt. "I'd be the fudge between two vanilla wafers."

Danielle controlled her panic enough to evaluate her situation. She was a doctor, after all, and knew better than anyone where the human body was vulnerable. She took a deep breath, then with all her strength brought one heel down on the man's foot while her right hand clutched and then twisted his genitals.

He did not react. *At all.* It was like she had grabbed mere leather, or something that felt no pain.

"Quit that," he hissed, and squeezed her face hard for emphasis. Her TM joint clicked inside her head as it popped and she immediately stopped fighting. To Olive Mark said, "Where's Leo and Fauvette?"

"Leo's back with his white boys. I thought Fauvette was with you."

He frowned. "No, she left before we did, said she wanted some alone time and she'd meet us here." Her absence was a surprise and, after what happened to Toddy, seriously worried him. "I think just to be safe we better get out of here."

Olive stamped like a petulant child. "But we just got here! I'm not through!"

Mark sighed. "Christ on a stick, Olive, you've still got that guy in the back of the truck to go through. And we'll bring this one," he added with chilling casualness; Danielle knew he meant her. She renewed her fruitless struggles and tried to scream.

"Dammit," Mark muttered as she fought him. As if he didn't have enough to worry about. He spun her to face him, holding her by the shoulders. She drew a deep breath for a shriek. But it never emerged.

Instead she looked up into the boy's eyes and simply, completely, froze. He was handsome, sure, if young and rather soft-looking. But something seemed to reach inside her and wrench feelings that had been completely untouched for too long. It was a level of response Danielle never thought she could experience, and it hit so hard she was thoroughly incapacitated. *Aroused* didn't capture the feeling, nor did merely *horny*. It was desire that went beyond merely physical response, although it certainly included that as well, to an embarrassingly wet degree. Somehow, with no warning or explanation, pleasing this total stranger had become not only the most important thing to her, but the *only* thing. She had instantly become his willing slave, and the certainty was so total she wanted to cry.

"Not a word out of you," Mark warned when he saw the change in her expression. Danielle nodded eagerly, like a child trying to win a brutal parent's approval. She stood with her fists against her thighs as he pushed past Olive and with a single motion slammed Billy's skull back against the stone mausoleum wall. The hollow *thwock* sound made Danielle wince, and clinically she wondered if he'd seriously injured that sweet, clueless boy. But considering the lust raging inside her for her captor, she could spare no more than a passing thought about Billy. She wanted to throw herself on this tall stranger and beg him for it, but that might annoy him, and she didn't want that. No, not that, ever. Perhaps if she *crawled* to him . . .

"Hey!" Olive whined as Billy slid to the ground. "He was mine! I caught him!"

Mark grabbed Olive by the ear and lifted her onto her toes. "Go get Leo," he hissed. "We're getting out of here."

"Why?" Olive said, drawing it out in a petulant whine and swatting at him. "Because of Fauvette?"

"No, because of Toddy. Something's going on, and I don't want to be caught out in the open."

Olive pushed out her lower lip in a pout; blood trickled down her chin. "Okay, fine," she said, and Mark released her. She turned to go, but Mark spun her back and wiped her bloody lips with his hand. She grinned, delighted, and took off into the night.

Then he returned his attention to Danielle. She looked so pitiful to him, wracked with a need she could neither comprehend nor identify, that he felt sorry for her. "Look, you've really caught a bad break here," he said as he touched her cheek. She sighed, a shuddering cry that left no doubt what the contact had done to her. "You're going to die before sunrise, probably slowly and painfully, and believe it or not I'm really sorry about it. But it can't be helped."

Danielle swallowed, her breath shallow. She'd never experienced an orgasm like the one that just shot through her, and she could barely stay on her feet. "Please," she pleaded, although she could not be sure if it was for her life or for another climax like the last one.

"Yeah," he sighed. Forty years of seeing this should've rendered him more immune to it, but he still felt like a heel. Maybe someday it would no longer bother him.

Olive returned with Leonardo. "What?" Leo demanded belligerently, hands loose at his sides.

"Nobody's seen Fauvette," Mark said. "She should be here. After what happened to Toddy—"

"Will you shut up about that?" Leo said, annoyed. "That little cracker deserved what he got. No loss, if you ask me. And it *sure* ain't a good enough reason to call me off before dinner."

"Leo, think about it. Remember what the paper said? He just dropped over in an alley. Nobody staked him, nobody dragged him into the sun. And he didn't catch up on his lost years. Something weird is going on."

Even over the roar of her hormones, Danielle understood enough of the conversation to be astonished. Found in an alley, the reference to "lost years" . . . the coincidence was gigantic, but could this "Toddy" really be Todd Crealey? She gritted her teeth against the desire to touch the boy she helplessly lusted after and tried to summon the courage to speak aloud, to confirm her suspicions. She failed.

Leo scowled. "Yeah, I know," he said, his anger fading. "Crossed my mind, too. You think maybe somebody killed him in some new way?"

"I don't have a fucking clue. But until we know more, and until Fauvette shows up, I say we get back to the warehouse, take care of this girl"—he nodded at Danielle—"and lay low for a while."

Now Leo turned and looked at Danielle, far more intently than he had at the gazebo. The scrutiny terrified her anew. "Hey, who the hell are you, anyway? I know Billy and his pals. Never saw you before."

She swallowed hard. "My name's Danielle," she said.

"And what you doing here?"

She said nothing. Mark ordered wearily, "Answer him."

She struggled against the urge to blurt the truth; again she lost. "I'm looking for a new kind of drug."

Leo chuckled. "One more rich honky chick thinking she can get high with the niggers," he said darkly. "Or maybe you *are* a narc." He looked at Mark. "Ask her."

Mark met her eyes. She could deny him nothing. "Are you with the police?"

She shook her head.

"What are you?"

She tried with all her will not to speak, to lie, to do anything but tell the truth. "I'm a doctor," she said.

"Bullshit," Olive said. She patted Danielle's behind. "She ain't old enough to be a doctor, she's just a baby."

Mark sighed. This just got better and better. He rubbed his temples. "Are you really a doctor?"

"Yes." *Now please touch me,* she wanted to scream. "I'm thirty-one."

"Are you married? Boyfriend, family?"

She shook her head.

"Hell, with knockers like that?" Leo said. "She's bluffing. Somebody'll be looking for them. I mean, for her." He grinned.

"Either way, that's one more reason to get off the street," Mark said. "Come on, Doc."

They moved so quickly through the dark that if Mark hadn't taken her hand, Danielle would've never been able to keep up. As it was, she had to run, and she was too out of shape to do so easily. By the time they reached another gap in the fence and slipped through it she was drenched with sweat and her chest was on fire. If she survived this, she'd never smoke again.

They emerged onto Neptune Street, less populated than Decatur had been. The pools of darkness between streetlamps were larger, and the traffic considerably lighter. Danielle wanted to scream for help, but she couldn't do it. Holding on to Mark's hand was now her whole reason for living.

Olive sang nonsense to herself as she bounded up the sidewalk ahead of them. Leonardo dropped into step beside Mark and said, "Makes you wonder what she was like before she got turned, don't it?"

"No," Mark said.

"You really think somebody deliberately killed Toddy?"

"I know what's supposed to happen to us when we die. It didn't happen to Toddy."

"That don't mean he was *murdered*, does it? We're kind of hard to kill, you know."

Praline's screams echoed in his memory. "Not if you know how."

They went behind an antiques shop, where a battered pickup with a camper shell was parked. Olive reached it first, opened the window above the tailgate, and peered inside. "Are you still quiet as a mouse, my darling?"

In the truck bed lay a very handsome Hispanic teenager. He looked up at Olive with anguished hunger, as if he needed her permission to move or speak. She climbed onto the bumper, leaned over the tailgate, and touched his lips with her fingertips. "Soon, my doll baby, soon as we can. This'll be all over."

Mark scanned the shadowy spaces between the buildings for Fauvette. They'd planned to meet in town, just like the old days before things got so unpredictable. She'd left early, saying she wanted to get some new clothes; what the hell had happened to her? Was she sprawled in some dark corner like Toddy, to be revealed by the sunrise?

Olive closed the window and hopped down. She'd been a virgin when she died, so not only did she lack sexual experience, she had virtually no sexual feelings. Conversely, her nosferatic ability to inspire them in others was incredibly powerful, which is why she could hold this boy immobile in the truck while she amused herself with Billy in the cemetery. She maliciously loved to mimic flirtatious, teasing behavior, but had no concept of the agony she made her victims feel.

Now Olive circled Danielle and lightly ran her fingers around the bare skin at Danielle's waist. The icy tips made Danielle shiver. She brushed the hair from the back of Danielle's neck and nipped it playfully. Danielle, eyes locked on Mark, yelped in response. She wanted to scream, to run, but he'd told her *not* to . . .

"Leave her alone, Olive," Mark snapped. To Danielle he said, "Get in the back, sit down, and stay quiet."

She scurried to obey. The inside of the camper smelled of sweat, decayed meat, and the unmistakable odor of blood. She sat in the corner against the tailgate, knees drawn under her chin. She watched Mark ravenously through the stained, scratched window. The Hispanic boy beside her was breathing heavily, his erection obvious inside his tight jeans.

Leonardo put a hand on Mark's shoulder as they got into the truck. "Hey, seriously, man, relax. Fauvette's a big girl, she be okay."

"Like Toddy?" Mark snapped back.

Leonardo shrugged and scooted into the middle of the seat. Olive packed in next to him, still humming. Mark took one last look around. He envisioned Fauvette drifting from the shadows as she had when he first met her, lithe and unbelievably attractive, a mixture of scared little girl and sensual exotic danger. She would be irresistible to mortal men; she almost was to him. But she did not appear.

In the back of the truck, Danielle managed to tear her gaze from Mark. She met the eyes of the immobile Mexican and saw more terror and longing in them than she'd ever imagined eyes could express. *We're going to die*, his eyes seemed to say, *and they're going to make us want it.*

Silently, because it was the only way she could express herself, Danielle began to cry. Who were these people? What had they done to her, and how? And what would happen to her?

She tried to think it through scientifically, logically. The girl Olive seemed to have bitten Billy in the throat, and swallowed some of his blood. Was this some gang that behaved like movie vampires? And yet, if they were just kids playing games, why was she filled with desire not just to have sex with the boy driving the truck, but to grant his every wish? She'd crawl naked through broken glass without hesitation if he asked her to.

The certainty of that, coupled with the intense sexual arousal, made her wonder if the marijuana she'd smoked had been the new drug she sought; certainly something that could do this would be incredibly popular. Yet they'd all smoked it, and only she and Billy seemed to be affected. Had the tall boy somehow hypnotized her? Or was he truly so handsome, so charismatic, that her long-denied body finally overruled her common sense?

She wiped her eyes. If she died tonight, she'd never water her plants again, wash the dishes inherited from her mother, or wear those incredibly comfortable sweats she'd kept since college. No more lying in bed on Sunday with the paper and a cup of coffee. Never again would she use the cutters on a rib cage, or weigh the contents of a stomach. She wished she had taken more time to appreciate those things before.

But like a tightened watch spring, fury curled under her fear and lust, awaiting the chance to snap. If the thing they'd done to her slipped or lessened enough for her free will to function, then these monsters would learn just what a pissed-off coroner could do.

CHAPTER 13

FAUVETTE AWOKE.

Fuzzily she realized how odd that was. The way she became aware of herself each sundown was nothing like the waking she remembered from her long-ago mortality. She tried to move, and something burned and sizzled in her head. *Pain.* That was also odd. She hadn't hurt anywhere other than between her legs for half a century.

Suddenly she remembered, and understood what happened. Someone had *knocked her out.*

She sat up. Her body would mend after a night's dormancy, but now she was terrified. Where was she? How long was it until sunrise? Who was strong enough to cold-cock a *vampire?*

She had left the warehouse alone, intending to take her time before joining the others in the cemetery. The effects of the gray powder had subsided even more, and she wanted to experience the night with some of the old wonder. She had gone along Second Street past the car dealerships, flirting with lone men perusing the latest vehicles. None had appealed to her, and so she moved into the darkness toward the cemetery and . . . then nothing.

Now she lay on a wide, hard bed. A single candle burned on the nightstand, next to a telephone, a clock radio, and a Gideon Bible. That brought a grim smile; did her attacker expect the Bible to keep her from using the phone? A red light flashed intermittently on the curtains from outside the window.

She picked up the handset and almost yelped at the loudness of the dial tone. She dialed the first number to the warehouse phone, the second —

"Before you summon rescue, I'd prefer we spoke first," a new voice said.

At the foot of the bed now stood a man she'd never seen before. He radiated the kind of aristocratic air she imagined exclusive to royalty or the truly wealthy. His wavy black hair shone in the candlelight, and a neat beard and mustache bordered his mouth. His eyes were dark and inscrutable. He wore a black silk shirt buttoned all the way up and new denim jeans. Although he was not tall, he exuded power. She instantly knew he was a vampire, and that she was in big trouble.

She carefully put the handset back on the cradle.

"Thank you," he said. His voice rippled with the slightest accent, something European. "I am Rudolfo Vladimir Zginski. I have a family title, but in this world it seems extraneous. I have brought you here to acquire some information, and if you give it to me freely, there will be no need for further difficulty."

Fauvette scooted back against the headboard and drew the sheets up to her chin. She still wore the tank top and baggy bell-bottoms she'd stolen earlier, although the platform sneakers were gone. She stared, eyes big, and made no attempt to answer. She had not been afraid in so long, the feeling was actually rather intoxicating.

"And you are?" he prompted after a moment.

"Don't you know? You just whack a girl upside her head

without even knowing her name?" When it was obvious he could wait her out for a real reply, she said simply, "Fauvette."

"Lovely," he acknowledged. "*La Petite Fauvette* is a wonderful composition, for piccolo, I believe."

She shrugged. "I wouldn't know a piccolo from a pepper plant."

"You have no family name?"

She said nothing.

"Your silence merely prolongs your discomfort. Is your family name such a valuable secret?"

"My mama wasn't sure who my real father was. Said if you run through the briars, you can't tell which thorn scratched you. She put 'Gilliland' down in the family Bible."

"A bastard," he said, and his lips curled in the most minimal smile.

"Bastard's a boy. Ain't no word for a girl, except maybe 'love child,' and that sure didn't apply."

"In our world, the circumstances of birth carry little significance. Don't you agree?"

She nodded. He moved around the bed, almost gliding. The candle's flame twinkled in his dark eyes as he loomed over her, and she sank back into the pillows.

"I apologize for my rudeness," he said gently. "The ambush, the attack . . . not the conduct of a gentleman. I am in your debt after taking such liberties."

"Are you going to hurt me?" she asked in a small voice. She had not uttered those words since the night she died.

"No, I have no plans to do so, if you cooperate."

"Why did you bring me here?"

He paused thoughtfully, composing his words. "I have been . . . away . . . for a very long time. Half a century. Now I wish to regain my prior station, but to do so I must comprehend the way this new world works for our kind." He nodded at the bed beside her. "May I?"

Again she slowly nodded. He sat on the edge of the mattress. "I will not harm you, Fauvette," he said gently. "I wish you to teach me about our place in this time, about the changes in the world. I assure you, I learn very quickly, and you will seldom need to repeat things. Will you do this?"

She licked her dry lips. "Do I have a choice?"

"No," he said calmly. "Help me, or I will destroy you."

"Like you did Toddy?"

He frowned. "Who?"

"My friend. You killed him because he wouldn't help you, didn't you?" If this super-vampire had been able to sneak up on *her*, surprising the always-distracted Toddy would've been easy. All the recent events now made sense.

"I give you my word, I have killed no man since I awoke in this time," Zginski said.

She bit her lip thoughtfully. Maybe he hadn't. And if he *had*, he didn't seem the type to just dump the body where it would be found and attract attention. "Then I reckon I have no choice. I'll help you."

He nodded acknowledgment. "And in return, I will grant you any favor you wish that is within my power."

That drew a wry, humorless smile. "There's nothing I want."

He tried to delicately brush a strand of hair from her face, but it was so heavy with accumulated grime that he had to pick it up and tuck it behind her ear. When his fingertips touched her bare skin, she trembled. "My dear, not even one such as you can have everything you want. If that were true, you would not seem so sad."

"Stop calling me that," she snapped, unable to hold his gaze. "I ain't your 'dear.' I'm nobody's dear."

"I stand corrected. Well . . . sit corrected."

She glanced up, saw his smile, and risked one of her own. "Just call me Fauvette, okay? Not 'my dear,' and not ever 'Miss Gilliland.' Just Fauvette."

They both looked up as a key turned in the door. Lee Ann entered, carrying two brown paper shopping bags. She stopped when she saw Zginski on the bed with Fauvette, and for a moment jealous anger flashed across her face. Then she met Zginski's gaze and seemed to have trouble catching her breath for a moment. The ever-present glow of the sign bathed her in red, alternating with the yellow glow of the porch light.

She closed the door with her foot and walked over to the small table. "Y'all got it dark enough in here, don't you?" she muttered without looking at them. She put down the two paper bags. "These ought to fit your friend. They ain't the most stylish stuff, but at this time of night, it's hard to be picky."

"Excellent," Zginski said approvingly. Lee Ann blushed from the compliment. "Fauvette, this is Lee Ann."

Lee Ann nodded. "Hello."

Fauvette said nothing.

"Lee Ann has brought you fresh clothing," Zginski said. "No offense intended, but if you're to be seen with me . . ." He touched the tank top's shoulder strap where it was ripped halfway through. "Changes must be made. I'm sure you understand. Lee Ann will attend to you, and help you with your ablutions."

Both women looked at him oddly. "What the hell is an 'ablution'?" Lee Ann asked.

"I wouldn't mind knowing, either, if I have to have one," Fauvette said.

Zginski hid his exasperation. *Peasants*, he told himself, *remember they're peasants*. "Bathing. Cleaning your hair. Helping you dress."

Fauvette's eyes opened wide. "She's going to *bathe* me?"

Zginski answered, but his eyes were on Lee Ann. "Yes, because I wish it. She will cater to your every need."

Fauvette saw Lee Ann's expression go in an instant from

outrage through defiance, submission, and resignation.

"Sure," Lee Ann said. "Do you want a bath or a shower?"

"A bath," Zginski said before Fauvette could answer. "I suspect she will need to soak."

"Fine. I'll get it started." She opened the bathroom door and turned on the light. It cast a bright slash across the foot of the bed.

When she heard the water running Fauvette turned to Zginski. "Who is she?"

"She is my . . . I believe the closest English word is 'victim.' You may share her tonight, if you wish."

"Victim? You use the same victim more than once?"

Zginski frowned, then recalled the way he'd witnessed her feed on the boy in the bed of the truck. "Yes. It is not necessary to kill a victim each time you feed."

"But . . . if you don't, they'll tell people."

He smiled paternally. "I see there are things I may teach you as well. Your first lesson will begin tonight: you may feed on Lee Ann, but only enough to sustain your existence. I will be very upset if she is permanently harmed."

Before Fauvette could reply, Lee Ann emerged from the bathroom. She leaned wearily on the doorjamb. "The water's ready. I have lots of soap and shampoo."

Fauvette scooted across the bed and went quietly into the bathroom. Zginski scowled at the imprint of grease, dirt, and insects left on the bed. Lee Ann looked at Zginski for a long moment, but said nothing. Then she followed Fauvette.

Lee Ann closed the bathroom door. It was tight in the little space, and the smell from Fauvette quickly filled it. Lee Ann turned on the vent fan, which whined like an electrocuted cricket. "Okay, first thing is to get you out of those clothes."

Fauvette removed the jeans, then the tank top, and placed them in a plastic garbage bag Lee Ann held. She wore no underthings. Lee Ann tied the bag, opened the door, and tossed it outside. Then she gestured at the tub. "Climb in."

Fauvette tentatively stepped into the water, which came up to her ankles. Then she lowered herself all the way. A sheen of oil quickly covered the surface as it sluiced off her skin along with other debris, some of it still living. Lee Ann wrinkled her nose. "Christ, when's the last time you had a bath?"

Fauvette drew her knees to her chest and wrapped her arms around them. "Cleanliness is next to godliness, so what's the point?" When she looked up again, Lee Ann had pulled off her blouse and was stepping out of her jeans. "What are you doing?"

"I don't want to get whatever's in that water all over my clothes," Lee Ann almost sneered. In bra and panties, she knelt on a folded towel beside the tub, soaped up a washrag, and began running it roughly over Fauvette's back.

"I'm not another of his victims, you know," Fauvette said after the fifth hard scrape of the cloth across her spine. "I'm not your competition."

"Save it," Lee Ann said. "I don't know whether *I'm* feeling something, or he's making me. Maybe he wants me to be jealous, I don't know." She squeezed out the rag and applied more soap. "Man, this time yesterday I never would've believed any of this. Now look at me. Boy, was my mom right."

She rubbed the rag over Fauvette's face, revealing the corpse-pale skin beneath the dirt. She made no effort to be gentle. Fauvette turned and glared at her. "He *told* you to take care of me," she snapped.

The change that came over Lee Ann was extraordinary. She looked like a child just told her parents had died. "No, please, I'm sorry," she said urgently. "Don't tell him, okay? You can do anything to me, you can beat me up or cuss me out or piss on me or anything, just don't tell him."

Fauvette couldn't help staring. She had seen victims

aroused by vampires, but never anything like this. Somehow Zginski had inspired not only mere physical lust in Lee Ann, but something that looked, and felt, very much like *love*. The girl's expression conveyed such naked emotional need that it was almost painful to see. "I won't," Fauvette said, and looked away.

Lee Ann washed her with careful delicacy after that, even cleaning her toenails. She attended to her intimate parts with gentle discretion. Then she helped Fauvette to her feet and opened the drain, letting out water the color of slate. A gritty residue remained in the tub. "It'd be easier on you if we washed your hair in the shower," she said.

Fauvette sat on the closed toilet wrapped in a towel while they waited for the shower to warm up. Lee Ann stripped all the way, and Fauvette noticed the girl's neck was unmarked. "Didn't he feed on you?" she asked curiously.

Lee Ann put one foot on the side of the tub. On the inside of her thigh, near her groin, were two small punctures that went straight into the femoral artery. A thin trickle of blood oozed from the scab over one of them.

At the sight of the fresh bite, Fauvette suddenly felt her own hunger surge anew. She stepped into the shower, and felt Lee Ann behind her. She closed her eyes as the water cascaded over her, and stood very still while Lee Ann shampooed and rinsed her hair. She felt the girl's hot, blood-filled nude body brush against her own, and clenched her fists to keep control. Finally the water began to grow cool, and Lee Ann said, "I think we're done."

Fauvette turned to face her. "We're not done," she practically growled.

Lee Ann swallowed. She blushed beneath her sea of freckles. "He s-said not to hurt me."

"I won't," Fauvette said, stroking the other woman's face. She had not fed from a woman in years, but now the hunger, and a victim so young, beautiful, and helpless, made her ignore such considerations. "Get on your knees," she said.

Lee Ann knelt in the shower before her. With the now-icy water cascading down on her back, Fauvette tilted Lee Ann's head to one side and exposed the delicious jugular.

CHAPTER 14

THE DIRT DRIVEWAY to the warehouse wound needlessly through the overgrown field around the building, a security measure so no one could approach unheralded. Scattered throughout the weeds were various bits of mechanical debris to disable any vehicles that tried a more direct approach.

Mark parked the truck in the back next to the loading dock. In its heyday workers piled cotton bales and produce onto lines of eager flatbeds. Age and weather had long ago collapsed the tin overhang, and Mark had carefully arranged it to hide the truck in a deep pool of shadow. The battered vehicle itself completed its own camouflage.

Mark turned off the ignition and watched the cavernous dock openings. He desperately wanted Fauvette to appear from the shadows, her white skin shining like ivory, with a perfectly reasonable explanation for her no-show in town. Then they could all enjoy the two victims in the camper in a vicious orgy of sanguinary consumption. But nothing moved except the wildlife that shared the warehouse with them.

Mark opened the truck's door and climbed out. A possum

hissed at him, then scurried away into the crumbling foundation. "Fauvette?" he called.

"She ain't here, bro," Leonardo said quietly as he climbed out. He patted Mark on the shoulder with genuine sympathy. "Just accept it. She went her own way tonight, like always. It don't mean nothing. You got to stop feeling so responsible for everything. We all plenty old enough to make our own decisions about things."

Olive opened the window over the tailgate and peered inside. "Hello, my little giblets. Ready for the last night of your life?" She looked at the Hispanic boy and crooked her finger. He sat up and almost leaped from the truck, gazing rapturously at her. She cupped his groin and giggled.

"Well, most of us," Leonardo corrected.

Danielle wanted to move, too, but that would mean disobeying her new owner, and she couldn't do that. *Owner,* she thought in astonishment. The word had simply appeared in her consciousness with no forethought or choice. It certainly seemed appropriate, given how she was responding to him. Could she muster the strength of will to fight his influence?

She looked down at her foot, barely visible in the darkness, and willed it to move forward toward the open window. If she could do that, then she could move both feet, and maybe make a break for freedom. All she had to do was move her right foot, proving she could overcome her owner's commands.

Nothing happened.

All she had to do . . .

Infinitesimally, her foot slid forward, the rubber sole squeaking softly on the metal.

Mark suddenly appeared in the window. "C'mon," he muttered, and she jumped to obey, scrambling over the tailgate with the same humiliating alacrity. She stood outside the truck looking at him, desperate for his attention yet terrified of receiving it. She wondered breathlessly if he would grope her as Olive had done with her captive, and the worst part was that she *wanted* it. She *had* to break this obscene hold; whatever these kids were, she knew that continuing to follow his orders would soon prove fatal.

Olive took her young man by the hand. "Can I play with her, too?" she asked, nodding at Danielle. "She's pretty."

"What? Oh. Sure," Mark said distractedly. He turned to Danielle. "Go with Olive and do whatever she says. You're hers as much as mine now."

The sensation that followed these words was almost unbearable. Danielle felt something inside her, some emotion she never knew she possessed, wrench like a cramping muscle; suddenly the fascination she felt for this boy was now shared by the pudgy black girl, and it was both disorienting and nauseating. She knew some women enjoyed sex with other women, but she had never even considered it before, let alone with a black. Now, though, she had the same physical response for Olive that she did for Mark.

Olive knew it, too. "Ain't that a sight," she said with a grin; it displayed the elongated canines behind her full lips. "Come on, you two, it's time for all of us to get better acquainted."

Mark shoved the door aside, and it screeched on the track where he'd bent it earlier. The full moon cast long blue rectangles on the littered floor. He immediately headed toward the stairwell that led down to the boiler room. "Don't forget," he called over his shoulder, "leave some for me."

"We won't forget," Leonardo assured him.

"Forget what?" Olive asked in all seriousness.

Mark stepped into the boiler room. "Fauvette?" No response. He opened the door to the boiler itself. Fauvette's coffin was empty.

He picked his way through the rubble around it, looking for some hint where she'd gone. It didn't appear she'd taken anything in preparation for a long trip. Then again, what did a vampire truly need except a small amount of grave dirt and a place to hide from the sun? But her coffin still rested on its cinder blocks, surrounded by piles of musty, crud-covered garments.

He noticed the dust on one particular pile of clothes had been disturbed. Finger marks were plain in the dirt and grime.

He carefully poked under them, ignoring the protesting screech from a mouse nursing her young somewhere in the folds of fabric. He felt the loose edge of a metal plate, hooked his fingers under it, and lifted. The mouse shrieked as she and her brood tumbled through a hole in the boiler floor.

This exposed a small cavity in the boiler bottom. He groped inside, dislodging two large roaches and a snake, and felt a plastic bag at the far reach of his fingers. Carefully he worked it forward until he got a good grip and pulled it out.

The bag held some sort of gray powder, so light it left an ashlike film on the inside of the bag. Yet it was clearly granular, with a consistency somewhere between baby powder and salt.

A dry, musty scent escaped when he unwrapped the metal tie. He sniffed carefully, intrigued by the odor, which seemed somehow both compelling and familiar. He licked his fingertip, touched it to the powder, lifted it to his tongue, and took a quick, experimental taste.

Danielle and the boy followed Olive into the big open space of the warehouse, moving through the huge squares of moonlight on the floor. Olive danced to a nonsense tune she hummed, then stopped and looked at the two entranced victims. "Well. A pair of real beauties here, aren't you? So let's have a look at you."

She nodded at the boy. "You first. Let's see you."

The boy quickly whipped off his shirt. His chest was

sharply muscled, and his abdominals stood out in cut relief. He slid down his pants and underwear all at once, allowing his erection to bob free. It cast a significant shadow, and Olive's eyes opened wide. He kicked off his shoes and socks and stood naked except for a St. Christopher medal.

"Not bad for a white boy," Olive said. "What you think, Leo?"

Leonardo laughed from somewhere overhead. "Looks like my little brother on a cold day."

Olive turned her back to the boy and stuck out her behind. "Like this, white boy? Like a little double-dip of chocolate?"

The boy trembled so hard that when the first drops of milky ejaculation shot forth, they fanned out in a spray in the moonlight. It wasn't a full climax, just a hint of one, enough to madden him even more. Yet he did not move or speak, other than a low, keening whine.

Olive slapped her hip and strutted over to where Danielle stood, similarly immobile. "I think I'd like to see them big ol' white titties," Olive said, and winked.

Danielle managed to resist the command for a full second. Then she reached behind her neck, untied the halter, and let the front fall. She had never exposed her breasts anywhere this public, and the roiling mixture of shame, excitement, and fear made her nipples harden. She pulled the garment over her head and dropped it at her feet.

Olive stepped closer and slapped lightly at Danielle's breasts. "They ain't so big when they're flopping loose, are they?" she said with a laugh. "Big enough for you, Leo?"

Leo dropped from the ceiling beside her, landing with the barest impact and making Danielle jump. He bent down and licked her closest nipple. His tongue was as cold as his touch, and she whimpered at the mix of disgust and arousal. "More than a mouthful's a waste, isn't that what they say?" He tousled Danielle's hair the way he might pet a dog.

Olive turned to the boy. "Come on over here and give these a suck, why don't you? Then tell us what you think."

Oh, my God, Danielle thought, *he's going to put his* mouth *on me.* She watched the boy approach, preceded by his erect penis; a thick droplet dangled from it and swayed when he walked. He did not look at her face at all, only her breasts, and when he was close enough he took her by the upper arms and bent his mouth to the same nipple Leo had licked. With no preliminaries he sucked it hard into his mouth, his clumsy teenage teeth painfully raking it.

"Ahhhh!" Danielle cried, and squirmed in his grip. She watched Olive's face scrunch up in concentration, while Leo just continued to smile. The boy did not let up, sucking hard and using his tongue with apparently all his strength. Danielle wanted to beg him to stop, beg Olive to *let* him stop, but she could not muster the words. She grabbed on to his wiry forearms to keep from falling over.

"That's enough," Olive said at last. The boy pulled his mouth away with a pop, and Danielle cried out again. She cupped her breast with both hands, wincing at the pain. Even in the half-light, she could see the hickeylike bruise already forming.

She had no time to recover, though. "Okay, Snow White, on your knees," Olive said. "Show our friend a little hospitality, too."

Danielle's eyes opened wide as she realized what Olive meant. She tried with all her might to speak, to resist, to say, *"Hell,* no." Suddenly the whole room tilted, and her field of vision swung crazily. She thought she might be passing out from stress, but it was simply her legs obeying the girl's command, folding and lowering her. They seemed to be completely disconnected from her conscious will, like every other part of her body. Now she was kneeling, looking up at Olive, aware that the boy's manhood bobbed in front of her face.

She wouldn't turn to it, she wouldn't look at it, she couldn't *possibly* . . .

She turned and looked at it. It was pale in the moonlight, and the tiny droplet still hanging from it glimmered. It came closer, and then Danielle realized it was *she* who was moving, leaning toward it. She clenched her teeth and pursed her lips. She wouldn't, they couldn't make her, it was something she'd never done, not even in college . . .

She opened her mouth and swallowed the head of his cock.

Olive slipped behind the boy and pressed her breasts against his back. She stood on tiptoe to lick his earlobes and whispered, "You know what I'm thinking about?"

He shook his head.

She ran one hand through his black hair. "I'm thinking about how I wish I could see the look on your face when I do *this*!"

She bit down on the side of his neck. Her jaws crunched as they pinned his jugular against her fangs and penetrated through skin, muscle, and arterial wall.

He cried out as the mysterious control was suddenly broken and scrambled to throw her off. In the process he kneed Danielle in the head, knocking her backward onto the floor. Olive grabbed a handful of his hair and easily pushed him down, holding him in a half-crouching position, her mouth still affixed to his throat. Thin ribbons of blood leaked out and trickled down his chest, and he screamed in loud, high-pitched wails. For an instant his eyes met Danielle's and he screeched, *"Madre Dios, por favor!"*

Danielle's skull rang from the blow, and bits of glass cut into her bare back. She shook her head, almost gagging at the taste left in her mouth, and then realized with a start that she was no longer held by their vile influence. This was her chance.

Olive rode the boy down to the ground until he sprawled limp and lifeless, the black girl still attached to his neck. His eyes rolled back, and he fully climaxed as he died, his erection twitching.

Heedless of her state of undress, Danielle jumped up and ran as hard as she could for the loading dock. She could hide in the field until daybreak, and then worry about finding more clothes and getting back to town. The most important thing now was getting away from these monsters.

With no warning Leonardo appeared in front of her, dropping from the rafters overhead and landing with barely a sound. His hand was around her throat before she even saw him move, the cold fingers like iron. "Don't be a jive turkey, sweetheart," he said warningly. She grabbed his arm and fought with all her strength, kicking at his knees and groin. He merely smiled.

Olive huddled over the boy, drinking the last possible bit, until finally she released him and staggered back. She wiped the blood at her mouth with the back of her hand and tugged her tube top back into place. "Wow," she gasped. "I love them last drops." Then she looked around. "Hey! Where's Snow White Titties?"

Leonardo pushed Danielle backward until they stood beside Olive. Danielle glanced down; the boy was unmistakably dead. The only visible wounds were the two punctures at his neck, from which slight trickles ran down under the curve of his body and dripped onto the floor.

The sight sent her into a frenzy, and she teared at Leonardo's arm and fingers. Not until that moment did she fully admit the truth: these teenagers, these *kids*, were genuine blood-drinking *vampires*. And she was their second course for the night.

Suddenly Olive grabbed her chin and turned her face so that she looked into the black girl's dark eyes. "Behave yourself, honky," she said seriously.

And with an inner scream, Danielle felt the fascination reassert itself, wrapping her in desire for this child. She whined in defeat, and when Leonardo released her she didn't move.

"Be right back," Leonardo said. He grabbed the boy's body by the ankle, dragged him to the loading dock, and kicked him over the edge. To dispose of him for good they'd drive down to the riverbank and dump him after cutting him up so it looked like he'd been caught in a propeller. He'd wash up two hundred miles downstream, partially decomposed, another John Doe corpse.

For good measure, Leonardo drove his middle finger straight into the boy's heart. It wasn't as satisfying as when he did it to a white person, but that couldn't be helped.

He looked at the boy's slack face in the moonlight for a long time, pondering things that once would've made him laugh.

Mark stumbled up the stairwell, every step taking what seemed like an hour. He felt weird, lethargic, apathetic. He had never been drunk as a mortal; was this what it felt like? The idea of continuing to walk, even to *move*, filled him with both exhaustion and, oddest of all, despair. Had just the slightest touch of the gray powder done that?

He leaned against the concrete beside the door. Despite having not fed since the inept robber at his store, he felt no desire for blood *at all*. This was what had killed Toddy, and probably Fauvette as well. The decay of his lovely Princess of the Night suddenly made sense: the powder erased the hunger for blood, and somehow made the very thought of feeding appalling.

He had to warn the others. He pulled open the door and walked uncertainly into the warehouse. Olive and Leo stood around the woman from the cemetery, who was topless and understandably terrified. Distantly he recalled that she had been his victim, and they were saving her for him. Also, wasn't she someone important, a cop or lawyer or something . . . ?

"I . . . you guys . . ." he started to say. He could barely stay on his feet. Leonardo frowned at him, but Olive paid no attention.

He sighed and shrugged. "Ah, forget it. Do what you want with her." He turned and stumbled back toward the door to the old warehouse offices.

"What was that all about?" Leonardo asked after the door slammed.

"Who cares?" Olive said brightly. She pulled down her tube top and pressed her own breasts against Danielle's. "Do you like this?" Olive giggled.

"Y-yes," Danielle breathed, eyes closed. The other boy, the one who'd first enthralled her, had just made a brief appearance, but she now totally belonged to Olive. The girl's big breasts cushioned her own, the dusky skin like a cold, soft compress.

"How 'bout this?" Leonardo suddenly whispered right in her ear. She gasped as she felt his body against her back. He slipped his hands just inside the waistband of her jeans. Then she felt his lips against the skin of her shoulder blades, his hands snaking up under her arms to fondle both her breasts and Olive's. She almost sobbed, anticipating the teeth in her neck.

Olive unsnapped Danielle's jeans and slid them down her legs, kneeling as she went. She lifted one of Danielle's feet, then the other, out of the pants. She trailed her icy tongue up Danielle's leg, then bit through the thin strip of material where her panties crossed her hips. The garment slid down her other leg.

"Hey, what's this? The little butterfly's got herself a

stinger." She ripped the knife free from Danielle's calf and studied it. "Is this your favorite scalpel, Dr. Snow White Titties?" She tossed it into the darkness, where it landed with a clatter.

Danielle stood helpless, and moaned in a thin, trembling whine. This was it.

Olive turned her and knelt, cold hands massaging her rear end. "Like sucking ice cream through a straw," she said. "But that's usually sweetest."

"And make sure we leave some for Mark," Leonardo agreed. He knelt beside her, fondling Danielle's other buttock.

Danielle could not find the will to turn, and her gaze was drawn to the moon shining through the window. She whimpered as they painfully kneaded her flesh, their cold hands immensely strong. She would be bruised all over, if she lived long enough for them to form.

She felt cold lips on the soft skin of her right buttock, followed by a sharp stinging sensation. Her eyes opened wide and she let out an involuntary *"Aggh!"* She cut her eyes as far as possible to see what had happened—were they giving her an injection?—but she saw nothing in her limited field of vision. Then she felt the same thing on her other hip.

Oh, God, oh, sweet Jesus help me, she prayed. These disgusting creatures, these unhuman beings, were *biting her on the ass.*

The sharp stings faded to a dull ache, a painful sucking as they drew blood through the thick gluteus muscles. The cold lips began to warm, and something hot trickled down her leg. She whimpered again, tears of pain and fury running down her face, but she could not move or speak or resist. Their icy mouths felt like the maws of giant leeches, and the wet sounds they made as they *drank her blood* filled her with disgust.

The moon had crept several degrees along its arc by the time she looked at it again. She covered her breasts and sobbed, the pain in her rear now fading to sore numbness. She thought she heard Olive laugh, a wet, slimy sound emitted through a mouthful of blood.

She felt a cold hand slide up between her thighs. She couldn't tell which of her tormentors it was, but they sought her wet center with unerring accuracy. She gasped as her body responded, leaving her trembling on the edge of release but never quite making it.

Then with no warning Olive psychically released her. And finally she screamed.

Zginski held up his hand. "That is sufficient. I believe we have established with certainty that the world is now very complicated."

He and Fauvette sat on either side of the motel bed. They were both fully dressed. Fauvette's new clothes consisted of brown corduroy bell-bottoms and a peasant blouse that hung low and loose. Lee Ann slept between them, snoring lightly, still naked under the covers.

Fauvette folded the newspaper and said, "I reckon so."

She looked at the window. For the last hour the red light had been growing more diluted as the dawn approached. Soon—too soon—it would be sunrise. "It's almost morning," she said guardedly.

"Yes," he agreed. "Perhaps we should go to the river and watch the sunrise over the city?"

Fauvette's eyes opened wide. "You're kidding, right?"

He looked genuinely surprised. "I beg your pardon?"

"We'll burn to chitterlings in the sun."

Now he frowned. "I have no idea what a 'chitterling' is, but . . . you believe the sun will *destroy* you?"

"And you, too, smart guy. Everybody knows that."

"Where did you get such an absurd idea?"

Her certainty faltered. "Well . . . all the movies have it in there."

"The movies . . ." he repeated. Lee Ann had used that same word earlier. "What are they?"

"Moving pictures," she said impatiently. Getting him up to speed on modern terminology would take a while.

"Ah. Cinema. Films."

"Yeah, all the cinema films have it in there."

"And you never tested it for yourself?"

"Testing burning to ashes didn't seem like a good idea."

With no condescension he said, "Fauvette, please tell me. How do you believe we can be destroyed?"

She sighed. If true death waited for her at sunrise, at least it wouldn't be long. "We can be destroyed by a stake through the heart, being caught without the dirt from our graves, burning, or exposure to sunlight."

He leaned over Lee Ann's prone form, and his voice was almost kind when he took her hand. "We are most powerful in the dark, true. But the sun is always shining somewhere in the world. The sun weakens us, diminishes our powers, but it cannot destroy us."

"Yeah, well, maybe in your day that was true, but this is the seventies."

He walked around the bed and took her by the wrist. When she realized what he intended she began to struggle. "No, please, I don't want this," she pleaded. "I did what you wanted, let me *go*!"

Another guest pounded on the wall for silence. "It's six o'clock in the morning, shut *up*!"

Zginski wrapped one arm around her upper body, effectively pinned her hands, and dragged her to the window. The curtains were now white with the full glare of the sun. "No, please!" she shrieked, crying in fear.

With his free hand he yanked the curtains open.

CHAPTER 15

FAUVETTE HELD ZGINSKI'S hand as they strolled through the riverfront park. It was not a romantic gesture; Zginski was the one thing she was sure of at the moment, and she wasn't about to let him go.

Sunrise joggers passed them, causing Zginski to momentarily wonder what pursued them until he grasped the truth. On the river, a chain of barges drifted downstream, surrounded by hovering gulls. Smaller boats buzzed against the current, bouncing off of or cutting through the barges' bow waves. He tried to make out the cargo on the big flatboats, but at this distance, through the haze, all he saw were what looked like piles of refuse.

Mosquitoes and gnats hovered in shafts of light, but ignored him and Fauvette. Neither did the heat and humidity affect their essentially inert physical functions. It occurred to Zginski that not sweating would attract attention, and he began pondering ways to overcome that.

Fauvette was beyond such mundane concerns. Birds sang in the trees along with cicadas and stubborn crickets not yet ready for sleep. She had not truly heard birds sing in nearly half a century, nor had she adequately recalled the many luminous shades of green sported by leaves. The buildings shimmered in the sunrise, the light bouncing off glass windows to cast hot spots of reflection. It hurt her eyes, but she did not look away.

Zginski couldn't repress a smile at her expression of wonder. "Do you see?" he asked softly.

"Oh, yes," she breathed. He referred to the prosaic truth about the sun's effect on them, but she meant something more. For her, the world had opened in a way she thought ended with her last living heartbeat.

Earlier, when Zginski opened the curtain, Fauvette had been sure she was about to die. Since the window faced east, the sunlight came straight at her, seared her eyeballs and singed her skin. She screamed and struggled, but Zginski held her firm, and after a few moments she realized she wasn't burning, she was *warming*. Her eyes gradually adjusted to the brightness, and instead of gray cliffs of metal and concrete towering over dark glittery streets, she saw a wonderland of bright abstract shapes and hazy towers.

Zginski released her, and she walked to the glass. She put her hand flat and felt the heat against the surface. He reached past her and opened the window, and she reached out into the arms of the sun.

Now she also watched the barges drift down the Mississippi as the morning haze dissipated, and smiled like a child on Christmas morning. "I *forgot*," she said in wonder.

"What did you forget?"

"Everything. How beautiful it all is by day."

He smiled and put his arm across her shoulders. "Let's sit down," he suggested, and led her to a bench under a large pecan tree. Squirrels scampered, paused, then scampered again across the flat park ground, before disappearing up the branches of a big live oak.

"How is this possible?" she asked. "I always thought sunlight would destroy us. It's like that in all the books and movies."

"Those stories were written by the willfully deceptive, to inspire confidence in their own abilities among the ignorant masses. Priests, magistrates, philosophers. *Scientists*," he said with particular venom, recalling Sir Francis Colby. "We are no stronger than anyone else during the daylight hours, and the sun is rather hard on our eyes. But we can only be permanently killed by destruction of the heart, decapitation, or burning. Often all three, although any one would suffice. As they would for any other creature."

"What about needing dirt from our graves?"

"A luxury. A comfort, if you will. But ultimately all we really need is a regular supply of blood."

"I never knew," she said and shook her head. "Forty-five years of skulking in shadows, sleeping in coffins . . ."

He turned her chin toward him. With clean, shiny hair and suitable clothes, she could pass for his daughter. "Fauvette, how were you made?"

She told him about the old man, and about the Scoval brothers who'd raped her dead body. She explained how she awoke in her coffin and clawed her way out, found her first victim—the elder of the Scovals, who wet his pants and died begging for mercy—and left Kentucky, first for Atlanta, then other cities in the South. She lost track of current events at the end of the Second World War, although she noticed that from 1967 on it was easier to find victims on the streets.

"So you were never taught what we are, or what we can do?" Zginski said when she finished.

"No. At first I watched some movies and read some books. But I had problems accepting some things."

"Such as?"

She looked down at her hands, clasped demurely in her lap. "Well . . . I was raised in the Church. Hard-core Pentecostal. I believed that everything was either of God, or of the devil. Since I had become one of the walking dead, it was pretty clear God had denied me the comfort of His heaven. So I figured I belonged to Satan."

"Do you still believe that?"

She shrugged. "I don't know. I haven't seen much evidence of God *or* Satan." She looked away for a moment, then back at him. "Enough about me," she said with forced levity. "I'm just a Kentucky hillbilly. What about you?"

Zginski considered this for a moment. He had resolved not to repeat the mistakes that led to his imprisonment in limbo, and one of them was trusting people. Still, this girl was also of the nosferatu, and she'd demonstrated considerable integrity. Plus there was something about her, a compelling innocence that nullified his baser instincts for self-preservation.

"Very well," he said at last, with no trace of his inner uncertainty. "Do you know anything about the history of Europe?"

Fauvette shook her head.

"In 1825, a group of Russian army officers who called themselves the Decembrists attempted to prevent the ascension to the monarchy of Czar Nicholas I; they failed. Nicholas then became a fanatic opponent of revolution in *any* form, seeing in the existence of royal bloodlines evidence of the true will of God. Your Pentecostals, no doubt, would approve. He went to great lengths to protect himself, up to and including the use of magic and other arcane practices."

Fauvette nodded, even though she had no idea what every third or fourth word meant. She felt the same way talking to Mark sometimes.

"At any rate, in an attempt to consolidate his own position, he more or less bought the power of his noblemen, exchanging their right to help rule the country as a whole for an almost total control of their own lands, which included the peasantry. Thus each nobleman ruled what was essentially an independent community of slaves, much like the plantations of this very region, and left national decisions to Nicholas."

Fauvette nodded again.

"So as these events unfolded in 1841, I was in Belgium attending the demonstration of Adolphe Sax's new invention — the saxophone, it was quite popular in its time — when I heard that Nicholas had allowed the Kiselev Reforms to become law, thus freeing the peasants from individual serfdom to their lords. This had little practical effect for them, but an enormous one for me. Formerly, serfs could be bought or sold as individuals, much as slaves, but now they could only be sold collectively. So I purchased an entire village."

She blinked as the words registered. "You bought a whole *town*?"

"Not the town, the people. I was . . . ahem . . . entrusted, shall we say, with a large supply of Japanese *maki-e* artwork, smuggled out just before that country finally opened its ports to the West. It was technically the property of a Chinese shipbuilder, who was too overwhelmed with the Opium War against the British to give much thought to black market art dealing. I agreed to transport it, using my own standing as a nobleman to avoid any unnecessary scrutiny, but then decided to use it to purchase the peasants."

She frowned in concentration. His big words hid what seemed a very simple truth. "So . . . you *stole* it?"

He scowled. "In a manner of speaking. I appropriated its value, shall we say."

"And what were you going to *do* with a whole town full of people?"

"That's the clever part, if I do say so myself. I intended to take them to Ireland."

Her eyes opened wider than they had all morning. "You were going to take *Russians* to *Ireland*?"

"Yes. You must understand, no one was or is better at making an existence out of the most inhospitable conditions imaginable than a Russian peasant. Ireland was in the midst of the Great Famine, and whole areas were abandoned as the families left or died off. I intended to bring my people in, use them to stake my claim, and then when the famine ended as I knew it eventually must, I would own vast chunks of the Emerald Isle." He smiled proudly, his fangs neatly slotted beside his lower canines.

"Heck of a plan," Fauvette agreed. "So what went wrong?"

"A woman," he said simply, although the mere word did not begin to capture the feminine flesh and desire that now filled his memory. Earthy scents of loam and sweat mixed with spices and incense, and the steady rumble of blood provided the rhythm for strange incantations and malicious laughter. "One of my peasants, who claimed to be a sorceress. At first she appealed to my . . . ahem . . . physical senses, but she was a *vyrдolak*, a vampire who sought the blood of those she loved best. That was the source of her apparent supernatural powers."

"I didn't know there were different kinds of . . . us."

"There are not, really. It's a matter of self-identification. She was what she believed herself to be. And, like yourself, she had an imperfect knowledge of her own nature."

Fauvette scowled, annoyed by his vaguely condescending tone. "So she turned you into a vampire?"

He nodded. "Eventually. And I believe, inadvertently. She did not feed on me, because it was not I that she best loved, a fact I ignored out of mistaken belief in my own cleverness. She merely used me to acquire power within her own tribe, as the favored companion of their purchaser. Unknown to me, she positioned herself so that all pleas had to pass through her before they reached me."

He paused, sorting through feelings he'd thought long extinguished. "When I discovered this, and confronted her and her lover"—and again a memory, of the hairy young Cossack's mocking laughter, his neck marked by *her* fresh bite, came to him with surprising vividness—"that was when she killed me. She did not intend to make me as she was, but as you can see, things did not go as she intended."

"But you didn't become a *vyrðolak*."

"No. That is a choice, not a state of being. Fortunately this occurred as we crossed the Austrian-Hungarian countryside, so the local folklore provided me with all the necessary information about my new condition. I learned I can appear as mist, as a wolf, as a shadow within a shadow, or as you see me now. I can summon the storms and the beasts that prowl the night. And I never practice . . . trust."

"Can you turn into a bat, too?"

He blinked in surprise. "A *bat*? Why on earth would I want to?"

"Well, I mean, in all the books and movies . . ."

"A bat is a rodent, like a rat or mouse. I can certainly command their actions, but to *become* one would be rather undignified."

She shrugged, annoyed at both his disdain and her own provincialism. "And that was over a century ago?" she said at last.

He nodded, and for a moment his voice turned wistful. "For men time is a river, with a beginning and an end. For us it is an ocean with an infinity of shores. It is often difficult to measure the progress of a journey with no end." He smiled and shrugged. "But no matter."

Fauvette nodded, but inside she wondered how much of this was true. Could he really transform into a wolf, or summon a storm at will? And if he could . . . could he also teach her to do it? After all, he was right about the sunlight. "So how did you end up here?"

"Ah, that is interesting. And there are parts of the story I do not yet know or fully understand. One man truly defeated me, long ago, in the hills of Wales. Sir Francis Colby." He produced the crucifix dagger from his pocket. "He drove this into my heart, believing its nonsensical religious significance would destroy me. It did stop me, and sent me into oblivion as he wished. However, I was revived when the object was finally removed, after much time had passed."

"You got a *knife* in the *heart* and it didn't kill you?" she said with disbelief. "Why?"

"I do not know for certain. I believe, based on what I know of our physiology, that the dagger was simply too thin and sharp to do enough raw damage. But I do not know for sure, and may never know."

She licked her lips and leaned close. Quietly she asked, "Did you go to hell?"

He could think of no way to describe the terrifying void in which he'd spent the previous sixty years. It was certainly not the prosaic hell taught of in Christianity. "Yes," he said simply. "But it was not as the Bible described it."

"And how long were you there?"

"I was sealed in a coffin for almost sixty years. I awoke only days ago."

"Wow." She started to reach for his hand, but caught herself and shook off the sympathy. "Well, at least you had some money stashed away."

He smiled. "No, my dear, I had no money."

"Then how did you afford that motel room and all these clothes?"

"I am a predator. I take what I want."

"Oh," she said in a small voice.

"May I ask *you* another question?" he said. "I first observed you in the alley behind that social club near your warehouse. You appeared . . . ill. I assumed that was the reason you kept feeding until your victim died."

"You were spying on me?"

"I was observing you. You were the first vampire I encountered, and your conduct was so odd it attracted my attention."

"Oh, and I suppose you don't ever kill your victims?" she snapped defensively. "You just brainwash them like that girl at the motel?"

His tone remained smooth. "In one sense I suppose I am like a *vyrðolak*. I wait for approval, tacit or otherwise, from the young ladies on whom I feed. And judging from the response of my current paramour, Lee Ann, that consent is much easier to obtain now than in Victorian times. But I have also found that blood given freely is the sweetest blood of all." He turned serious. "Despite your valiant effort, I have not forgotten my earlier question. What was wrong with you that night?"

She shrugged. "I was just tired, I guess. And then Toddy gave me some of this gray powder, and it made me even more depressed."

"Gray powder?"

"Yeah, like sugar or something, except it tasted bitter."

"You consumed it?"

She nodded.

"And if *affecteð* you?"

She nodded again. "I don't know how to describe it, it just kind of made the hunger go away, so I didn't want blood anymore. And it also made me feel more . . . aware of myself. In a bad way. I *felt* like a real walking corpse, like something dead, unclean, un*holy*. So I stopped caring."

Zginski leaned closer, his concern obvious. "Where did your friend acquire this gray powder?"

"He never told me. Then he died."

"He *ðieð*? How?"

"He just . . . died. They found him one morning in an alley, dead. Mark said he read it in the paper. He still looked like he did when he first became one of us, so it attracted a little attention."

"Had he also consumed this gray powder?"

"Yeah. It didn't seem to depress him like it did me."

Zginski frowned in thought. The greatest danger vampires faced was discovery by a world quite content to deny their existence. If this substance caused vampires to drop dead almost willingly, it was a threat to them all, including his biggest priority, himself. "Do you have any of this powder left?"

She nodded. "I have some back where I sleep, at the warehouse."

"Will you take me there?"

She bit her lip before answering. "Uh . . . Mark, he's kind of our leader, doesn't like it when strangers show up."

"I will deal with him."

"No, that's not what I mean, I just mean he . . . worries a lot. But I suppose you have to meet him sometime."

Zginski stood and offered Fauvette his hand. His smile was warm, friendly, and genuine, with no hint of his true thoughts. He would learn more about this gray powder and, if necessary, eliminate any who knew of it, including Fauvette. But all that could wait a bit. "Fauvette, you have helped me immensely. As a reward, we will wander the streets of this Memphis just as Antony and Cleopatra might have done their own, and judge the qualities of people as they did. Then we will go to your warehouse before sundown, so that we may be there to greet your friends when they emerge, and learn the truth of this gray powder."

She wanted to insist that she go to the warehouse first and explain things to the others, but he held her eyes until she nodded. For a moment Fauvette had relaxed, believing Zginski liked and trusted her; but now she knew she was as much his prisoner as if he held her in a cage.

CHAPTER 16

THEY EMERGED FROM the park and strolled down the sidewalk as the streets filled with early-morning traffic. Few people actually worked in downtown Memphis, so the grid-lock was brief and intermittent. For Zginski the noise and stench from the combustion engines was overwhelming, worse than even the coal-burning furnaces he remembered in European cities. That smoke had been heavy and almost tangible; this was thin and scalding. He wondered what evo-lutionary changes man might make to continue existing in such filth.

Still, he got no sense of wild joy from these vehicles the way he did riding with Lee Ann. These drivers looked sullen and miserable, as if resisting the urge to speed from place to place, hair blowing and music turned up loud, had killed something fundamental in them.

Fauvette discreetly observed a pair of prostitutes totter-ing down the street, talking animatedly about their night just like any other workers at the end of their shift. Both gave Fauvette a cursory, contemptuous glance. They assumed she was a runaway teen with her first john, and it was never too early to defend your territory. If they'd known she was merely entranced by the colors of their spandex and sequins, they would've been even pissier.

At the corner, the headline inside a newspaper rack proclaimed *Joint U.S.-Russian Space Flight On Schedule*. Zginski knelt to peer through the machine's scratched plastic window. An illustration showed a spiderlike craft against a background of stars, with a hammer-and-sickle on one side and an American flag on the other. It took several moments for the story to register on Zginski's consciousness, and when it did, he felt his stomach drop. Man had *left the planet*. America was now going into space on a regular basis, and apparently the Russians were there as well. Technology had leaped so far he could now barely comprehend it, and for the first time he wondered if he could ever truly fit in again, let alone regain his previous stature in society.

Fauvette watched a pigeon land on the sidewalk to peck at a discarded half donut. The birds lived in the warehouse, of course, and she'd seen them startled from their sleep many times. But this was the first time she could recall seeing one going about its normal business, head bobbing in blank-faced determination. It struck her as incredibly beautiful.

"Hey, other people might want a paper, too, y'know," said a wide-shouldered black man clad in stained coveralls with CITY WORKS DEPARTMENT stenciled on the front pocket. He scowled in annoyance, clearly used to his physical size doing most of the work of intimidation.

Zginski stood and faced the man with narrowed eyes. "Did you speak to me?" he said in a tone of supreme, complete authority, despite being a good eight inches shorter.

It had the expected effect. "You need to borrow fifteen cents, is that it?" the man said, sarcasm dripping from the words. "Nothing smaller than a twenty-dollar bill in your pockets? Well, maybe you shouldn't come downtown where the po' folks are."

Fauvette took Zginski's arm. "Come on, let's go—"

Zginski did not move, but merely fixed his gaze on the bigger man. "I am not finished," he said through tightly clenched teeth. "When I am, then *you* may have access to this machine."

The man's eyes opened wide in surprise, hostility, and amusement. A fight was clearly what he wanted. "Hey, you think you be Jerry Lawler or something?"

By now a half-dozen people surrounded them, most black, all amused at Zginski's impending smack-down. "You should treasure your ability to speak to me this way," Zginski said, his voice barely loud enough for the man to hear. "You should look upon this moment as a gift from your tribal gods."

"Tribal gods?" the black man said, now puzzled as well as angry. "The fuck you talking about, honky mofo?"

"I'm sorry, he's from Europe," Fauvette said, still trying to tug Zginski away.

"He's about to be from my motherfucking-foot-in-his-ass Arkansas, when I kick him across the river."

"You're making a scene," Fauvette whispered to Zginski. She did not want to die on the first morning she'd seen a sunrise in almost half a century.

Zginski fought to control his temper. It was one thing to accept in the abstract that people of inferior races now behaved with impunity, but another to confront it so unexpectedly. He craved the confrontation, if only to force the big Negro to his knees where he belonged. But Fauvette was correct, drawing this much attention was dangerous.

Without a word Zginski turned and strode away down the sidewalk, tugging Fauvette behind him. The man's laughter rang in his ears, quickly joined by the other bystanders'. They turned the corner and continued down two more blocks before Zginski finally turned left into an alley, yanking Fauvette after him.

She twisted from his grip and snapped, "*That* was brilliant."

He whirled to face her. The rage in his eyes made her gasp. "That primitive had no right—"

"*Yes, he did!*" Fauvette hissed. "The world isn't like it was sixty years ago! Skin color doesn't matter anymore, everyone has the *same* rights. Now get a hold of yourself!"

His glare intensified, and suddenly Fauvette's knees wobbled as a surge of physical need for him swelled within her. She practically leaped into his arms and hungrily kissed him before even knowing her body was in motion. The pain she knew she'd feel if they consummated this moment was nothing against the agony of not feeling him inside her.

Then like a switch it was gone, and she was gazing into his eyes, breathing like a goldfish discarded on a countertop. "Never forget your place," he said in a soft, dangerous whisper.

She felt tears run down her face. "You bastard, I've tried to help you," she whimpered, the physical effects of his power taking far too long to fade. "You didn't have to do that."

He continued to glare at her, but she noticed something new and unexpected as well—he looked *tired*. The effort of controlling both himself and her had worn him out. She pushed him away, and he did not resist.

"That was unfair, and mean, and creepy," she continued, wiping her eyes. Her lips still tingled from the kiss. "I am not your victim. If you want to yank some girl's chain, go back to the motel."

" 'Scuse me, little miss, is this fella botherin' you?" a new voice said.

They both turned in surprise. A police car was parked at the far end of the alley, and one of the officers sauntered toward them, his uniform armpits already stained from the heat. He had short blond hair, a thick mustache, and the cocky air of a schoolyard bully. He looked muscular enough to bench-press his patrol car. "You know this fella?" he added.

Fauvette wiped roughly at her eyes. "Yes, sir, I know

him," she said in her best little-girl voice. "We were just arguing. He's not bothering me."

The cop's name tag read BARKER. He looked down his nose at Zginski with a half smile, and disdainfully flicked a strand of Zginski's long hair. "This your father?"

"No," Zginski said. It was only one syllable, yet loaded with complete contempt.

Barker's smile faded. "You best learn the words 'yes, sir' and 'no, sir,' you plan on hanging around Memphis too long," he said. "I got a funny feeling about you. Let's see some ID."

Zginski looked blank. "I beg your pardon?"

Before either Fauvette or Zginski could react, Barker slammed Zginski back against the wall, the nightstick pressed across his throat. "You're going for a little ride to the station, smart-ass. Trolling for illegal poontang, and I'm betting this little sleaze pot is a runaway, too."

Zginski, startled, reached up to grab the stick and was about to hurl the man across the alley when Fauvette suddenly spoke up. "Officer?" she said in a small voice.

Both men looked at her. She had her chin down, and her big eyes looked up at him pitifully from beneath her bangs. She had tugged down the front of her blouse so that the adolescent curves of her breasts were exposed. "He wasn't hurting me," she said, fixing her eyes on the cop. "But if you'll let us go . . ." She nodded toward the dark space behind a nearby Dumpster.

Barker smiled, and then looked puzzled as Fauvette's daylight-weakened but still potent nosferatic powers took hold of him. He released Zginski, punctuating it with a little shove to remind him who was in charge, then waved an okay sign at his partner down the alley.

"I'll meet you around the corner in front of the movie theater," Fauvette whispered to Zginski, her eyes locked on Barker. Zginski clenched his fists to control himself, then turned and stalked away. Fauvette led the cop into the shadows.

On the next street Zginski found the theater she'd mentioned. The Malco sported a wedge-shaped marquee visible from either direction on the street, announcing an "early bird summer matinee double feature." Although he was furious, the vivid posters behind the glass penetrated his rage and got his attention.

One was for a film called *Vanishing Point*. Printed across the top was the line, "Tighten Your Seat Belt. You Never Had a Trip Like This Before." The image showed a stylized circle of young people in what looked like ritual ecstasy, clad in odd clothes and holding what seemed to be musical instruments. Bursting through the center was a modern automobile, surrounded by streaks to indicate motion.

The second poster, though, pushed aside all thought of his earlier encounters with the peasantry and focused his attention where it needed to be, on his immediate problems. It showed a hirsute Negro with his mouth open, displaying the unmistakable fangs of a vampire. He was about to drive them into the throat of a lovely young white woman in a nightgown.

Blacula, the poster proclaimed. "Dracula's Soul Brother!" ran the blurb across the top.

He lost track of how long he stared at the poster before Fauvette appeared beside him. Her hair was disheveled and her eyes blazed with fury. "We should *really* get you off the street," she snapped, "until I can explain some things to you, like how to talk to cops."

"So you finished that arrogant constable?"

"If you mean by 'finish' that I gave him a blow job to get him to go away, yes," she said bitterly. "I hate doing that, you know." And it was no understatement; once she, the backwoods good girl, had grasped the concept of fellatio, she spent three years doing little else to lull her victims before killing them. The power it gave her over men made her head spin, until she realized she could get the same result without touching them, and without the disgusting smells and aftertaste.

Zginski was too distracted to notice her mood. He tapped the glass over the *Blacula* poster. "We must see this cinema."

She did a double take at the poster. "You're kidding, right?"

"No," he said firmly.

"Why?"

"Because I need to understand how this era expects beings like ourselves to behave. If this is a serious attempt at showing a vampire in this modern world, I *must know*."

"But you said everything the movies told me was *wrong*," she pointed out.

"They were wrong about *us*, yes. But they will show us exactly what the *mortals* currently believe about us."

"I suppose I have to go, too?" she sighed.

"Of course."

"Great," she muttered as they went to the ticket window. No matter how powerful he was, she had almost reached her limit of being Zginski's pet.

CHAPTER 17

DANIELLE OPENED HER eyes. The sunlight blinded her, and she quickly closed them again.

Every part of her body hurt. Each joint, even the hinge of her jaw, felt clogged with ground glass. She tried to move, but the pain made her stop, and she managed only a pitiful whimper.

She took a moment to sense the world around her. She lay facedown, and felt hard concrete all along her body, which meant she was still naked. Her hips from waist to knees felt numb and sore, particularly her buttocks, although for the moment her scrambled memory could not recall why. Her mouth was excruciatingly dry, and her head thundered like buffalo wanted out of her skull. She smelled the odors of decay, garbage, and metallic by-products like oil and gasoline. She was also, despite the summer heat and the sunlight evidently shining on her, very cold.

Again she tried to move, but she simply lacked the energy to overcome the pain and numbness. She sought a diagnosis, an explanation of the symptoms, but her disjointed brain just wouldn't work on that level. With a long, soft whine of surrender, she allowed herself to pass out again.

For an early-morning show the theater was surprisingly full, mostly with black people. Zginski and Fauvette sat in the last row, which gave them a good view of both the screen and the sea of Afros and caps before them. Zginski was too absorbed by his own thoughts to sense the tension around them; Fauvette heard comments pass among the other patrons about the "crazy honkies" in the back row and slid down in her seat as people turned and glared at them.

At last the lights dimmed and the red velvet curtains drew back. The scratched trailer for snacks in the lobby appeared, accompanied by tinny, blaring music. Then the screen filled with a huge ampersand against the sky and the words "American International presents."

As *Blacula* began, Zginski was enthralled not so much by the story, but by the sheer intensity of the visual presentation. The cinemas he recalled were indistinct, dreamlike experiences in flickering shades of gray; this was in perfect detail, glorious color, and, most amazingly, featured the *voices* of the characters. The actor playing the Negro prince, especially, had a rich, full, and commanding baritone. Compared to Zginski's memories of silent films, this was like looking through a window on the affairs of giants.

He realized the gray-haired man treating the black prince with contempt was supposed to be Count Dracula, the titular villain of Stoker's famous novel. Zginski had read the book, of course, and been impressed with its accuracy. He certainly never pictured the Count as this foppish, hamfisted buffoon.

Then Dracula's vampire followers appeared, looking like befanged refugees from a bad primary school production of *A Midsummer Night's Dream*. Zginski's chuckles grew louder. When Dracula evidently drew out all of the black prince's blood in an instant, Zginski began to laugh in earnest, big guffaws that echoed in the theater and caused many angry faces to turn toward him.

"Will you *shut up!*" Fauvette hissed. "They think you're laughing at the hero!"

With great effort Zginski controlled himself. After this introductory scene the titles began, weird animation that reminded him of Dr. Wiene's German film about the carnival hypnotist. After that, he sat in silence, mouth open, unable to believe what he was seeing. The vampires presented in this film were ludicrous in both their appearance and behavior. The female vampire racing in slow-motion toward the camera might frighten a nervous child, but no one else. Yet there was no hint that these proceedings were intended to amuse; for all intents, the story was grimly serious, and the depiction of vampires meant to terrify.

Not that it frightened the audience around him. As Fauvette said, they saw the black prince as a hero, and whenever he took a life they cheered and catcalled at the screen. Conversely, they also cheered whenever the mortal Negro protagonist was rude to his white superiors. It took a few occurrences before Zginski understood this: they simply enjoyed it when any black character triumphed over any white one. He wondered if this film was, in fact, made by Negroes for their own kind, or was it a white enterprise designed to give them a vicarious outlet for their passions.

And yet, despite the foolishness, the African prince-turned-vampire earned Zginski's sympathy. Here was a man who was a ruler in his own kingdom, turned revenant against his will and, like Zginski, locked away in a coffin without benefit of being truly dead. Like Zginski, he emerged ravenous and seized on the first source of blood he found, although Blacula was not careful enough; discarded like so many empty wineskins, his victims formed a veritable band of vampires without his knowledge or interest. Zginski, at least, was pickier about his companions and far more careful with his victims.

Finally, though, the black prince was undone by the sentimental weakness of love. Dispirited, defeated, he staggered into the sunlight, denying his enemies the satisfaction of dispatching him. The ending brought a chorus of "boos!" from the crowd.

Beside him, Fauvette huddled in the stiff seat, knees drawn to her chin, softly crying. Despite all that had happened to him, and all the evil things he had done, the black prince had known love, both as a mortal and as a vampire. In that sense he was blessed. She felt the pain of his loss in the great unloving, unloved emptiness of her own heart.

That brought up the memory of the gray powder's deadening peace. If she'd had the bag with her at that moment she would've consumed it all, Zginski be damned. So what if it meant her final destruction; what purpose did her empty existence serve anyway?

She risked a glance at Zginski. He was enraptured by the images on the screen. She felt even more alone.

Then the second feature started. Bulldozers rumbled up to block a desert highway. Grim, dusty people watched from nearby buildings. And at the first roaring engine, Zginski sat up, eyes wide.

He had some trouble following the story; the time frame seemed to be disjointed, so that scenes from the past followed those from the present. Yet the individual sequences enthralled him, especially those that featured the main character's automobile in action eluding the constabulary. The Polish driver seemed to be one with his vehicle, handling it with calm efficiency even in the direst of circumstances, much as the great Towarzysz Husaria horsemen had once done.

In the driver's travels, Zginski also saw an America he'd never imagined: flat arid landscapes, verdant mountainsides, ocean-pounded beaches. The Pole did not move among the upper classes, but navigated with impunity through the dregs of society, both white and colored. A black man spoke into machinery that transmitted his voice to the hero through the same device Lee Ann's car sported, and Zginski went colder than normal at the memory of Sir Francis's signalman broadcasting his demise that long-ago day in Wales. A woman lived naked in the desert, her display of flesh considered neither unseemly nor even unusual. People had all sorts of motorized transportation devices, some with only two wheels like bicycles.

He grew more confused as he watched. Was this Pole actually driving through the same world, the same culture, that had also produced *Blacula*? Could one time period contain such disparate concepts as old-world superstitions and up-to-date vehicular technology? Or had society stratified into those who believed the ludicrous suppositions of *Blacula* and those who strove for the mechanistic future world implied by *Vanishing Point*? If so, then where would he, Zginski, belong? For that matter, in which world was he *now*?

And then, the end: car and driver, in a last act of defiance or madness, crashing full speed into the bulldozers seen in the first moments of the film. No triumph, no explanation, just an end that seemed inevitable. The point had vanished, indeed.

And in the silence following, the voice of one patron, speaking no doubt for many: "Say *what*?"

The auditorium doors opened, sending bright shafts of sun down the aisles. The overhead lights came on. The audience members filed out, muttering and laughing, many of them pausing to glare at Fauvette and Zginski. No one said anything, though, for which Fauvette was immensely grateful.

"Can we go now?" she said wearily. "I'm exhausted."

"Yes, we shall return to the motel. Then we shall rest until evening, when we will meet your friends."

She put a hand on his arm before he could stand. "Wait a minute. I want you to promise me something. I know you can kill us all. I know you'd kill me without a second thought. But I want you to promise you won't."

"Kill you?"

"Kill *them*."

He smiled at her utterly serious expression. "And what would my word be worth to you?"

"I'm betting a lot. I think that under that arrogance you might still have a shred of honor. These people are my friends, and if they die because of me, I'll be forced to seek justice for that. Which means I'll die, too, I'm not kidding myself. And I don't want to, not like that, not after all this time. So I'm asking for your word that it won't come to that."

Zginski couldn't hide his surprise. The strength of her conviction, emanating as it did from a young teen's body, took him off guard. He saw no need to point out that she was wrong, that his honor had died when his physical self did and his priorities, now as always, extended very little past his own skin. Instead he nodded and said, "Very well. They will come to no harm through me." In a pinch, he could always claim that he actually meant "k-n-o-w" instead of "n-o."

CHAPTER 18

ZGINSKI UNLOCKED THE motel room door. It was hotter inside than out, although heat had no effect on him or Fauvette. Lee Ann sat in the middle of the bed still naked, the sheets wrapped around her, crying softly.

He closed the door and said sternly, "What's wrong? Why are you still in bed, we've been gone for hours?"

"Because I can't get out of it," she whined. She had the collapsed, defeated look of a prisoner of war.

"What do you mean?" he snapped, and she winced as if from a blow.

"I *mean,* you didn't tell me I could get up," she whimpered. She glowed with sweat and the smell permeated the room. "I'm starving, I'm dying of thirst, and I *really* have to pee, but I can't get off the bed."

"Attend to yourself," he said absently, closing the curtains. Although the sun was now behind the building, the early-afternoon light was still intense and he was weary of it. Lee Ann clutched the sheets around her and rushed into the bathroom; a moment later they heard her immense sigh, followed by the sound of her urination.

Fauvette crossed the room, closed the bathroom door,

and stood against the wall, arms folded. She was truly tired as well, but there was no way to return to her coffin and rest. "You're mean to her."

"Yes, that was thoughtless," he agreed. "I had no idea her will was so weak. Perhaps she will not do as a long-term companion after all."

"What will we do until dark?"

"First we will feed," Zginski said. "Then we will rest."

"Rest here? What, in the *bed*?"

He nodded. "It has its dangers, but with Lee Ann on hand, we should be safe enough." Anyone discovering them in true rest would think that they were dead bodies, so it was useful to have a mortal human to stand watch. Not that he could count on Lee Ann's resourcefulness or initiative, apparently.

Lee Ann emerged from the bathroom, the sheet now tied under her arms. She was still sniffling, and her eyes were red from crying. "So where did you go?" she asked demurely.

"You do not question," Zginski said, and Lee Ann's demeanor again crumpled. She sat on the edge of the bed, head down, her shoulders trembling.

Fauvette scowled at Zginski and went to Lee Ann. "I'm sorry. We went to a movie. We should have left you . . . freer."

Lee Ann nodded. "It would've been nice. Is this what it'll always be like?"

"I don't know," Fauvette said.

Zginski took off his shirt. His skin was pale, his body lean and hard. There were rapier scars from his mortal life across his chest, and what looked like a burned emblem, a brand, that had been obliterated by a second, later burn. "Come, Lee Ann," he said as he sat on the other side of the bed. His meaning was instantly clear.

"Oh, God," Lee Ann whimpered.

"Not yet," Fauvette said. She traced a finger along Lee

Ann's still-perspiring face and neck, around the bite she'd left there earlier. "She needs a shower."

"What?" Zginski said blankly.

"Look at her; she's been sitting in her own sweat all day. Let her clean up a little first." She took Lee Ann's hand. Lee Ann looked apprehensively at Zginski.

Zginski shrugged. "If you wish."

Fauvette pulled Lee Ann to her feet and into the bathroom. "And turn on the air conditioner," she said before the door closed on them.

Fauvette pulled off her own shirt. "Set the water however you like, it doesn't matter to me."

"You can't tell the difference between hot and cold?" Lee Ann said, twisting her hands together nervously.

"I can, it just doesn't matter," Fauvette said, slipping the jeans down her legs.

Lee Ann started the water and, as they waited for it to warm up, said, "Are you going to kill me?"

Fauvette shook her head. "I'm just trying to be nice. You were nice to me before."

"B-but you . . . you *drank my blood* before."

"Did it hurt?"

"A little, at first. Then I felt really tired afterward." She stuck her hand into the water to check the temperature. "But you . . . I mean, vampires . . . you kill the people you suck blood from, don't you?"

"I always figured we did," Fauvette said wryly. "But lucky for you, *he* looks at it differently."

"Differently how?"

"What do you know about him?"

"He left some papers on the nightstand. I got so bored I read them. They talked about how he was killed in Wales or Welshland or someplace. Is that true?"

"As far as I know."

"Then he can be killed," she breathed in disbelief.

"Everyone can," Fauvette agreed.

Lee Ann's hope faded almost at once. "But not by me. I can't even fight him enough to go to the bathroom."

Fauvette smiled faintly. "Lee Ann, I'm sorry. This must all be very difficult for you, and I should've stood up to him more for your sake."

"But you're just like him."

"No, we have a lot in common, but he doesn't care any more about me than he does you." She ran her fingers through Lee Ann's hair, longer and finer than her own. "I guess that makes us sisters, of a sort. Now check that water again."

It was warm enough, so Fauvette followed Lee Ann into the shower. When Lee Ann reached for the soap, Fauvette stopped her hand. "It's my turn to do you."

Fauvette picked up a rag and began washing the taller woman's back. She was careful and gentle, especially around the bites on her neck and thigh, as she continued to the rest of her body. She caressed her with her other hand, not sexually but with soft, slow strokes along her arms, hips, and legs.

"The water's getting cold," Lee Ann said finally.

"Then we're done," Fauvette said, and stood on tiptoes to kiss her on the cheek. "Let's get you dried off now."

Lee Ann turned off the water, and the two women stepped from the shower. Fauvette took a towel from the rack and, beginning with her hair, rubbed Lee Ann dry. "Can I ask you something?" Lee Ann said. "How old are you?"

Fauvette did not pause in her work. "What year is it again?"

"1975."

"Reckon I'm closing in on sixty, then."

"How old were you when . . ."

"Fourteen."

"And you'll always look like you do now?"

"I suppose."

"That's pretty cool." She said it in the same defeated, limp way, but her admiration was apparent.

"I suppose," Fauvette repeated after only a slight pause.

"You're real pretty."

"Thanks."

When they were both dry, Fauvette again took Lee Ann's hand and led her into the other room. The air conditioner had made little dent in the heat, but for Fauvette what was important was that Zginski had turned it on at her command. The two naked women stood before him holding hands while he inspected them with blatant appreciation from the bed. He was still shirtless, and had also removed his shoes. Fauvette suddenly recalled the forced kiss in the alley and realized, despite herself, that he was a supremely attractive man in ways that had nothing to do with his ability to overpower her. Her body tingled in response to his scrutiny.

In her mind, she repeated a phrase she'd heard Leonardo use on occasion. *Eyes on the prize, girl.* He'd kill her in an instant if it suited him. Right now she wanted him to think her as weak and helpless as Lee Ann.

"This is a sight many a man would savor," he said. "Alas, my need is too great for such a luxury." He gestured to the bed. "Come to me, Lee Ann."

"She needs to eat something," Fauvette said. "Look at her."

"No, that's okay," Lee Ann said to Fauvette. Then she crawled onto the bed and stretched out beside him. She snuggled into his embrace, and he brushed the hair from her neck, revealing Fauvette's earlier bite mark. She ran her hands over his chest and shoulders, suddenly breathing heavily.

"You are a beauty, Lee Ann," he whispered. "You command the attention of all men who see you. All would envy me if they knew of your presence in my arms. Your beauty gives you such power."

"You're so cold, Rudy," she whispered. "Can you feel me touch you?"

"I can feel every living inch of you," he replied softly.

She sighed with arousal. His hands traveled lightly over her skin.

"I chose you for your exquisiteness," he continued, but his eyes met Fauvette's. She remained beside the bed, heedless of her nudity, working hard to keep her expression neutral. "I treasure your charms because they are given freely, without any resistance."

"Yessssss," Lee Ann breathed in response. "Oh, yes . . ."

He slid down the bed until he was on his stomach between her legs. She moaned and tossed in anticipation. He lifted the thigh he'd bitten before and positioned himself over the same marks. When his mouth closed around it Lee Ann's body jolted like she'd been shocked and her hands clutched at the mattress.

Whether deliberately or not, Zginski's seduction of Lee Ann had also affected Fauvette, and she now needed the same thing he did. Her plan, tenuous at first, began to coalesce as she crawled onto the bed and reclined beside Lee Ann. The girl looked at her with wide eyes, breathing in rapid gasps as Zginski's mouth made soft, wet sounds against her thigh, and Fauvette's cold body molded itself against her. She was both terrified and aroused at being the center of all this attention.

Fauvette stroked Lee Ann's face and smiled. "You won't die, I promise," she whispered to the fear in the girl's eyes. "We both need you too much right now. *Sister.*"

Then Fauvette gasped, too, as Zginski's hand traveled up her leg. In the tangle of limbs he might have simply mistaken her for Lee Ann, but knowing that did nothing to still the unfamiliar tremor that ran through her. His power was so great she responded even when it was inadvertent.

She turned Lee Ann's head to one side, exposing her

neck. The tiny scabs were soft now from the shower. "He's right, you *are* beautiful . . ."

"Are you going to bite me, too?" Lee Ann managed to ask.

Fauvette pressed herself against the girl's hot, full body. "Yes, ma'am," she said.

And when Fauvette put her cold lips to her own previous bite, Lee Ann experienced a sexual release greater than her simple mind ever imagined.

Danielle awoke again. The light was no longer shining directly on her through the broken glass, but the heat was murderous. She was thirstier than she'd ever been in her life, and weaker than she would've thought possible. Yet this time she was able to get her hands beneath her body and lift her torso enough to look around.

She met the eye sockets of the dead hobo, fiddle still clutched in his hands. She'd seen many corpses in a similar state, so this did not frighten her. Nor did the flies buzzing around it, or the maggots visible in places where the skin allowed access to what remained beneath it. The stench made her gag, but that was a response to her overall nausea more than anything else.

She turned her head the other way. The wall beneath the window was streaked with old, dried blood in a pattern she easily recognized as an arterial spray. Someone's throat had been cut near the very spot she now occupied, and she grabbed her own throat to verify the wound hadn't been hers. But her skin remained intact.

The agony had now localized in her hips, specifically the big gluteus muscles of her rear end. She looked back and saw that it was literally purple, a mass of bruises radiating out from central spots on each cheek. Those spots each sported two holes, puncture wounds that were now scabbed over.

The bruise pattern directly around those pairs of holes looked familiar, like . . .

A mouth.

And then it all came back to her. And she tried to scream, but her throat was so dry she managed only a pitiful croak.

CHAPTER 19

LEE ANN STOPPED her car in the overgrown field behind the warehouse just as the radio played the intro to "Kung Fu Fighting." After spending an hour relating what little she knew of the historical facts behind "The Night Chicago Died," she was relieved she wouldn't have to also explain Asian martial arts.

Zginski rode in the passenger seat, while Fauvette sat in the back. Lee Ann drove with one hand, while the other picked tiny Krystal hamburgers from a bag between her knees and shoved them greedily into her mouth. She was weak and still shivery from the hours spent between the other two, a passive plaything for their sensual, but not carnal, pleasure. She had felt like taffy being slowly and deliciously pulled in two different directions, her life incrementally drawn from both her neck and thigh. Now both the girl and Zginski seemed to have power over her, to the point that even their slightest request felt like the most important task in the world. She wondered if she'd ever feel normal again.

Gnats swirled through the dust disturbed by the car's arrival. Mark's truck was parked in its usual spot, which told

Fauvette they had returned the previous night early enough to take the standard precautions. Had they not even bothered to look for her? Surely Mark wouldn't just abandon her.

"You live *here*?" Lee Ann asked as she looked over the building. The old warehouse looked leprous in the sun, corners and edges fallen or torn away by time. Only the concrete slab of the loading dock appeared solid enough to hold weight. "It looks like the old barn my grandpa hasn't used in twenty years."

Before Fauvette could explain, Zginski stroked one finger lightly across Lee Ann's forehead and she drooped forward, making the horn bleat once as her weight hit the steering wheel. Her mouth hung slack, one corner stained with mustard. Zginski pushed her back against the corner of the seat and door.

"What the hell?" Fauvette gasped, and leaned over the back of the seat to look. Lee Ann's eyes were closed and saliva already trickled from one corner of her mouth. "Did you *kill* her?"

"Hardly," Zginski said impatiently. "I merely put her to sleep. She will stay that way until I awaken her."

"Christ, how can you *do* that?"

He shrugged. "It is a simple trick." But he did not elaborate.

Outside the sounds were all organic: wind, birds, squirrels, insects, and the river in the distance. No highway traffic reached this far. A raccoon disturbed by their arrival emerged from beneath a weed-choked packing skid and waddled off into the grass, the only overt sign of life.

Zginski looked at something on the ground. "What is this?" he asked disdainfully.

The Hispanic boy's corpse swarmed with insects in the heat, although the smell was relatively slight. Ants trailed in and out of the hole punched into his chest. "Someone brought him here last night, I imagine," Fauvette said.

"And you just toss them aside like empty containers?"

"Mark or Leo probably plan to dump him in the river tonight."

"Revolting," Zginski sneered. Then he gestured for Fauvette to precede him up the steps to the loading dock.

Fauvette led Zginski into the warehouse, but she stopped in the loading bay opening. She'd never seen the place during the day, and even its junk-filled interior became a magical sea of shapes and colors. The birds, rats, and insects looked more like fairy-tale creatures than common pests. Even the way dust floated in the shafts of sunlight, so different from the moonbeams she knew, seemed beautiful. She wanted to clap her hands in delight.

Zginski took it in slowly, with much less enjoyment. "This is your home," he said with no inflection.

"Yes," she said, still enraptured.

In truth he, too, had spent a month hiding in a ruined castle before learning that his true nature did not require him to share the haunts of the dead. A castle, though, even in ruins, retained its dignity and grandeur, the nobility of its original purpose. This utilitarian structure had no grace at all.

Zginski picked his way through the debris, growing more repulsed with each step. The place was filled with the rot of both meat and metal, and it appalled him that Fauvette would consider it a suitable home. The girl was certainly a bundle of contradictions: intelligent and naive, worldly and innocent. In a way, he realized, it made sense, given how she'd degenerated before he found her, that she would bury the rose of her undying beauty in this manure of her civilization. He felt a surge of smug satisfaction that he'd helped her bloom anew, and that she might yet prove worthy of the effort.

Then he found the hobo's corpse, source of the vilest of the many stenches, and his optimism soured. This was intolerable; only the basest creatures lived in their own filth, and apparently Fauvette's friends were on a par with dung beetles. He looked back at her. She stared up at the sun coming through cracks in the tin roof, amazement in her eyes.

Then something moved in the corner of his vision. He whirled toward it.

Danielle rose on her elbows and stared up at him with blank, feral terror. "Please," she whimpered, her voice ragged with thirst. "Help me. I'm a cop, I'm from the city, I've been attacked . . ." The "cop" bit was a stretch, but Danielle was in no mood to explain her real job description. She was convinced at first that she'd dreamed the sound of the car's engine outside, and now the reality of rescue brought tears to her eyes. Whoever this pale, handsome stranger was, he and his daughter had arrived just in time.

Zginski stared back, deciphering the story from the wounds visible on her body. She was another plaything from the previous night, not finished off like the boy outside but too weak to escape.

He turned to Fauvette, who had joined him. "What is a 'cop'?" he asked softly.

"A policeman."

"You allow women to be police officers?"

She shrugged. "Some are."

He pondered for a moment. "This is unfortunate."

"Why?" Fauvette asked. The naked woman now stared at her, relief fading to uncertainty as neither she nor Zginski made a move to help.

"The peasant boy outside is one thing, but a police officer, especially a woman, will be missed," Zginski explained. "If she is found dead, the effort to identify her killers will bring more scrutiny than we wish."

"What do we do with her, then?" Fauvette asked.

He knelt and looked into Danielle's face. "Tell me the full

truth," he said to her, and she shivered. "How did you come to be here?"

For a moment she successfully resisted the overwhelming urge to do as he said. Then she answered, "I'm not really a cop, I'm a doctor. I'm an assistant coroner for Shelby County. A boy was found dead of causes I couldn't identify, and I was trying to find out if there was a new drug being used by the local teens."

"Toddy," Fauvette said.

"And who brought you here?" Zginski asked.

"A tall white boy, and two black kids."

"My friends," Fauvette said.

Danielle looked at the girl, a fresh jolt of fear going through her. How had she not noticed the girl's pallor, and the sharpened canines when she spoke? "Oh, God, you're with them, you're *one* of them . . ."

Zginski touched a distinctive red smear at the corner of her lip. "Is this your own blood?"

Danielle suddenly flashed back to the pressure of the black boy's cold lips on hers. "Hey, taste your own ass blood, white girl!" he had said, and pushed the fluid into her mouth with his thick tongue. She snarled and bit at it, and he jumped back, wincing at the sensation. "Wow, this one bites back!" he said with a laugh as she vomited.

Danielle tried to answer, but was too scared to speak. Zginski stroked her across her forehead, causing her to collapse like Lee Ann. Fauvette shook her head. "You've *got* to show me how to do that."

He ignored her and looked around. "There are her clothes," he said. "They appear undamaged. We shall dress her, and send Lee Ann to take her home."

"Just like that?"

"Yes, just like that. Lee Ann will obey any instruction we give her now; she is fully under our power. And I can control this woman well enough to get her home, where her tales of vampires will no doubt inspire the same ridicule as they did in *Blacula*."

"But she saw us. She knows where the warehouse is."

"It is of no concern. If she is smart, she will count herself lucky that she survived this experience at all."

Fauvette looked down at the woman. Even in her forced sleep she looked terrified, not lucky at all.

❦ On the radio later that day, Memphis's own Al Green pleaded with his girlfriend to stay together. Seated in Lee Ann's car outside Danielle's apartment building, the two women felt the irony of that sentiment. Despite their mutual wish to be far away from each other, they resolutely, impotently stayed together.

The engine idled and the windows were rolled halfway down, so in the afternoon heat the vehicle was an oven. Flies and sweat bees buzzed inside, attracted by the salt on the women's skin. Neither woman made any move to shoo them away, instead gazing silently straight ahead. A UPS deliveryman looked askance at them as he left a package outside the building's entrance but made no comment. Other than him they saw no one.

For Lee Ann, it was a matter of exhaustion. She was simply too tired to move, no matter Zginski's wishes. His orders were the only things keeping her conscious, but even the compulsion to obey them couldn't get her going. She needed food, and sleep, but could acquire neither while the other woman sat in her car. *Take her home,* he had said, *make sure she gets inside, then wait for me at the motel.* But the bitch just wouldn't leave.

It was different for Danielle. She *wanted* to fling open the door and run away screaming, but her body would not respond. The last thing the long-haired man had told her was to obey the other woman, and until Lee Ann ordered her to go, she could literally do nothing. Worse, her injuries made sitting agony, and the sweat from the hot car only added to the pain.

She couldn't believe no one stopped to ask if they needed help. The parking lot was almost empty; her neighbors, all professional people, were still at work, and since the building did not take couples with children, there were no housewives home to notice her. Even the deliveryman, faced with two attractive women sitting in a car on the hottest day of the year so far, had not said a word. Perhaps he thought they were on drugs.

Finally Lee Ann cleared her throat and said in a monotone, without looking, "Hey."

"Yes?" Danielle answered, eyes still fixed straight ahead. Her voice was ragged from both screaming the night before and the recent enforced silence.

"Can I ask you something?"

"Yes."

Lee Ann took a long, deep breath. Speaking took every bit of strength she had left. "Why are you still *here*?"

"I think you have to tell me to go," Danielle said.

"What? That's *it*? Then go."

With a burst of energy, Danielle threw open the car door and ran up the stairs to the building entrance. She burst through the breezeway and up the steps, sobbing at the pain in her legs and rear. No one appeared from any of the other apartments to offer aid, and at last she reached her door.

Then she remembered her apartment keys were still locked in her car downtown.

This final defeat was too much, and with a whine of submission she slid to the floor, huddled against her door, and cried quietly until she passed out.

Outside, Lee Ann tried to put the car in gear so she could

return to the motel and sleep, but her fingers lacked the strength. Her task completed, she passed out slumped over the wheel, and slowly slid off until she fell across the front bench seat, half on the floorboard. Within moments she was snoring in harmony with the car's idling motor.

CHAPTER 20

THE SUMMER NIGHT took forever to arrive, but eventually the sun dipped below the trees, then the horizon. Stars appeared in the east as the day's glow faded. Fireflies sparkled in the tall grass.

Olive emerged first, slinking out of the shadows, humming to herself. She was dressed in a bright green tube top and jeans low on her hips, with a wide green belt.

"Hey, Olive," Fauvette said. She leaned against the warehouse wall beneath one of the windows.

Olive did a double take. "*Wow.* Chile, I forgot how nice you clean up. What size are those Levi's?"

"Where's Mark?"

"I dunno. Guess he's not up yet. He'll be late for work, and he hates that." Then she looked around. "Hey, where's the white girl we left out here?"

Fauvette ignored the question. "What about Leo?"

Leonardo dropped from the ceiling next to Olive. "Right here, you fine ladies." He grinned when he saw her. "Damn, Fauvette, you look like a vanilla shake with *all* the sprinkles." Then he looked around. "Hey, where's our mayonnaise princess from last night? She was like Thanksgiving turkey, you just knew the leftovers would be better the second day."

"I have dealt with the young woman," Zginski said as he sauntered from the loading dock, hands casually in his pockets. He knew how to make an entrance, Fauvette thought; he stopped just short of the moonlight that would've shown his face. "She was a police officer, and if luck is with us, she will keep all this embarrassing nonsense to herself and your animalistic actions will have no further consequences."

Leonardo frowned at Zginski's superior attitude and shifted to a belligerent, cocky stance, his chest thrust out. "And who the hell is *this* honky mofo, calling me an 'animal'?"

"He's with me," Fauvette said quickly.

"I am Rudolfo Zginski."

"You about to be Rudolfo the Red-Nosed Reindeer," Leonardo said, and threw a punch that could've knocked down a tree. Zginski calmly blocked it with his forearm and struck back with a quick, effective jab to the neck. He swept Leonardo's legs out from under him with one foot and dropped atop him, a knee on the boy's sternum, an index finger jabbed straight down against his chest. A little more effort would send it straight through his heart.

"You will crumble to dust, or whatever your kind becomes, if you provoke me again," Zginski snarled.

"*Fuck* you!" Leonardo bellowed raggedly, clutching his throat. "Get your ofay-lookin' ass off me!"

"Please!" Fauvette cried. "Leo, stop it. He's not kidding, he can do it."

"Assume your place and hold your tongue," Zginski said. "Or perish. I have no preference." For emphasis he pressed his finger against Leonardo's sternum.

"All right!" Leonardo snapped. "Anything you say, *massah*. God *damn*."

Zginski stood and Leonardo, glaring ferociously, got to his feet. He brushed off his T-shirt and stepped back to stand beside Olive. "We'll just wait over here at the back of the bus, honky," he said. "But you best know I got a *long* memory."

Zginski ignored Leonardo as he noticed Olive for the first time. "You."

"What?" she said guardedly, and backed up a step.

"I know you. You are the one I saw in the paper, photographed in the crowd at the scene of some crime."

"Oh, yeah, last week," she said proudly. "My eye shadow looked really good, didn't it?"

"Only a fool lets herself be photographed," he said. A photo taken now could be compared with one taken in a hundred years, and the discrepancy—or lack of it—could prove fatal. In the days of painted portraits, it was much easier to raise doubts. "Vanity is a fatal indulgence."

Olive sniffed haughtily. "Well, says *you*. I think I looked *bad*."

Zginski turned to Fauvette. "You said there were three others. Where is this 'Mark'?"

"Don't you drop a dime on him, Fauvette!" Leonardo warned. "That boy's been good to you."

"Shut up, Leo, until you know what you're talking about," she said wearily. She pointed toward the offices, a walled-off section of the main room. "He sleeps in there."

Zginski strode toward it. Fauvette rushed to catch up. "Let me talk to him first," she said quickly. "He might get mad if—"

"His anger does not concern me," Zginski said as he reached for the office door.

Suddenly a metal folding chair struck him with vehicular force across the back of his head. He fell to his knees, dazed by a blow that would've decapitated a mortal. Leonardo raised the chair again, but before he could strike Zginski shoved him against the nearest wall hard enough to crack the cement.

"No!" Fauvette screamed and grabbed for Zginski a moment too late.

Zginski hit Leonardo again at full speed, ramming him back into the wall. The crack traveled up to the ceiling and dislodged an old light fixture that crashed beside them. Leonardo's hands were around Zginski's throat, while Zginski held Leonardo under the arms, his feet off the ground.

"Stop it!" Fauvette shrieked. Neither acknowledged her.

Then Olive struck Zginski across the back with a two-by-four. The wood snapped like a dry twig, and Zginski pivoted, using Leonardo's dangling feet to knock Olive aside. He then threw Leonardo the length of the huge room, this time into the sliding metal door. Olive rushed to his aid.

"Leo, please!" Fauvette cried. "He's just playing with you. You don't know what he's *capable* of!"

"I don't give a fuck," Leonardo said coldly. "*I* ain't playing, and he's about to find that out."

Zginski smiled at this. "You are right, Fauvette. They do not know. Let me demonstrate."

And then suddenly he was gone, and a huge wolf stood in his place. There was no gradual change of shape, no moment of transition. One moment a man stood there, and the next an animal. Its fur was black, and its eyes reflected the moonlight. Its lips peeled back and it growled, a deep rumble that vibrated in their chests.

Leonardo and Olive froze under the animal's gaze. Fauvette gasped, her eyes wide.

"This is some jive-ass trick," Leonardo said, but his voice was barely more than a whisper. "It ain't real."

The wolf padded toward him. In the night's silence, the sound of its paws on the concrete rang through the warehouse. A broken bit of PVC piping clattered as the wolf pushed it aside. It stopped again and growled low and deep.

"Can't nobody turn into no wolf," Leonardo said, his voice even softer. His eyes never left the animal, and he stayed pressed into the metal door where he'd landed.

Then, just as before, Zginski stood in place of the wolf:

no puff of smoke, no flash of light, just suddenly there. "*This* is some of what I am capable of," he said calmly. "Do you need more?"

"That wasn't real," Leonardo insisted, his voice rising as he pulled himself free of the metal. "And I ain't puttin' up with this massah bullshit, even if he turns into goddam George Wallace. He best start treatin' me with some respect."

As Zginski opened his mouth to reply, Fauvette stepped between them and said, "He's right. You treat Lee Ann better than this. Leo is my friend, and if you don't respect him, then you don't respect me."

Leonardo snapped, "Hey, I don't need no white honky bitch to—"

"You do right now," she fired back.

Zginski nodded toward Leonardo. "To gain my respect, he must control his attitude."

"Do you mean 'shut up'?" she asked.

Zginski nodded. "That is a start."

She turned to Leonardo. "Leo, I'm asking you as a personal favor to me, as payback for that time I shared that van full of hippies with you, to please stop talking for a while."

"Leo, the man just turned into a goddam husky right in front of us," Olive added.

"That was a *wolf*, Olive," Leonardo sighed wearily. But he finally nodded.

Fauvette sighed with relief. "Thank you."

"Hey, shouldn't all these balls clacking together have woken up Mark?" Olive said. "He's usually out here if one of us blinks too loud."

"She's right," Fauvette said to Zginski. Without waiting for his permission, she opened the door to the old office.

The enclosed space was neater than anywhere else in the warehouse. Mark's books were stacked on shelves, and his clothes arranged in the huge desk's drawers. His coffin leaned against the wall at a forty-five-degree angle, blocked from view by a filing cabinet. It wasn't as secure as the coffins in the basement, but a casual look would not spot it.

"So this is where your leader lives," Zginski said disdainfully.

"Yeah," Fauvette said.

"Then I shall meet him." Zginski pushed the coffin lid aside. Fauvette gasped.

Mark had vomited blood in his sleep, and the dark liquid had dried down the side of his face and soaked into his clothes. His cheeks were sunken and cadaverous. A vampire at rest mimicked a fresh corpse, but Mark looked truly, genuinely *dead*. Losing Toddy had been sad, but to lose Mark would be a genuine tragedy; in a tiny, trembling voice Fauvette said, "Mark?"

He slowly opened his eyes and turned his head as if the effort overwhelmed him. When he saw Fauvette, he smiled. His teeth were coated with dried blood.

"Hey," he croaked. "You came back."

"What happened to you?" she said, brushing disheveled hair back from his forehead.

He smiled again. "I was a bad boy. I went prowling and found your stash."

She felt her stomach drop. "*No*, Mark . . ."

"I just took a taste, just a *taste* . . ."

"Of the gray powder?" Zginski asked.

Mark nodded, then frowned. "Hey, who's this guy?"

Fauvette ignored the question and reached for his arm. "C'mon, you need to get cleaned up."

He laughed weakly. "That's a switch, isn't it? You saying that to me . . ."

Fauvette helped Mark from his coffin and into the old desk chair. He slumped over, elbows on his knees, as if he'd pass out any moment. "That stuff is some heavy shit," he said. "I never felt anything like that. It was *awful* . . . but *sweet*, too."

"Where is the powder now?" Zginski asked.

Mark looked up suspiciously. "And exactly *who* are you?"

"He's okay," Fauvette said quickly. "And he's smarter than us about some things."

"I want to identify the powder," Zginski said, "and find its source. Its properties are clearly a danger to us all."

"I dunno . . . maybe it's all for the best, Fauvette, like you said. We *are* dead, after all."

Zginski started forward impatiently, intending to assert himself with Mark as he had with Leonardo, but Fauvette grabbed him by the collar and pulled him back. *"No,"* she hissed, "you will *not* hurt him."

"I will have my answers," Zginski said, and slapped her hand away.

"Yeah, you will, but first we'll make sure Mark's okay." She trembled a little, but she'd finally had enough of his snotty continental attitude. "Unless you intend to throw me around like you did Leo."

Slowly Zginski smiled and bowed his head. "Very well. Let us first attend to your friend."

They stood him up and walked him around a little to clear his head. Fauvette got him a clean shirt, and he washed the dried blood from his face. He phoned the store to tell them he was sick. He would need to feed soon, but otherwise he appeared past the crisis.

Then he removed the bag of gray powder from his pocket and handed it to Zginski. "Don't try it," Mark warned. "Not even a taste."

"I have no intention," he said.

"Who are you again?" Mark asked.

"He's Rudy Zginski," Fauvette said. "He's been around for centuries, and he knows a lot more about things than we do, trust me. A *lot* more." She couldn't wait to tell Mark about the sun, and the sweet taste of blood willingly given. But this was definitely not the time.

"That a fact," Mark said, and weakly offered his hand. "Well, then, pleased to meet you."

Zginski ignored him as he studied the texture of the powder in the bag. "I have never seen anything like this," he said softly. "And none of you has any idea of its origin?"

"If you mean where it came from," Leonardo said from the office door, "all I know is that cracker nut-job Toddy showed up with it about a month ago. Never said where he got it."

"Then we must know its nature in order to know its source," Zginski said, turning the bag in his hand and watching the flakes catch the moonlight.

"And how do we do that?" Mark asked. "Toddy's dead. The *real* kind of dead. Who do we ask?"

Zginski smiled a little. "You will enjoy this, Fauvette. I am about to admit that I have made . . . an error."

# CHAPTER 21

DANIELLE AWOKE FACEDOWN again, only this time it wasn't hard concrete beneath her but a soft familiar mattress. She rose up with a start, looked around, and saw that she was in her own bedroom, lit only by the glow from the streetlamp through the window. Her old teddy bear, complete with surgical mask, watched her from atop her dresser. For one brief, blessed instant she thought that perhaps the whole experience had been a dream inspired by a bad barbecue sandwich. Then she tried to move and felt the same tight, aching pain in the muscles of her rear end and knew it had been real. She clutched the lace-edged pillow and began to cry.

The bedroom door opened a crack, and a sliver of yellow light cut across the floor and the foot of the bed. Someone peered into the room and said softly, "Danny?"

"Leslie?" Danielle whimpered.

Leslie entered the room and turned on a lamp by the door. She was still dressed for work, which in her case meant she looked like a cross between Perry Mason and Foxy Brown. She placed a glass of wine on the nightstand before kneeling and taking Danielle's hand.

"Hey," she said gently. "Welcome back to the land of the living."

Danielle looked around, as if the walls might dissolve into those of the awful warehouse. "How did you . . . ?"

"They found your car downtown. I'm friends with one of the patrol boys, so he let me know. Your office said you hadn't been in today and hadn't called in sick, so I came straight here. I found you passed out at your door and brought you inside. You looked like Evel Knievel had dragged you behind his motorcycle."

Danielle nodded; Leslie did have the spare apartment key. "Did you see anyone else? A man with long hair, or a skinny teenage girl?"

Leslie shook her head. "No, you were alone." After a moment she added, "I haven't called an ambulance, but I think it's a good idea. You're hurt. Were you . . . ?"

The question hung for a moment before Danielle's fuzzy brain deciphered it. "No, I don't think so," she said. "I mean . . . not how you mean."

"It looks like you've been stabbed in the ass with an ice pick," Leslie said. When Danielle looked at her in surprise she added, "I undressed you. Those punctures could be serious."

"I'll look at them in a little while," Danielle said wearily.

Leslie picked up the glass. "I brought you a drink."

The sight of the red fluid made her stomach churn. "No thanks."

"You never drink . . . wine?" Leslie said in a Lugosi accent, trying to lighten the mood.

Danielle's eyes opened wide, and she began to shake. Then she began to scream.

By the time she stopped, Leslie had crawled onto the bed with her and held her tight, trying to calm her down. A neighbor pounded on the wall for silence. "Whoa, Danny, it's okay, it's me, no one can hurt you now," Leslie repeated firmly, stroking her friend's hair. When she saw Danielle's eyes had lost their glassy look she said, "Shit, girl, what was *that* all about? I'm calling that ambulance."

"No!" Danielle cried, and clung tightly to her. "Don't leave me, please."

"I'm not leaving you, sweetie, but you need medical help. Then we can talk about whatever happened to you." She reached for the phone beside the bed. "Every cop in Memphis will want in on this. Whoever did it won't get far."

"No!" Danielle repeated, only this time with an inexplicable edge of anger. Leslie jumped, then looked at her friend with shock.

"Wow," she said softly. "I'm just trying to help, you know."

"Jesus, will you just shut up?" Danielle said. She untangled herself from the sheets and climbed off the bed. "Just wait here, I'm going to go inspect the damage."

Leslie nodded, continuing to stare at her.

Danielle turned the light on in the bathroom and shut the door. In the harsh illumination her pale body looked filthy, smeared with grime and blood. She turned so she could examine the wounds to her rear end, and saw that the bruises had faded quite a bit; how long had she been out? The actual bites were small and scabbed over, with no red streaks indicating any kind of infection.

She turned on the shower and, while she waited for the water to warm up, allowed herself to remember what had happened to her. The obvious truth, that she'd been assaulted by teen vampires, was too ludicrous for words, Occam be damned. Clearly these kids *thought* they were vampires, or enjoyed pretending to be, and they'd attacked her as if they really were. But vampires were fairy tales. The strange, overwhelming attraction she'd felt could've been simply the effects of the marijuana on her squeaky clean, and no doubt repressed, psyche.

Finally she stepped into the water. She turned it as hot as she could stand it, then began scrubbing from the top of her head down. She shampooed three times, then lathered up with disinfecting soap from work and rinsed her body until she felt less like a piece of rotted garbage. The puncture wounds stung, but did not reopen or bleed. If anything, they seemed to be closing up with surprising swiftness.

She stepped out, toweled herself dry, and brushed her short hair back from her face. She wiped the mist-covered mirror and saw the dark circles under her eyes and the red splotches all over her white skin. Still, she did not look too badly battered now, and if she continued to heal as quickly, she would be fine. She'd get herself checked for diseases, of course, but since she had not actually been raped, the chances of transmission were slight.

She let out a deep, long sigh. Maybe this would turn out to be nothing but a well-learned lesson. She began to feel giddy, realizing her unbelievable luck.

She pulled on her blue terry-cloth robe. It felt sumptuous against her skin, and she felt a flutter deep inside at its touch. *That* was weird, being turned on by just a bathrobe. The feeling passed, and she wrote it off as some delayed aspect of shock.

When she opened the bathroom door, the light fell across Leslie, who remained in the same spot on the bed. She looked up at Danielle with a puzzled, frightened expression, but said nothing.

"Sorry for snapping at you," Danielle said as she went to her dresser. "I saw some crazy stuff last night, and I think I just barely avoided the ol' 'fate worse than death' our moms always told us about." She pulled out a pair of her baggiest, most comfortable cotton panties and pulled them on. "Guess I should pay more attention to my smart friends like you, huh?"

Leslie neither moved nor spoke. Her eyes were wide with

what looked like terror, yet she said nothing. "Are you all right?" Danielle asked.

"I can't move," Leslie said in a flat monotone voice.

Chills ran down Danielle's spine. She knew that tone, because it had been the very one she had used when under the influence of those . . . those *people*. She swallowed hard and had to take a deep breath before speaking. "Leslie . . . are *they* here?"

"No," Leslie answered. "No one's here but you. You told me to shut up and wait here. It's all I can do." Her full lips trembled, and her eyes grew shiny with unshed tears.

Danielle stood very still as she absorbed this. She looked away from Leslie, took a deep breath, and said, "Leslie, stand up."

Leslie scooted to the edge of the bed and stood up. She did nothing else, her hands dangling at her sides. In the silent room, her rapid, panicky breathing was as loud as a furnace.

Danielle was suddenly at war with herself. Her decent side, the one that made her a responsible adult human being, told her to free her friend, apologize for her actions, and seek medical help. Whatever was happening wasn't natural, and she had no guarantee it wasn't also fatal. Yet the rush of power was intoxicating, more than the marijuana had been, more than any alcohol. Had surviving the previous night's assault somehow gifted her with this ability? She felt no compulsion to drink Leslie's blood, but the thought of *controlling* her . . .

No! her conscience demanded. *Leslie is your friend, has been for years, she came over to help you, you can't treat her like this.*

Danielle licked her lips. Leslie's fear was turning to anger, although it showed only in her eyes. Her hands swayed slightly as she fought to exert control over her body.

Just then, the phone beside the bed rang. Danielle picked it up and said, in a trembling voice, "Hello?"

"Boss?" Skitch said. "Is that you?"

"It's me."

"I heard you'd been . . . that you had some trouble. Are you all right?"

He sounded so worried it almost made her smile. "I'm fine," she said. She imagined Skitch in the lounge at the morgue, hunched over the counter as he spoke, his scrub pants firm against his fine tight ass. She'd listened to the other women at work talk about how cute he was, and for the first time she realized she agreed with them. Now, if she controlled a hunk like *him* . . .

Then she did smile. It couldn't hurt to try.

"Skitch," she said carefully, "are things busy tonight?"

"No, haven't had a call. Why?"

"Come over here. Be here in fifteen minutes. Don't tell anyone where you're going. Do you understand?"

"Yes," he answered, in the same marvelously flat tone. Then he hung up.

Danielle put down the phone. A photo of her mother stood beside it, and she carefully placed it facedown on the nightstand. Then she turned to Leslie. "We're about to have company. Another friend." She stepped right up to Leslie, who still did not move or speak. A single tear ran down her dusky cheek. Softly Danielle added, "I'll make sure you enjoy it."

CHAPTER 22

"SOMETHING HAS HAPPENED," Zginski said. He stood outside on the loading dock, looking up at the stars. The nearby city's glow erased all but the strongest of them. He had sent out a mental command for Lee Ann to return to the warehouse, and she'd had plenty of time to do so. She lacked the willpower to resist, so circumstances must have interfered.

Fauvette stood beside him, watching him the same way he did the sky. "What do we do?" she asked.

Zginski scowled. "I should have had the woman tell *me* where she lived and not just Lee Ann. Now that we have need of her scientific expertise, we have no way to reach her."

"Your error?" Mark asked.

"Yes," Zginski agreed, seething. He despised his own mistakes more than anyone else's.

Fauvette leaned close and said softly, "Would you be willing to accept some help?"

"In what way?"

"Well, I fed from Lee Ann, too. I have the same connection. If you show me how to use it, maybe the two of us together can get her attention."

"I am strong enough," he said. "Something is actively preventing her, I'm certain."

"Maybe, but if not, this might make the difference. If I'm wrong, no harm done." *Except,* she thought, *that I've learned one of your tricks and some of your limits.* But she kept her expression open and guileless.

Zginski pondered this for a moment, then nodded. "Very well. Come with me. The rest of you, please excuse us."

"Oh, *now* he says please, when he wants to be alone with the white girl," Leonardo said. Olive smacked the back of his head and pulled him into the warehouse. Mark met Fauvette's eyes for a moment, then followed the others into the building.

Zginski led Fauvette into the grass, so that they stood in the open beneath the sky. He faced her and took her hands. The moonlight cast dark shadows beneath his eyes and cheekbones.

"What I am about to share with you will bind you and I more than you may wish," he said gravely. "I do not know the full ramifications of it, because I have never done this before. It is a ritual that exists in the tales of our kind told deep in the European mountains."

"Then why do it now?" she asked before she could stop. *Just shut up and learn,* she berated herself.

He smiled. "Because there is a quality about you, Fauvette, that intrigues me. This will also allow me to examine it more closely."

"What quality is that?"

"Your belief in an objective right and wrong."

She shrugged. "That's just my momma's doing. She made sure we were all well churched."

"Whatever its source, I wish to know more. And this way I will."

Before she could ask any more questions, he suddenly

lifted her into his arms and sank his fangs into her neck. He pressed her head against his own jugular, and instinctively she bit him as well.

✠ Danielle gazed down at Skitch, who grunted with the effort of lifting her with his pelvis. She straddled him, and had discovered another amazing facet to her new ability: she was able to keep Skitch from climaxing indefinitely. He'd been hard for two hours now, despite his best efforts. He looked up at her and gasped, "God, I'm exhausted. How long have we been at this?"

She bent and rubbed her breasts against his face, enjoying the scratchy stubble. The bedroom reeked of their activity. "I'm the boss, I give you permission for overtime."

"It's just . . . maybe this wasn't too bright, since you *are* my boss, and me being married and all."

Danielle closed her eyes and gritted her teeth as an orgasm shuddered through her. Skitch grunted and drove up into her, desperate for his own, but she held it in check until he fell back, breathless, keening in disappointment. "Shh," she whispered, "just keep doing what you're doing and I promise it'll be worth it."

"Is this going to make work awkward?" he said, his hands closing around her breasts.

She casually slapped them away; she was no one's property tonight. "Nothing will be awkward," she assured him. "I'll take care of everything."

She realized she was thoroughly exhausted, having not eaten for nearly two days. She rode him for a few more minutes as he strove to reach his own release, almost laughing at his desperation. Then she put a hand on his lips and said, "You want to get off, baby, is that it?"

"Yes!" he practically shouted.

"I don't want you coming in me, I'm not on the pill. But I have a place for you."

She turned toward the bathroom door. As if summoned by an inaudible bell, Leslie emerged and stood in the dim light. She was naked, her skin gleaming and her Afro catching the illumination from the streetlight. She stared at Danielle with a weary, defeated expression.

"Leslie, you remember Skitch, don't you?"

Leslie nodded.

"Skitch will do anything you tell him to," she said. "Won't you?"

Skitch looked at Leslie uncertainly. "Ah . . . I don't know, Danielle, I mean, she's black."

Danielle slapped him across the face, so hard his head snapped back and bounced off the pillow. "Are you so picky right now?" she said, then raised herself off his erection with a tantalizing, slow movement. He groaned, the slap instantly forgotten, and by the time she stood up he was futilely masturbating.

"Leslie," she said dreamily as she stood and stretched, "tell Skitch what you want him to do to you."

Leslie was as helpless as Skitch, although she at least understood that somehow Danielle was responsible. "No," she whispered.

Skitch's arm was a blur, and he grunted with vain effort.

Danielle stood on tiptoe to kiss the taller woman lightly on her cheek. "I know he's white, but I also know those stories about black men aren't true. I see their bodies all the time. And he's very enthusiastic."

Leslie shuddered, her resistance gone. She met Skitch's eyes and said, "Move over."

He scooted aside, and she reclined on the bed. With no preliminaries he crawled atop her, positioned himself, and rammed into her, drawing a cry from them both. He pounded her into the mattress as Danielle watched, fighting not to giggle at his white ass between those dark brown thighs. They quickly found their rhythm and began fucking in earnest.

Leslie had an orgasm almost at once. Then she wrapped her legs around Skitch and grabbed his face, forcing him to stop. She whispered something Danielle didn't catch, and then Skitch, moaning as if in pain, disengaged himself from her, slid down her body, and lowered his head between her legs. She moaned, eyes closed, hands caressing herself.

Danielle curled up in the only chair and watched this with fascination. She knew of cunnilingus, of course, but had never experienced it, and during her time with Skitch had never thought to tell him to do it. Leslie tossed her head on the rumpled bed, her dark skin shining with sweat.

Then, at the moment she experienced another orgasm, she met Danielle's gaze. Danielle saw a mix of rage, helplessness, and undeniable pleasure in Leslie's eyes, as well as something that brought her up short—betrayal. No matter how good it felt, Leslie *knew* it wasn't right. And deep down, so did Danielle.

Now Leslie was on all fours on the bed, with Skitch behind her. Danielle drew her knees to her chest and felt her eyelids grow heavy with weariness. Her injuries no longer hurt, she was fully sexually satisfied, and the exhaustion at last caught up with her.

She closed her eyes. At the moment she lost consciousness Skitch finally had his orgasm, exploding into Leslie with a roar of release that drew more pounding from the irate neighbors. Leslie was seized with a mix of excitement and revulsion as he held her hips tight against him, twitching inside her as he emptied himself. Finally he released her and she scampered quickly into the bathroom, slamming the door behind her. Skitch collapsed onto the bed, exhausted. "Wow . . . nigger poon . . . is outta sight, man . . ." he said, and laughed.

In moments he was as sound asleep as Danielle. Neither of them heard Leslie crying.

꧁꧂ Outside in her car, Lee Ann suddenly snapped awake. She had heard both Fauvette and Zginski in her head, ordering her to return to the warehouse. Before she even realized it she was turning the key in the ignition.

Nothing happened.

She tried again, then remembered. She'd fallen asleep with the engine running and the radio on. Now the car was out of gas and its battery was dead.

Lee Ann jumped out and looked around frantically for help. The parking lot was now filled with other cars, but she saw no people. She had to get back to them, to *him*, and once again she desperately needed to pee.

"Oh, God," she said to herself, "they're going to kill me for this." She pushed her matted hair out of her face and tried to think.

She began trying the doors on the other cars, searching for an unlocked one.

CHAPTER 23

"WHAT," ZGINKSI SAID, "is *this*?"

Lee Ann stood beside the stolen vehicle in the field behind the warehouse. Its headlight beams cut through the dust raised by her arrival and its idling engine silenced the normal insects. "It's a 1972 Chevy El Camino with a 402 eight-cylinder engine," she snapped. "Does that tell you anything useful?" Between stealing the car and having to pee in the bushes beside the parking lot, she was in no mood for his disdain, no matter how great his hold on her.

He stared at the low, long vehicle with its empty cargo space behind the cab. It appeared to be a drab tan color, with darker brown highlights. "It is not aesthetic at all."

Lee Ann turned off the ignition and closed the door. In the sudden darkness, the scene became instantly menacing and creepy, and she felt goose bumps despite the heat. Zginski and the others, standing still in the moonlight, looked like stone sentries outside the warehouse's crumbling visage. "Yeah, well, it was unlocked and I found the spare key under the floor mat, that's all that concerned me."

"You *stole* it?" Fauvette said, surprised. "Why?"

Lee Ann glared at her. "You wanted me back here in a hurry, didn't you?"

"But you *have* a car."

"Ran out of gas. And the battery died."

"Both?"

"Yes."

"How'd *that* happen?" Mark asked.

"Mainly because I met him," she said with a nod toward Zginski. Then she looked from him to Fauvette and back. "There's something different about you two," she said guardedly.

"What do you mean?" Zginski and Fauvette said together.

Lee Ann stared. "Okay, that was weird."

Fauvette and Zginski looked at each other. The moment of connection they'd shared when their blood mingled had been brief but profound; Fauvette felt more naked to him now than she had when she stood before him unclothed. But she had learned little about him, except the vague feeling that he was hiding things. She needed no arcane ritual to tell her that.

For his part, Zginski was trying very hard to ignore the emotions Fauvette had roused in him. They weren't the ones he expected, not lust or desire or rage. Instead he felt sad, and wistful, and almost profoundly aware of beauty he'd never noticed before. She was, despite everything, still an inherently innocent creature, and their bond had shared that quality with him. He could not wait for these sensations to fade.

"We should get going," Mark said. "It's nearly midnight, and summer nights aren't very long."

"I will go alone," Zginski said.

"Why?" Mark asked, eyes narrowing with suspicion.

"Yeah, why?" Leonardo echoed. He watched from back near the entrance, Olive beside him.

"Because a single man arriving at a woman's door in the

middle of the night is indiscreet, and decent neighbors will look away," Zginski said. "If half a dozen people arrive, those same neighbors will blatantly stare."

"How do we know you'll come back?" Mark said.

As he answered Mark, Zginski turned to Fauvette. "She will know if I betray you."

Fauvette said nothing. Basically she *felt* nothing, either, but she kept that to herself and simply nodded.

Zginski turned to Lee Ann. "Take me back to the woman's home."

"But that's where I stole this car," she protested. "If I drive up in it—"

"I will handle any difficulties. We shall return it none the worse, and the good doctor will provide any further transportation we need."

Danielle awoke suddenly, as if startled by a noise. She sat in the dark listening, but except for the normal city sounds outside, all was silent. Had it been a gunshot? A car backfiring? A scream?

The noise came again. It was a knock at the front door. Firm, no-nonsense, yet soft enough to avoid startling the neighbors.

She uncurled from the chair in her pitch-black bedroom. Her lower back and inner thighs protested; the muscles were as sore as if she'd run a marathon. Her robe lay on the floor, and she snatched it up as she went into the living room. Images from sleep remained fresh in her brain, a vision of Skitch and Leslie, of all people, making love on her bed. What had she eaten for dinner to give her such weird dreams?

"All right, I'm coming," she said, and had a strange déjà vu moment where she remembered saying almost the exact same thing to Skitch. She seemed to recall looking down at him, his bare chest and sweaty face visible beneath her . . .

She turned on the lamp beside the door. *Wait a minute,* she suddenly thought, *why was I sleeping in the chair?* Before she could puzzle this through, the knock came again. "Who is it?" she said.

A deep, commanding voice said softly, "I met you at the warehouse earlier today."

And then it all came back to her.

She sank to her knees, her empty stomach roiling as it sought in vain for something to vomit. She began to hyperventilate as every moment, from the cemetery to the warehouse to the events of that very night, hit her like a sledgehammer to the stomach. She looked at her bedroom door in terror, wondering what she would find when she turned on the bedroom light.

The knock came again. "I will break down the door if necessary," he said quietly.

Danielle stood and undid the chain lock, then turned the dead bolt. When she opened the door, the man who had rescued her—if she could call it that—stood in the hall. He was as pale as she remembered and also as handsome, clad in tight jeans and a black button-down shirt. His long hair fell around his collar, and the neat beard outlined his strong jaw and inviting lips. "Good evening, Dr. Roseberry," he said.

"Who are you?" she said, clutching her robe closed with one hand and the door with the other. Her voice was ragged again. "*What* are you?"

"I am Rudy Zginski. I am exactly what you think I am, as were the ones who accosted you at the warehouse. I have need of your expertise."

"It's late, come back in the morning," she said, desperate for any reason to refuse. It sounded lame to her own ears.

He smiled. The tips of his fangs showed. "Do not dissemble. May I enter?"

"I have to invite you, don't I?" she said, with a moment of hope. A vampire could not cross a threshold without an invitation. Then he put one hand firmly on her sternum and pushed her back until he was inside. He closed and locked the door while she sank onto the sofa.

"Folklore is seldom accurate in its specifics," he said. "Now, to the point. I need your scientific know-how to tell me what this is." He held out the bag of gray powder.

Danielle barely heard anything he said as she went through recent events anew. "I'm sorry . . . what? You want me to what?"

Zginski knelt before her and looked into her eyes. There was nothing kind or human in his own, just dark and surging will. "Most immediately, I want you to pay attention to me. At the moment, you are more valuable to me alive, as you are, than either dead or under my control. That can change. So please, give me your attention."

Suddenly he frowned and looked toward the bedroom. "Is there—?" he started to ask, then abruptly got to his feet and strode from the room. After a moment Danielle followed.

He stood in the middle of her bedroom, looking at the bed as though he could see it plainly in the dark. She turned on the light, saw what he did, and drew breath for a scream. His hand slapped over her mouth before she could emit it.

Skitch lay on the bed, naked. His pallor told her instantly he was dead, and had been so for at least a couple of hours. His eyes were open but foggy, and his mouth had oozed saliva and blood onto the pillow. More blood, from his freshly cut throat, soaked the bedclothes, and despite herself Danielle's professional mind instantly assessed the wound: from beneath the ear to the base of the collarbone, opening the length of his jugular. Not a wound he could give himself.

Memories of what she had done with him, done *to* him, flooded her mind. She'd had sex with him, and hit him; had she also killed him?

"This man is dead," Zginski said. He'd sensed the

distinctive presence of death the moment she'd opened the door, but thought at first that it was merely some carryover from the woman's job. "As is the Negro woman in the bathroom."

Danielle froze again, then tried to pry his hand away.

"Do not scream," he warned softly. Then he released her.

She rushed to the bathroom and turned on the light. The sight that greeted her burned itself into her brain in every detail. Leslie's nude brown body was slumped forward over the edge of the bathtub, stark against the white tile and porcelain. Her arms lay in the basin, wrists slashed with a blade taken from Danielle's razor and discarded on the rim. Blood ran in an almost straight line down the length of the tub into the drain.

Danielle sagged against the door frame. She could barely breathe. Leslie had killed Skitch, then herself, because of Danielle. Because of what her best friend had made them do.

If any man ever rapes me, Leslie had told her more than once, *I'll kill him, then myself. Neither of us would deserve to live.*

That's insane, Danielle always said. *You'd be blaming yourself for being a victim.*

Maybe, but that's how I feel. Call me old-fashioned.

"This is unfortunate," Zginski said behind her.

She threw herself at him with a shriek of fury, but he easily wrapped her in his arms and immobilized her. "They're dead," she whimpered. "My *friends* are *dead.*"

"Yes," he said with no emotion. "If you wish to join them, continue to be difficult. If you would like to survive this night, then listen to me and *be quiet.*"

She was in shock, so it took very little for her to nod in agreement. She was also freezing cold, but his embrace gave her no warmth at all.

Mark stood on the loading dock and looked out into the night, following the flights of bats as they swooped and dove after insects. They were a constant, and it was nice to see them on a night when so many things had apparently changed.

After his brush with the powder, he no longer wondered why it attracted first Toddy, then Fauvette. For a brief time under its influence, he actually lost the craving for blood that defined his existence. It wasn't easy for an inherently decent person to accept a new identity as a blood-sucking fiend from beyond the grave, and the powder took away his need to do so.

But the powder also seemed to magnify the latent guilt he felt over his existence. He saw himself as something disgusting and repulsive, something *evil* living on those good and pure enough to embrace the sunlight. He had *chosen* to become a vampire, after all, and that decision marked him as one of the bad guys. An indefinite, meaningless living death followed by either the torments of hell or the horror of nonexistence was all he could look forward to.

Whatever Zginski's doctor friend discovered, Mark already knew enough to understand some things. The powder somehow acted to bring out the weakest parts of their personalities, where all the self-doubt and loathing festered; coupled with the way it killed the desire for blood, it was a miracle Toddy lasted as long as he did. Then again, Toddy probably didn't have any guilt to bring out; depth wasn't his overwhelming trait.

So where had he gotten it? Who knew about vampires, and hated them so much, and was smart enough to come up with this stuff?

And what had happened between Zginski and Fauvette? If he was honest, *that* was what really bothered him. Watching her gaze adoringly at Zginski made him want to start breaking things. Were those *bite marks* on her neck? Surely not . . .

Like a shadowy breeze summoned by his thoughts, Fauvette appeared beside him. "Hi. Want some company?"

He was, as always, glad vampires didn't blush. "Sure. I was just thinking about you, anyway."

"Good things?" she said shyly. "Or are you mad? Because I couldn't blame you."

"Nah, I'm not mad. Just thinking about stuff, watching the bats."

She took his hand. His long fingers threaded between her much smaller ones. "I really am sorry about the powder and everything. I never expected you to try it. You're always so . . ."

"What?"

"Well . . . careful."

"Yeah." He saw Zginski's bite on her neck, two dark punctures in pale unbruisable flesh. They would remain until she slept again, then they would vanish. Would the newcomer's influence over her go away so easily? "Learned it the hard way, though. Did I ever tell you how I became a vampire?"

She shook her head. "Just that you were from the Midwest originally."

"You remember the Dust Bowl in Oklahoma in the thirties? Well, my family were farmers, so it wiped us out. I was buddies with this guy we called Praline, because he was crazy about the candy. He skipped out on his family real early in things, right after the stock market crash in '29. His dad eventually went nuts and killed the rest of his family, so maybe Praline did the right thing. *My* family hung on to our land as long as we could, but eventually the dust got us. We were starving, homeless, getting ready to head to California, when one night Praline shows back up. He tells me he knows a way out of all my problems, and makes it sound really good: live forever, always young, super strength, everything. Since I hadn't eaten in a week, I didn't need much convincing."

"Reckon not," Fauvette agreed. The Great Depression had also hit Kentucky just before she died, and her extended family had spoken of it in the same reverent, terrified whispers as they did God.

"But he left out two things. One, being a blood-sucking demon isn't real good for your conscience. And second, he had some snake-handling Bible thumpers on his tail, convinced he was the devil who had brought all this famine down on us. Between the time he took me, and the time I woke up as a vampire, they caught him."

"What did they do?"

"Well, he'd buried me a long way off, which was lucky. They dragged him out of his coffin while he was still sleeping and nailed him to a wagon wheel. When he woke up, they set him on fire before he could get away."

He scowled at the memory. "It wasn't so much the fact that they killed him that got to me, it was the way they waited for him to wake up so he'd know it. So I ran. Never really stopped, I guess. And I became very, very careful." He turned and smiled at her. "Okay, now you have to share one of your secrets."

Fauvette bit her lip indecisively, then took a deep breath. "You know . . . I haven't told any of the others this . . . but Zginski can walk in daylight."

Mark looked at her sharply. "You're kidding."

She shook her head. "Nope. I've seen it."

"And how did you see it?"

She took a deep breath. "Because, Mark . . . I did it, too."

He stared. "Fauvette—"

"Mark, I'm serious, I saw the sunrise this morning. After forty-five years, I saw squirrels, and birds, and colors. And he told me we can summon the powers of the storms, and turn ourselves into things." She shook her head. "He knows so much more about what we are than *we* do."

"Yeah, and he's a jackass."

She took both his hands and gazed intently into his eyes. "He can teach us, Mark. He may be the only one left who can. What if there are no other vampires around who know this stuff?"

"Then we'll just plod along on our own. I don't trust him." He paused. "You really went into the sun?"

She nodded. "And I didn't die. But I would recommend sunglasses."

He smiled. But he recalled the moment, days before, when he'd contemplated the ability to become a mist, and then thought he saw himself transparent on the shoplifting mirror. Was it possible? And was learning it worth putting up with Zginski?

Fauvette snuggled back against him and pulled his arms around her. He didn't resist. The bats continued to dance in the air.

CHAPTER 24

"WHAT ARE *YOU* doing here?" Lyman Newlin asked.

Danielle looked up from the mortar and pestle. The rest of the building was deserted except for old Mallick, the elderly security guard who watched the main entrance and alerted staff to "deliveries." She had entered through the side door unnoticed and gone directly to the lab while trying to avoid all the signs of Skitch's recent presence: new *Sports Illustrated* in the lounge, half-full cup of coffee on the examining table, his desk calendar with his wife's birthday encircled by a heart drawn in heavy red marker. She had immediately set up the lab to run basic tests on the gray powder, not even stopping to put on her lab coat and hoping no deliveries arrived before she finished. She looked awful, her hair askew and nose red from crying, but she couldn't very well step over Leslie to take a quick shower.

And now, out of the blue, Newlin. After driving two of her friends to murder and suicide in her own apartment, the sight of a homicide investigator almost made her giggle.

"I usually stop in to shoot the bull with Skitch when I'm up this late," he said. "I thought the whole point of being the boss was that you didn't have to work graveyard."

"I'm not the boss, Jerry Francisco is," she said wearily. "And this is *all* graveyard shift, remember?"

"You're *Skitch's* boss." He idly walked through the lab, tapping various glass and metal objects with his fingernails. "Where is he?"

"Indisposed," she said, trying for flippant.

"If that wife of his finds out he's been indisposing around, she'll give him a permanent attitude adjustment." He pulled one of the stools up to the worktable and sat. "His car's still out there in the lot."

Faced with the choice of taking Skitch's or Leslie's car, Danielle had chosen the one she had never ridden in before so it would contain no memories. "Is it? Maybe his date picked him up."

"I heard they found *your* car down by Elmwood Cemetery."

"Yeah," Danielle said with forced casualness. "Broke down on me. Meant to get it towed. Were there any hubcaps left?"

"Do I look like a traffic cop? I didn't see it, I just heard about it." He picked up a pair of tweezers and clicked them experimentally. "Not a part of town where you find many educated professional white women. Would it be out of line to ask why you were down there? And how you got back here?"

She looked at him. Had the bodies in her apartment been discovered? Zginski promised to take care of them, but what if he didn't? Was Lyman just trying to trip her up, catch her in a lie before arresting her? Or was she just that much closer to paranoid delusions? "It would be rude, Lyman, but nothing's out of line for a cop, is it?"

"Getting more and more wealthy white folks interested in smack. Causes them to cross a lot of socio-economic lines to get it."

She barked a single, loud laugh. "Lyman, be serious. If I was on heroin, would I be at work in the middle of the night?"

He shrugged. "Can't say. Never tried the stuff myself, and by the time I meet 'em, most junkies tend to be unemployed."

"Lyman, that's sweet. But there's no mystery. The truth is, I'm a coroner, and sometimes I just . . . visit cemeteries." She pretended to be embarrassed. "You can understand why I wouldn't talk about it a lot. And I got a cab home, and then took the bus down here to work. I've been sick, so I'm pretty far behind."

He looked at her steadily. Finally he said, "I reckon. Well, tell Skitch I'll catch him later." He sauntered out as casually as he entered. Danielle remained absolutely still until his footsteps faded and she heard the distant front door slam shut.

She had to try three times to get her hand to stop shaking enough to light the burner beneath the test tube. But as she watched the prepared solution of gray powder begin to boil, everything receded except her considerable scientific curiosity. What the hell *was* this stuff? It had the physical texture of cremation ash that had been granulated, but the spectrum analysis was all wrong. Well, not *all* wrong, but definitely off-kilter.

She quickly prepared another sample. Where had she seen a similar response before? Not since working here, certainly. Very seldom did she get called on to verify that ash remains were human. It had been years ago, while she was in school . . .

It was a simple matter to confirm her suspicion. Then she sealed up the bag and dumped the evidence of her tests down the sink. She stood in the shadows just outside the side door and made sure Lyman Newlin wasn't staking her out before scurrying to Skitch's blue Gran Torino and heading back to her apartment. Despite every awful thing that had happened, she was genuinely intrigued by the mystery she'd discovered. Her conscience could damn well sit in the corner.

Leonardo perched on a beam near the warehouse ceiling. It was his favorite spot, high above the world and among the bats, birds, and other flying things. If he could've thought of a way to get his coffin up here, he would have.

Through a gap in the roof, he saw a band of stars occasionally blotted out as bats flitted in and out of the building. He wondered if the asshole Zginski could also turn into a bat, like the vampires in movies. If so, Leonardo might spot him and crush the life out of him before he could transform back. Yeah, that would show the stuck-up mofo.

He smiled, amazed at his own prejudices. Did skin color really matter to vampires? Mark, Fauvette, and Toddy were all white, yet none of them had ever made him or Olive feel less than equal. The human world, of course, continued to beat blacks down, offering them drugs and violence instead of education and jobs. But as a vampire, he was immune to drugs. And he didn't need a job, just victims who had one. So what else did he need to know? The troubles of mortal blacks shouldn't concern him at all.

And yet here was Zginski, also a vampire, who seemed determined to maintain the mortal world's racial attitudes. His arrogant perpetual sneer made Leonardo want nothing more than to pound his face with his bare hands, and normally nothing would stop him.

But the man had turned into a wolf right in front of him. A *wolf*. A real, physical animal. And then turned back. No matter what, Leonardo wanted to know how that had happened. If it meant biting back the urge to kick ass and take names, he supposed he could do it.

He snatched a bat out of the air and held it for a moment, admiring the perfection of its tiny, needle-sharp teeth as it fought his grip. Then he released it.

Yeah, he could keep his cool. That's a natural fact. Until it wasn't needed anymore.

Below on the loading dock, Fauvette suddenly trembled in Mark's embrace. "What?" he said.

"We have to go," she said. She walked to the edge of the platform and stood there, fists clenched, as if something unseen might pull her over. "Zginski needs us in town."

"Why?"

She shook her head. "I can't tell. Just . . . it's urgent."

He frowned. "Has something gone wrong?"

She whirled and snapped, "*Fuck*, Mark, I don't *know*! We just have to go!"

Olive emerged from the warehouse and put her hands on her wide hips. "Whoa, Ms. Got-the-Body, what's up with you?"

"Her new paramour has sent out the signal," Mark said dryly. "We're being summoned."

Olive frowned. "What the hell is a 'paramour'?"

"A really classy boyfriend," he said with all available sarcasm.

"Oh, stop it," Fauvette snapped. Then she added, "Can we go? Now?"

Leonardo appeared beside Olive. "Where we going?"

"To hell, most likely," Mark said as he headed toward his truck. "Did he tell you the address before he left?"

She nodded. "But I won't need it." The urge grew stronger the longer she denied it, and by the time they were actually driving away she was ready to scream.

・ ・ ・

Danielle turned the key in her lock an hour before sunrise. She entered tentatively, hyper-conscious that when she'd left, two dead bodies had been present.

Nothing in the living room appeared out of place or disturbed. A single lamp glowed over the kitchen table where Zginski sat. He appeared unruffled and nonchalant. The half-light made him devastatingly handsome. "I assume you have answers?" he prompted casually.

"I . . ." She kept glancing around. Surely something was different. "I found out some stuff. But it sort of raises more questions." She put her keys on the hook beside the door. "Did you—?"

He gestured around the apartment. "Please, inspect the place. I insist."

She stood in the bedroom door, and noted that fresh sheets covered the bed. She walked into the bathroom, took a deep breath, and turned on the light. The place was spotless, cleaner even than it had been before. Zginski had kept his word. She went back into the kitchen and poured herself a glass of wine.

"Does it meet with your approval?" Zginski said.

She nodded. "Yeah, looks great. What did you do with . . . ?"

"Do you truly wish to know?"

She nodded.

"They will be found in situ together in the backseat of her automobile outside. I have it on good authority that such illicit trysts are commonly held in such places. There will be no indication of any 'foul play,' as it is termed. When the lightning strikes the vehicle and sets it ablaze, the authorities will be satisfied."

"How do you know lightning will strike?"

"Because I summoned the storm. It will do my bidding."

216 | Alex Bledsoe

As if for emphasis, lightning and thunder crashed almost simultaneously.

"That's a good trick," Danielle said sourly. The sky had been entirely clear as she drove home fifteen minutes earlier. "Can you do it on command?"

Without smiling, Zginski snapped his fingers. Lightning and thunder struck immediately, just outside the window.

Something icy and cold clutched Danielle's heart. "Do you have to burn them?"

"The less clear evidence, the better. As a medical examiner, would you not agree?"

Danielle closed her eyes. Leslie's father and Skitch's wife appeared before her, their faith broken, their idealism shredded. "Please," she said softly. "Don't burn them. Allow them some dignity."

"As you did?" he said with just a hint of amusement.

She looked up at him and forced herself to meet those cold, depthless eyes. "What's happening to me?" she asked, so quietly he barely heard.

"Nothing," he said. "Those of my kind who took you were clumsy and reckless. They inadvertently imparted a hint of our nature to you. It has fully faded by now. Not," he added with a shrug, "soon enough for your friends."

"Don't burn them," she said, big tears welling in her eyes. She'd seen many burned corpses, and knew what it would do to them.

He looked vaguely regretful. "The time for decision is past."

Another flash, much brighter and more intense, flared through the window. The muffled *whump* of an explosion rattled the glass, and she heard other residents moving around and opening doors.

"Oh, God," Danielle said softly. Wine splashed on the floor as her hand began to shake. "Oh, sweet Jesus, Leslie . . ." She leaned on the kitchen counter and, through the little window over the sink, saw the reflected orange glow of something burning around the building's corner. In the parking lot.

"And now to your report," Zginski said.

Before she could answer, someone knocked on her door. Startled, she dropped the wineglass into the sink. The police couldn't be here already, could they? Perhaps one of her neighbors had come to alert her to the fire.

Zginski calmly held up a hand. "I believe this will be my associates. I took the liberty of inviting them to hear your findings, as they have as much interest as I."

He opened the door. Mark entered, followed by Fauvette, Olive, and Leonardo. Zginski shut the door behind them and said, "Welcome, my friends."

"We his friends now," Leonardo muttered to Olive.

"There's a car on fire in the parking lot," Mark said. "And your girl chauffeur is out there with the crowd watching it."

"Yes, I know," Zginski said. "Your arrival is timely. Dr. Roseberry was just about to share her findings with me."

Danielle remained frozen at the sink. Even after everything these monsters had done to her, this felt like the greatest violation of all. The whole ghastly assault had occurred in *their* space, but now they were here, in her home. She felt fresh disgust and fury.

She stared at Mark. "You."

He smiled a little uncomfortably. "Uh . . . hi."

Her gaze shifted to Olive. "And you."

"What you eyeballing me for?" Olive said with a defiant head bob.

"What you . . . *creatures* . . . did to me . . ." Danielle spat.

"I know," Mark said. "Listen, believe it or not, I'm real sorry about what happened at the cemetery."

"'Sorry'?" she repeated. "*Sorry?*" Suddenly she ran at him, brandishing a Ginsu knife from the rack beside the sink.

"Actually, yeah," he said wearily, calmly catching her wrist and twisting until the pain made her drop the knife.

"Manners, Dr. Roseberry," Zginski said smoothly. "He is your guest." He took her hand and pulled her away from Mark. Leonardo emitted a sharp "huh" of amusement.

Danielle said nothing, but her glare took in Fauvette, who looked away; then Leonardo, whose expression was unreadable; and finally Olive again. "I swear to God," Danielle snarled, "if any of you *touch* me again—"

"Spare us," Zginski said coldly. "Any one of us can kill you with the effort it would take you to swat a fly. Or reduce you to the same quivering helplessness you felt before, and draw the life from you slowly. Would you prefer that?"

She looked down, defeated. "No."

"Good. Now. What can you tell us about the gray powder?"

She walked back into the kitchen, got a fresh glass, and poured some more wine. "Well, without going into a lot of technical detail, I can tell you that most of it is made of cremated human bodies. The ash is ground into powder which makes it heavier."

"Really?" Zginski said, surprised.

She nodded. "But there were some other trace elements I couldn't identify right away. Organic preservatives, of a very specific type."

"Which means what?" Mark prompted.

She raised her glass in a mock salute. "Well, my blood-sucking friends, it means whoever manufactured this powder made it from cremated Egyptian mummies."

CHAPTER 25

AFTER A MOMENT of silence Zginski repeated, "*Mummies?*"

Danielle nodded. "I studied them in school. The Egyptians were some of the finest embalmers in history. Their compounds keep corpses intact for thousands of years."

For the first time since any of them, human or vampire, had known Zginski, he seemed genuinely at a loss. "Is it . . . are you absolutely certain?"

"If I'm lyin', I'm dyin'," Danielle said sarcastically. "Yes, I'm sure."

"So how come powdered mummy dust makes us not want blood?" Mark asked.

"It does what?" Danielle said. "You mean you *eat* this stuff?"

"It has the effect of eliminating our immediate need to consume blood," Zginski said. "There are, unfortunately, undesirable side effects."

"Always are," Danielle said dryly. "And I'm sorry, I only know about dead people who have the courtesy to stop moving. I don't know anything about how you people work internally."

"Is there any other possible use for such powder?" Zginski asked.

She shrugged. "Maybe as fertilizer. But it wouldn't be very good."

"Then somebody made it specifically to fuck with us," Leonardo said. "Maybe the FBI, like they did black folks about ten years ago. Started selling heroin in the ghetto to keep us quiet."

"Oh, the FBI wants to get vampires hooked so we won't have a revolution?" Olive said. "That's just *dumb*. How we gonna revolt when we drop dead every morning?"

Zginski shook his head and paced to the patio doors. Now the red lights of a fire truck swept across the trees, and he heard the crowd gathered around the burning car on the building's opposite side.

He could not rationalize Danielle's findings. Mummies had been around for millennia, yet he'd never heard of them used in this way. As the Negro said, someone had to be manufacturing the powder with this particular effect in mind. This mysterious pharmacist evidently knew a great deal about vampires, including their physiognomy. Even Zginski didn't know much about that, because vampires never needed medical attention, and thus never visited doctors. And no one could acquire that sort of knowledge, unless—

"It must be another vampire," Zginski blurted as the thought hit him. "It is the only explanation. What other vampires do you know of in this city?"

"I've been here the longest," Fauvette said, "and I've never seen anyone other than us."

"These others may not be as unconcerned with detection as you are," Zginski said. "Most vampires wish to remain unknown even to others of our kind. Our power works best in isolation; when we join together, we attract too much attention."

"He mean us," Leonardo said to Olive, making sure everyone else heard. "We cramping his style."

"Hey, I *dig* attention," Olive said.

Zginski ignored them. "If only we knew where your friend Toddy initially acquired that powder. That would give us a starting point."

"Yeah, well, that sounds like your problem, not mine," Danielle said. She was bone-tired, and the wine had cut through her tension just enough to let her really feel it. "So now that you've done my favor and I've done yours, why don't you folks get out of my apartment and leave me alone with my hysterics, okay?" The memory of Leslie's tear-stained face kept floating before her.

Zginski turned and scrutinized her. "Yes . . . you kept your part of our bargain."

"Thanks. If I ever open my own practice, I'll call for an endorsement."

"But we may not be done with you."

Fear chilled Danielle from her spine to her heart. "Yes, you are," she said, but it didn't come out with nearly the force she intended. "Now leave."

"No, Dr. Roseberry. As this substance and its effects are complete unknowns to me, your medical training may again prove valuable. I may need to summon you at a moment's notice." He fixed his eyes on her. "Come to me."

"No, no more," she said in rage and horror, but the same sexual compulsion that immobilized her before rose inside her. Her heart pounded, her knees grew weak and her body wet and quivery. This time it was even more powerful, and made the feelings Mark and Leonardo conjured in her seem mere shadows of lust. A soft "Oh!" escaped her clenched teeth.

She grabbed the back of the couch for support, grateful for any physical barrier, however slight, between herself and Zginski. "Stop it," she hissed, and summoned all her willpower. "Stop it, no more, just stop it—" But her body surged toward him seemingly on its own, and her hands slipped from the couch as she rushed into his arms.

Touching him did nothing to ease the desire she felt, though; it quickened it, made it even hotter and more raw. She clung to his shoulders to keep from falling.

Zginski held out his left hand and, with the nail of his right index finger, cut a deep slice into it. Dark fluid oozed out, thicker than human blood. He held the hand out to Danielle, the liquid slowly pooling in his palm.

She gently cupped his hand with her own, and a tingle of something humiliating and delicious shot through her as their skin touched. Her whole body trembled with resistance, but she was losing, and she shuddered with anticipation as she delicately brought the oozing wound up to meet her lips.

"This isn't right," Mark muttered.

"Don't get involved, please," Fauvette whispered.

"Screw it, this isn't right," Mark repeated, and put a hand on Zginski's arm. "Whoa, wait a second, here."

Zginski blinked, his concentration broken, and Danielle felt a rush of relief, followed by a wave of nausea. She stumbled away from him and grabbed the couch again for support. The intensity of the emotions he called up in her, and the willpower it took her to fight even for those few moments, nearly exhausted her, and their sudden cessation left her disoriented. The odor of his ancient, rancid blood churned what little remained in her stomach.

Zginski whirled on Mark. "How dare you!" he snarled, his voice a whisper.

Mark was not intimidated. "Look, don't you think she's been through enough? You got that other girl outside on your leash, just leave this one alone."

Zginski grabbed Mark and rammed him into the nearest wall so hard the plaster cracked. Pictures fell all over the apartment. Then he yanked Mark down until the taller man was on his eye level. "These mortal beings are nothing to us.

The death of any of them should affect us no more than the sight of someone's mongrel dead along your roadways. We use and discard them as we do any of our inferiors."

Mark slapped Zginski's hands away, and blood splattered the wall from the wound on his palm. "Yeah, well, wake up and smell the diesel, blue blood, 'cause this is the twentieth century and you're not in a position to act like damn royalty." Then Mark rose to his full height. "And if you ever touch me again, you'll wish you were still back across the pond, or wherever the hell it is you come from."

Fauvette and the others stared; it was wholly out of character for Mark to lose his temper. For a moment it seemed Zginski would press the issue, but he closed his eyes, seemed to sink inward as he calmed, and then turned to the group.

"I apologize," he said flatly. It was impossible to tell if he was sincere. "I sometimes forget how much time has passed, and how much things have changed." He turned to Danielle. "My apologies, Dr. Roseberry. You have indeed honored your agreement, and I thank you." He pulled a white silk handkerchief from his pocket and pressed it to his palm. The cut would, of course, be gone by tomorrow. "We have completed our business here," he said to the others.

"Completed, hell," Leonardo said. "We still don't know where Toddy got that shit. We supposed to run around town looking for some vampire pusher?"

Before Zginski could reply, Olive volunteered, "I know where he got it."

Everyone looked at her. "You do?" Mark repeated.

"Sure enough I do," she said coyly. "Toddy used to tell me stuff he never told nobody else. Most of it was dumb-cracker talk, but that don't mean I didn't pay attention."

"Then why didn't you say something?" Zginski said tightly.

She shrugged dramatically. "Because none of you 'nilla wafers *asked* me."

Mark rubbed his forehead. With weary contriteness he said, "That was thoughtless of us, Olive. I'm real sorry. Where does the gray powder come from?"

Olive smiled, looked up at the ceiling, and clutched her hands under her chin. "From the stars above, baby." Then she batted her eyes and hummed an off-key rendition of *Also Sprach Zarathustra*.

"What does that mean?" Mark asked.

"You just keep that to yourself for now," Leonardo said suddenly. "It's almost dawn, and I want to make sure we don't get left to burn up in the daylight." He looked at Zginski as he spoke to Olive. "Fella figures he got no more use for somebody, he might not take very good care of them."

Zginski smiled. "Very well. I do not wish to cause dissent. We will continue this conversation tonight, when no one feels pressed for time."

Fauvette started to say something, but thought better of it. There was enough tension in the room. Waiting one more day wouldn't hurt anything.

They emerged from the building into a madhouse of flashing lights, screeching horns, and murmuring voices. Almost all the apartment building's residents, many in robes and pajamas, watched as the fire department continued to soak the burnt-out wreckage of Leslie's car. An ambulance drove away with the bodies, lights twirling but sirens silent. The night was humid, and the sky overhead shone with stars past the city lights' haze.

Lee Ann stood beside the fire truck watching the blasé firemen hold the hose steady. Water stood two inches deep beneath the car, overwhelming the few storm drains around the parking lot. It was lucky, she thought, that this car had been parked far enough away from everyone else so none of the other cars caught fire, too.

She stared at the uniformed police officers, and especially the one older man in a rumpled suit who looked so sad and kind. Surely if she approached him and told him she was being held against her will, he would help her. Zginski couldn't overpower all of them and drag her away, could he?

Then she turned, saw the others as they came out of the building, and ran to Zginski as if she might leap into his arms. At the last second, seeing his expression, she skidded to a stop and stood beside him, head down and hands clasped. "Did you do that?" she asked demurely, nodding toward the car.

"Why would you think so?"

"Lightning came out of nowhere. The storm lasted about a minute. Like it was brought here just to blow up that car." She raised her eyes to his. "That's what I told the police happened, because it's true. I answered all their questions honestly, just like you said. Now please, tell me: can you do that?"

He smiled. "That would make me very powerful, wouldn't it? And I would need replenishment after expending so much energy, wouldn't I?"

She gasped a little as the implications, and his power, took hold of her. She could feel his weakness, although he was still plenty strong enough to incapacitate her will. But a stronger woman might be able to resist him at this level. Maybe.

He put his arm around her shoulders. Grateful for the implied permission to touch him, she snuggled into the embrace, trying not to whine or whimper at the base need he had called up in her. "We have many things to discuss, Lee Ann. And we will need your help."

"Sure," she said, lacing her fingers together around him. He was cold as always, but she was hot enough for them both.

"We should get out of here," Mark said quietly. "We don't want to attract that attention you talked about."

"Very true. Lee Ann, come with us. We will attend to your vehicle later."

Zginski opened the hatch over the tailgate and gestured for Lee Ann to climb in. He followed her, and after a glance from him, Fauvette joined them. Mark scowled as he got into the driver's seat, while Olive and Leonardo piled in beside him. He headed back toward the warehouse, the thin light on the eastern horizon already stinging his eyes.

CHAPTER 26

LEE ANN SAT cross-legged with her back to the cab. Fauvette reclined against one side, her arm across a wheel well. Zginski knelt before Lee Ann and looked into her eyes, his fingertips brushing her cheek. The engine was loud in the hot, confined space.

"You have done very well," he said. "I am impressed with your resourcefulness."

"Thank you," she whispered. Then she noticed the bloody handkerchief in his hand. "Oh, you're hurt."

"It is nothing," he said. "It will be gone once I have rested." He ran his thumb over her lips. "Your concern is appreciated, however. And will be properly rewarded."

As if responding to an unspoken signal, she began to undress. Her movements were awkward in the tight camper, made more so by Mark's mad driving to beat the sunlight, but in moments she was nude. She spread her clothes over the truck bed's metal ridges and lay down on her back, her toes toward the tailgate. Then she raised the leg on which Zginski had fed before, exposing his scab-covered bite marks. All the while her eyes never left him.

Zginski smiled at her compliance. "Beautiful. But do not forget our friend."

Lee Ann obligingly turned her face away from Fauvette, displaying her earlier neck bite.

"Do you like her this way?" Fauvette said. "All passive and weak?"

"I prefer order. She knows her role. That makes it easier for everyone."

"Not for her."

"I don't mind," Lee Ann said. "Really."

"You do know eventually this will kill you," Fauvette said.

"I'm not afraid of that."

Fauvette scowled at Zginski. "Wonder why that is?"

"Her fate is sealed, to use a cliché," Zginski said. He stroked Lee Ann's nearest breast, and she let out a long, shivering sigh. "Sympathy for her is misplaced."

"What about kindness?"

The truck rattled over a particularly rough stretch of road, but Zginski stayed balanced. He ran his hand along Lee Ann's side and raised thigh. "I am kind to her," he said the way a man might refer to a pet. "She is in no pain."

"Please," Lee Ann said, her breath fast and shallow, "both of you, just . . . do it."

Zginski smiled triumphantly at Fauvette.

Fauvette stretched out beside Lee Ann, turned the girl's face to her, and kissed her lightly on the lips. "Thank you," she said sincerely.

"You're welcome," Lee Ann replied, looking away to Zginski.

Fauvette turned the girl's chin back to her. "No. He has nothing to do with this. It's *me* thanking you."

Zginski braced himself against the side of the camper as the truck turned off the highway and onto the secondary road. Fauvette looked up at him and said, "You could show them the day, like you did me. They might trust you more."

"When the time comes," he said. Then he crawled down to reach the bite in Lee Ann's thigh and, after a preliminary lick to soften the scabs, sank his fangs into the holes. Lee Ann sighed with contentment.

Fauvette turned the girl's head again and descended to her own bite, letting the warm fluid flow into her. Normally she would have closed her eyes, but this time she positioned herself so she could watch Zginski as he fed.

He held Lee Ann's soft thigh delicately with his strong, long fingers, and did not seem to be hurting her. If anything, her soft little moans implied she enjoyed being their mutual victim. But that could not really be the case; anything she felt was because Zginski caused her to respond that way. If her mind was clear, would Lee Ann still consent?

Lee Ann reached up and stroked Fauvette's hair. The gesture was so sisterly, so tender that Fauvette responded in kind. "Yes," she heard Lee Ann sigh, "oh, yes . . ."

Suddenly they all bounced off the truck bed and slammed back down as the vehicle jumped the ragged track and skidded to a halt behind the warehouse. As he jumped from the driver's seat Mark slapped the camper shell and said, "Get a move on!" Through the narrow plastic window, Fauvette saw the sunrise now truly coming from the east.

"Let them go," Zginski said languorously. "We will stay" — he rested a hand on Lee Ann's bare stomach, just above her navel, and caressed her slowly — "here with her." Then he settled into his bite again. Fauvette did likewise.

Mark, Leonardo, and Olive rushed into the warehouse. The faint hint of the sun seemed to scald the air around them. As Mark climbed into his coffin, his last moments of consciousness worked around Olive's mysterious comment about the powder coming from "the stars."

Shit, he thought, had Toddy gotten the powder from *aliens*?

An hour later, Danielle huddled in the corner behind her rocking chair, where it was dark and no one could see her. Her arms clutched her knees to her chest. She still smelled the awful blood from the older vampire's *(They really were vampires! Oh, God!)* hand, the one called Zginski. The odor seemed to permeate everything. She knew she was safe only as long as they did not need her, and with the slightest effort any one of them could reduce her to quivering servitude, which was far, far worse than merely drinking her blood. If Zginski had wanted to take her on the floor in front of his friends, she would've been on her back in an instant.

She was beyond tears or hysterics now. These fiends had ripped into her life and left it in shreds around her. There was nothing left to repair, no fragments to glue back together; the pieces were too small. The events of the past two days cut soul-deep into her, left her like some still-pulsing organ torn from the warmth of its host body. She could never return to normal.

Someone knocked at the door. Hard, insistent. Official.

"Danielle?" Lyman Newlin called through the door. "Wake up. I need to talk to you."

Numbly she stood and went to the door. Through the fish-eye peephole she saw Newlin's distorted face, and opened the door. "Yeah?"

He blinked in surprise when he saw she was still dressed. "You're up."

"I'm a ghoul, remember? Come on in."

He shut the door behind him, then stood with his hands respectfully folded. "You cut yourself?"

She looked up sharply. Droplets of Zginski's blood stained the floor and wall, a reminder of his reality. The dichotomy between the fantastic creatures that had stood there a mere hour earlier and the fully mundane man who did so now overwhelmed her. She had to bite the inside of her cheek to stay in control.

"No," she said, "I splashed some wine. Haven't cleaned it up yet." Danielle shuffled into the kitchen. "I'll make us some coffee. So what brings you around?" She poured some grounds into the top of the percolator.

He ran his finger along the cracked plaster where Zginski had attacked Mark. "So did you hear the sirens outside earlier?"

"Sirens? No, the building's pretty soundproof. You don't hear the street much back here. That's a mean left turn into the parking lot, though, an accident wouldn't surprise me."

He took a deep breath. "I, uh . . . have some bad news."

With her back to him, Danielle closed her eyes. "What?" she asked distantly, and hoped she could manage a fair approximation of surprise.

"It's about Skitch and your friend Leslie."

"What about them?"

"Well, we found them together tonight. Uhm . . . dead."

Danielle stood very still. What was the appropriate reaction? Hysterics would be *very* easy. She turned and looked at him. "Dead," she repeated.

"Yeah. In her car, parked right outside your building. Apparently lightning hit it. I've never heard of that happening to a car before, but there are witnesses."

Danielle just blankly stared. She could muster no feelings at all.

"Any idea why they were in the backseat of her car?" he asked.

"Why does anyone crawl into the backseat?" she said, hoping her horror came across as numb surprise.

"Any idea why they'd be doing it here, practically right outside your door?"

Danielle said nothing.

Newlin regarded her steadily. "So you knew they were having an affair?"

"*He* was having an affair. She wasn't married."

"But you knew?"

She nodded. One more lie on the pile. "They needed a neutral spot to meet."

Newlin sighed. "Well, I took the liberty of arranging for another M.E. to fly in from Nashville to do the actual autopsies."

This touched her deeply, and she had to struggle to hold her tears. "Thank you."

He walked into the kitchen and rested a fatherly hand on her shoulder. She fought the urge to recoil from his touch; she never wanted anyone to touch her again. "Do you want me to stick around?" he said softly.

"No, Lyman. It's just . . . a lot to absorb."

"Yeah." Just when she thought he was turning to leave, he stopped and looked down at his shoes. "I've known Leslie's dad a long time. One of the first black street officers in the department. He's gonna take this real hard. He was always so proud of Leslie, the way she made her own way and everything. I already had to tell Skitch's wife; she damn near needed a straitjacket. Had no clue anything was going on." He shook his head. "Well, I won't keep you. If the guys down at the M.E.'s office pass the hat for Skitch, let me know so I can pitch in. Leslie was a helluva girl, even though she was colored, so I can't really blame him for goin' after her, I guess."

After Newlin left, Danielle drank another glass of wine and watched the sun tinge the skyline. Where were the vampires now? she wondered. Where did the sunrise find them? Did they really sleep in coffins, and if so, where did they hide them?

And then she knew.

She very carefully finished her wine and placed the glass

in the sink. She poured a cup of coffee and left it to cool. Then she went into the closet and dug out her .38 pistol and the box of shells. As dawn broke over the city she cleaned and oiled the weapon, loaded it and spun the cylinder expertly. Once she had been a pretty good shot; and whatever her marksmanship, she was still very, very clever.

Bullets wouldn't be all she had on hand, though. Not against them. After she'd had time to prepare a special little surprise, things would go very, very differently.

It was full dawn by the time Zginski and Fauvette were satiated, and Lee Ann had long since passed out. They emerged from the camper and into the sunlight, Fauvette wincing and shading her eyes. Still, the sight was magnificent: acres of green-gold weeds with white and yellow flowers, the tall trees all around heavy with luxurious foliage, and a blue, cloudless sky.

"Why didn't you tell them?" Fauvette said. "They're hiding in the dark like animals. They could be out here with us."

He smiled at her, his eyes heavy with blood and satiation. He took her hand, raised it, and pulled her into a twirl that ended with her pressed against him, his other hand at the small of her back. "Because I do not know them, *ma petite* Fauvette. They are strangers, and strangers are inherently dangerous."

"They're *my* friends," she said, pushing herself firmly away. "*I* know them."

"And I know you?"

"You know me well enough. I won't lie to you, and I won't betray you."

With no warning, he pulled her back into his arms. "We have shared many things, yes. But not enough for me to consider you an ally. Not *nearly* enough."

He was so handsome, with his disheveled hair falling in

his eyes and his smile of superiority that Fauvette could only stare as he bent to her mouth. When his lips touched hers she kissed him back, tentatively at first, waiting to see if he would force her to want it the way he had in the alley. But she felt no external pressure, no uncharacteristic need for him. He was kissing her because he wanted to, not to prove a point or demonstrate his power.

And then she crushed her lips to his so hard their teeth clacked together and made them both giggle. She put her arms around his neck and ran her hands through his hair, grateful that he was closer to her height than Mark.

The sudden thought of Mark, kind and gentle and always looking out for her, brought her back to earth and she broke the kiss, turning her head. "No, wait," she said. She put her hands on his chest but did not push him away. "This . . . is way too fast. Way too fast."

He released her without a struggle. "The advantage to our condition is that we have a surfeit of time," he said with surprising kindness. "When you are ready, come to me."

He did not say *"Come to me"* in the same smoky, commanding tone he used with Lee Ann. This time it was an invitation to somewhere warm and safe, where arms waited to hold her in an embrace that did not involve causing someone pain. Just when she'd gotten used to him as an asshole.

She looked out at the waving grass. A quail shot up from cover, its wing tips slapping as it dashed for a new hiding place. Insects buzzed across the flowers. Zginski had given this to her; for a woman who believed herself doomed to the darkness, there could be no greater gift. "It'll happen," she said, and she believed it. "It will."

"Then, for now, let us rest," he said. "Tonight has the potential to be very eventful. We will need our strength."

"My coffin isn't big enough for both of us."

"We need only darkness," Zginski said, and she followed him into the warehouse. She felt a deep tingle of anticipation.

CHAPTER 27

THEY WENT THROUGH the main part of the warehouse and down the stairwell toward the boiler. When they were completely shielded from the sunlight, Zginski stopped and pulled her into his arms again. She was too startled to protest.

"I find myself drawn to the idea of touching you," he said softly, his accent making the words sound even more lush.

"So I see," she said. His embrace was firm but not over-powering.

"Your beauty is the kind that makes an existence like ours worthwhile. It will never tarnish or fade."

"I bet you say that to all the vampires you seduce."

"I've never seduced a vampire before."

"You're kidding."

"I am sincere. None has ever appealed to me as you do."

The next kiss was even hotter, and she felt his erection against her through their clothes. It seemed oddly incongru-ous that this powerful being who could command the storms was prey to the same base desires as other males, yet she also could not deny that her own body was responding as well. "Not bad for your first time," she said when their lips parted.

"I may not know the specific trail, but the forest is very familiar to me."

"I don't know if I like that. I can't tell if you're seducing me or hunting me."

"How about . . . I might not know the song, but I know the funk when I hear it."

She giggled. "You got that from Lee Ann."

"Yes," he admitted with a faux sheepish smile. "She calls what we do 'groovalistic.'"

"Also a little sadistic," Fauvette pointed out.

He nodded. "Sadistic and groovalistic." He paused, then said, "I will give you only the groovalistic part."

Again she giggled. "No more jive talk for you, okay?"

"Agreed."

He lifted her easily into his arms and carried her into one of the abandoned offices along the hallway to the boiler. Except for an old wooden desk the room was empty, its floor relatively clean of debris. He kicked the door shut without breaking their kiss.

Despite relishing his attention, Fauvette was thoroughly confused by his motives. He was a man who would use people, even other vampires, easily and willingly. Why was he suddenly so hot for her? She could ask, but how would she know if his answer was honest? And more important, given the sensations that he was conjuring in her body with just his lips, why did she care?

She turned her head slightly and said, "Wait. I need to tell you something."

"No," he said, and leaned in to kiss her again.

"Yes," she said, and her tone made him stop. *He's not forcing me,* she realized. *He's not making me do this.*

In the total darkness he saw her as one vampire sees another. "Do you not wish this?" he asked with a hint of his old arrogance. "Have I misinterpreted your response?"

"No, that's not it, I just need to tell you something first. Please."

He carefully set her down. She leaned back against the wall and caught her breath, an odd feeling since she did not normally need to breathe. When the blood stopped pulsing in her ears and other places, she said, "Do you remember when I told you how I became a vampire?"

He stood respectfully with his hands clasped behind his back. "Yes, of course."

"There's something I left out. I was a virgin when I was killed."

He immediately understood her meaning. Virgin vampires of either gender were normally asexual. Only the merest sexual response could be forced from them by a more powerful vampire, although they in turn could inspire them in others to a much greater degree. "I was unaware of that."

"I know what you're thinking, but there's more. I was raped after I died, but before I rose as a vampire. So I'm capable of feeling everything, yet my virginity returns each time it's taken. Just like that cut on your hand will be gone tomorrow, if we . . ." Suddenly she could not get the words out, and had to gulp big lungfuls of air. "If we make love tonight, I'll be a virgin again after I sleep."

His expression was unreadable. "I have never heard of such a thing."

"Yeah, well, it's no picnic, believe me."

"So to experience love with me, you will have to endure the pain of losing your maidenhead?"

She nodded.

"Every time?"

She nodded again, her head down. She felt ashamed and dirty.

He touched her chin and turned her face up to his. "I cannot change this, Fauvette. But I believe I can minimize it.

I have exerted only a small part of my power over you in the past. Its full influence would . . . alter your priorities."

"Would I be your slave, like Lee Ann?"

He shook his head. "No. I have never met anyone like you, Fauvette. I am far too intrigued by you to do anything to permanently change you."

"That sounds like a come-on," she said with a little smile.

"It is," he said as he leaned in close, "a promise." He kissed her lightly and said in a whisper, "With your permission?"

She licked her lips and, before she changed her mind, nodded.

Later she would have time to absorb what it had felt like to have her will and personality completely overwhelmed by a desire so strong it rivaled the blood-hunger. Zginski took her on the floor of the room, and she responded with a ferocity she'd never imagined she could feel. He broke through her intimate barrier at some point, but she had no clear memory of the moment amid the general thrashing, writhing, and moaning.

Guided by his hands and her own need, she descended into sex that was as ferocious as any attack. Her nails tore at his skin, flaying strips from his back and arms, while he left vicious bites on her breasts and shoulders. Finally they again sank their fangs into each other's neck, merging in a way she'd never imagined possible, and she experienced psychic sensations of his orgasm along with the intensity of her own. The mutual climax left her a weak, shredded thing limp in his arms.

Later she lay beside him on the floor and felt his body grow rigid as the true sleep came over him. His power over her faded as well, and she was back to her full self, aware and in control. She felt the blood between her thighs, and the soreness, but they seemed minor and inconsequential compared to the other feelings. And like the jagged wounds torn by his teeth, they would vanish after her rest.

In the darkness she studied his inert features. How much could she really trust him? Was this all part of some elaborate scheme to destroy her and her friends so he would have Memphis to himself? And how would she ever explain this to Mark?

But she didn't regret it. As her own deathly rest claimed her, she smiled at the memory. She had given, and been taken, and it was all right. Her body was a fair exchange for being given back the sunlight.

CHAPTER 28

ZGINSKI SAID TO Olive, "And so, my dear, please tell us where your friend Toddy acquired the gray powder."

They stood in the warehouse shadows shortly after nightfall, in a loose circle around Olive. She had on a hot pink tank top and white denim pants, and clearly relished the attention. With her hands on her hips she said, "I suppose I've kept you in suspenders long enough. Toddy got his stuff . . ."

She paused, then giggled. "Sorry, y'all just look so goddam *serious*. Anyway, Toddy got his stuff . . ."

Again she paused and giggled.

"Olive," Mark warned.

"Okay, okay, sorry. He got it at the Red Palace."

Mark and Fauvette exchanged a puzzled look. Leonardo said, "Say *what*?" Zginski merely folded his arms and waited for more.

"He went there for the laser shows," Olive continued. "He did love his hippie music. And I think he used to stay after everyone left to run around and mess with stuff. They got mummies there, you know."

"I take it this 'Red Palace' is a museum?" Zginski said.

"Yes," Mark said. "Downtown, by the river. They have

laser shows in the planetarium. Kids go to get stoned and watch the pretty lights."

"Is a 'planetarium' something like an orrery?" Zginski asked.

"An ornery what?" Leonardo asked.

"It displays the motions of the stars and planets," Zginski explained.

"Yeah, that's it," Olive said.

Zginski nodded. "And a laser is . . . ?"

"A really skinny beam of light," Mark said.

Zginski nodded, although the explanation meant nothing to him. "Then we should visit this Red Palace and its planetarium, and see what we may discover about your friend's activities there."

"All of us?" Leonardo asked, clearly a challenge.

Zginski merely smiled. "Of course. Friends can always be trusted." He offered his arm to Fauvette, and after refusing to meet Mark's perplexed gaze, she took it.

Lee Ann slept the day away in the back of the truck. She had pulled on her T-shirt at some point, but otherwise had not moved. The sun shone directly on the camper all afternoon, and the hot air had no way to escape, so she was covered in sweat and weaker than she could ever recall. Her dreams were almost-nightmares of clawing through choking dirt toward the distant air above, where something wonderful awaited her.

When Zginski opened the hatch over the tailgate she did not stir, and he had to speak her name twice before she awoke. Even then her eyelids fluttered for several moments before finally opening. She stretched, displaying far more bare flesh than she probably intended, and said through her yawn, "*Fuck*, I'm thirsty."

Then she stared at the faces peering in at her and clutched

the rest of her clothes to protect her modesty. "What's going on?"

"We are visiting the Red Palace," Zginski said.

"We are?" she said blankly. "Why?"

"For nothing you need be concerned with." He climbed over the tailgate and into the camper. Fauvette followed. Mark started to comment, but Fauvette caught his eye and shook her head. He scowled, but did not force the issue.

Zginski stroked Lee Ann's sweaty, tangled hair. "Fauvette has need of you, Lee Ann."

"What about you?" she said, reaching tentatively to touch his face.

"At the moment, I wish for you to give yourself to Fauvette as thoroughly as you do to me."

Lee Ann's disappointment was obvious, but she obediently began to remove her T-shirt. Fauvette put a hand on her arm. "That's okay," she said softly. "What I need doesn't require you to be naked." She guided Lee Ann back down and bent to her old bite on the girl's neck. The truck rattled to life as Fauvette replenished what she'd lost with Zginski.

"Thirsty," Lee Ann whimpered, so quietly it was lost in the road noise. "Please, I'm so thirsty . . ."

They returned to the apartment complex where Danielle Roseberry lived after filling a gas can, buying jumper cables, and letting Lee Ann drink a half gallon of orange Gatorade. The remains of the burned-out car had been removed, leaving only a patch of scorched pavement. Zginski considered asking Dr. Roseberry to join their expedition, but decided one less person to watch out for would be better.

Lee Ann's car would not start until she put some gasoline directly into the carburetor; then it rumbled to life. Zginski and Fauvette rode with her, while Mark, Leonardo, and Olive followed in the truck.

The route took them along the riverfront, past the bridge to Arkansas and the flat-topped, round form of the Mid-South Coliseum. At last they entered a genteel neighborhood of parks and manor houses, and turned down a winding driveway. Ahead the Red Palace waited, illuminated by safety lights and the parking lot's streetlamps.

The Red Palace was aptly named, since it had been constructed in 1920 out of red bricks, with its elaborate wooden trim painted a darker crimson. The parking lot faced the main entrance, located in the center of the rectangular five-story building. At the far end a round structure, like the dot atop a lowercase "i," stood set off from the main edifice. This was the Hoving Planetarium, attached to the museum itself by a single enclosed corridor. There were several cars already parked, and a group of teenagers waited outside the domed planetarium building.

Mark parked beside Lee Ann's car, and when Zginski emerged he and Lee Ann were in the midst of an argument.

"I don't *know* why!" Lee Ann snapped. "It's just a song on the radio!"

"But it makes no sense," Zginski insisted. "If he is in the desert alone, for apparently days, why would he *not* name his horse?"

"A problem?" Mark asked Fauvette.

"Culture shock," she replied, and rolled her eyes.

Zginski stepped close to Lee Ann. "Wait for us in the automobile."

"But—" she started to protest.

He touched the hollow of her throat, very lightly. She gasped. "Wait," he repeated, and she nodded.

Mark bent to Fauvette's ear and whispered, "Can we talk?"

"Later," she said, and patted his hand.

Zginski turned to the others. "I do not know precisely what we seek here. Perhaps someone who knew your friend, and can relate more of his activities. Perhaps the very person behind his death. I ask that you each keep your eyes open for anything that might provide us with a clue. I never met the late Toddy, so only you would know his potential behavior."

"And then we come tell you, is that it?" Leonardo said.

"That would be wise."

"Huh," Leonardo snorted.

Zginski fixed his eyes on him, but his tone stayed even. "The mind behind this is well aware of us. He understands more about how we exist than any of you do; perhaps even more than I. I would not choose to face him alone, and on his terms. It would therefore be unwise for you to do so."

"How do you know it's a 'him'?" Olive asked.

"I do not," Zginski agreed. "In fact, I know nothing, and will learn nothing out here. Come." He led them toward the sidewalk that ran along the front of the museum building, past its main entrance.

Leonardo touched Mark's sleeve as they walked, and Mark dropped back a few steps. "Dude seem a lot more mellow than he was?" Leonardo asked softly.

Mark shrugged. "Mellow how?"

"Like he got him some last night."

"We were with him until sunup," Mark said, bristling at the suggestion. "When would he have gotten it?"

"Dunno, man. Just sayin' what I'm seein'."

Ahead, Fauvette walked beside Zginski, their hands repeatedly brushing. Was Mark seeing things, or did they both spread their fingers to ensure the brief moment of contact?

They passed the four great columns that supported the balconied porch over the museum entrance. An informative bronze plate attached to one of them explained that the color scheme was the direct request of the man who put up the money for the construction.

Zginski suddenly stopped, turned, and went back to the plate. The others watched him read it again, running his fingers over a particular name. At last Olive said, "Hell, even I could've read all that boring shit by now. What's wrong?"

"Nothing," Zginski said distractedly. "A name I did not expect to encounter."

Olive peered past him and read aloud, "'Sir Francis Colby.' Friend of yours?"

"Hardly," Zginski said. Then he strode toward the planetarium so quickly the others had to rush to keep up.

Fifteen people gathered outside the double doors embossed with stars and ringed planets. All but two were male, and most had long hair, scruffy clothes, and glazed, red-rimmed eyes. A distinct, sweet-smelling smoke hung in the air. Many sported scraggly facial hair and T-shirts proclaiming things Zginski could not identify. He wondered at the cultural significance of Frampton coming alive; perhaps it was a religious cult built around the curly-haired messiah splashed across the girl's ample chest.

"Is it Zeppelin tonight?" one of the boys asked.

"Naw," his friend replied, chewing a mouthful of Frito's chips. "I think it's Parliament."

"Who?"

"One of them big funky bands, with the horns and everything."

"It's not Zep?" a third man asked, his voice rising with his outrage. "Or *Floyd*?"

"Shit," the first man said. "Parliament. Figures it'd be nigger music."

His friend jabbed him in the ribs and pointed to Olive and Leonardo. "It's cool," he said in exaggerated street talk, so that the final word actually came out "coo." They turned away with ashamed casualness.

"Stoned white crackers," Leonardo muttered. "I must not be living right if I got to hang out with them."

"You ain't living at all," Olive pointed out.

"That's a natural fact," he agreed. "Least the show should be good. *Parliament*," he said with a grin.

"Can you translate this conversation for me?" Zginski said softly to Fauvette.

"They're talking about different music they use during the show. Parliament is the name of a band."

"Ah. It's not the one who sings about nameless horses in the desert, is it?"

"I doubt it."

"Good."

An attendant, not much older than most of the kids, opened the door and began collecting admission. He exchanged soul handshakes with several of the patrons, obviously regulars. Zginski paid for them all with money taken from Lee Ann. The attendant stared at them as they entered, but said nothing.

"Did you notice the eyeball that boy gave us?" Leonardo asked Mark.

"Yeah, like he knew us. Did you ever come here with Toddy?"

"Course not. You?"

"No."

They milled about in the lobby, whose walls were painted with a panorama of the solar system. Tiny lights set within it twinkled to mimic the stars. The ceiling was domed in imitation of the actual planetarium, although it was decorated only with ridges that ran to a central point, like the vaulted ceiling of a church.

Zginski said to Fauvette, "The man who accepted our admission seemed unduly concerned with us. Do you think you can find out why?"

She shrugged. "Olive's a lot better at getting men to—"

"Olive is a fool. I have more faith in your judgment."

She shrugged again. "Okay, I'll see what I can do. Save me a seat inside."

The doors to the actual planetarium were opened by a middle-aged woman, who stepped wearily aside to let the kids enter. She had the same look of disdain for all of them, and paid Zginski and the others no special notice. They took up one whole row, with an empty seat between Zginski and Mark for Fauvette. The sweet-smelling odor grew stronger as homemade cigarettes flared to life all around them in the semidarkness.

Zginski sniffed, then softly asked Mark, "What is that?"

"Dope," Mark said.

Zginski blinked in surprise, then fired back, "Mucksnipe."

"No, they're *smoking* dope," Mark explained. A couple of people looked back and glared at him between tokes. More quietly he said, "Marijuana. It's like tobacco, except it gets you high."

"Ah," Zginski said, and nodded. He studied the elaborate projector mechanism, unaware or unconcerned that Mark continued to stare at him. *Wow*, Mark thought, *he has mellowed out. Maybe he's been smoking dope and just didn't know what it was.*

Fauvette leaned against the wall as the crowd entered the auditorium. She slipped her hands into her jeans's pockets and pushed out her hip, maximizing her seductive pose. She wore a white sleeveless jersey with a daisy design, and tugged down the front to show off her cleavage. She waited for the young man to notice her.

He closed the front doors, rattled them to make sure they'd latched, then turned and stopped. The doors to the auditorium closed as well, leaving him alone with Fauvette.

"Uh . . . can I help you?" he said. He fidgeted in place, first crossing his arms and then sticking his hands in his own pockets. He had a pimply neck and the kind of greasy hair that no amount of washing could fully contain. If he'd worn glasses he would've been a textbook nerd, but his eyes were big, green, and clear.

Fauvette pushed herself off the wall. His nervousness made her uneasy as well; she had exerted no power over him, and unless he was simply terrified of girls—which was possible—he had no reason to act this way. "I noticed you staring at me when I came in," she said, careful to keep her distance. She reached out with her power tentatively, to see if she met any resistance. "I thought you were cute, too."

He licked his lips, but did not appear to be succumbing; the front of his jeans remained resolutely unlifted. She took a step closer. "What's your name?"

"David," he said, and glanced toward the doors that led directly into the museum. A sign marked them for AUTHORIZED PERSONNEL ONLY. "My name's David."

"It's okay if you've got a girlfriend, David. I won't tell, and we can have plenty of fun."

He took a matching step away from her. He knew what she was, that much was clear, and seemed to be immune to her nosferatic power. Trying to seduce him would not accomplish anything. She could call for help, or . . .

What would Zginski do?

She flew across the room and pressed him back into the wall. He was almost as tall as Mark, but she closed one hand around his neck, while the other clutched his genitals. Both grips were like iron. She pulled him down until his face was level with hers, his gawky knees splayed wide.

"You knew we'd show up, David," Fauvette whispered. "Who told you about us?"

"Th-the old man," he hissed, his hands flattened against the wall. He was covered in sweat, and she worried he would lose bladder control as well. She'd seldom seen anyone so afraid. He kept looking at the door to the museum.

"What old man?" she asked, her voice still soft.

And he told her.

The lights inside the arena suddenly dimmed, and a sea of stars appeared on the ceiling above them. For a moment they were stationary, then they began to spin clockwise as music blared forth from hidden speakers. Someone yelled, "Yee-*hah*!"

The show was entrancing. From the zooming passage through stars and galaxies to the abstract patterns of narrow beams of light, Zginski watched with childlike delight. The music was tribal, primitive, and yet relentlessly upbeat, extolling the virtues of that mysterious "funk" and insisting that the band could "tear the roof off the sucker."

He glanced at the other patrons. Some were awestruck, some giggled, and some, he was amazed to see, appeared to be asleep. One girl ate a bag of potato chips with such gusto, he wondered if she had been on a religious fast.

Several minutes into the show Fauvette appeared, climbed past Zginski, and settled into her seat. Mark turned to speak to her, but she ignored him and leaned close to Zginski.

"There's some weird stuff happening," she said over the music. "We need to get out of here so we can talk."

He nodded. Although he hated to leave this spectacular presentation, he was far more interested in Fauvette's report. He stood, she followed, and after a moment Mark and the rest did as well.

In the deserted lobby the music was still loud, but they could speak without shouting. "What have you learned?" Zginski asked.

"David, that's the guy's name, said he was told to watch out for people who had the same look as Toddy," Fauvette said. "Pale, dark eyes, you know."

"He knew Toddy?" Mark asked.

She nodded. "Said Toddy was a regular, and used to sneak out during the show and prowl the museum. At first

David would chase him out, but then he was told to leave him alone."

"Told?" Zginski said. "By whom?"

"An old man who works nights in the antiquities collection. David only works here on the weekends to see the show for free and score some weed, so he doesn't know the man's name, just that he's important."

"Then I assume this old man in antiquities works weekends as well," Zginski said.

She nodded. "David says he's here every Saturday."

"Think he's our vampire pusher?" Mark asked.

"Possibly," Zginski said. "Did your friend describe him?"

"Said he was old, really old. Could barely move around. He has a big mustache and long white hair."

"And that is all?"

Fauvette paused. She'd read the story of Zginski's imprisonment, and seen his reaction to the name on the plate, so she knew how he'd respond. "And he's British."

"British," Zginski repeated softly.

"Yeah."

Zginski could not speak for a long moment. Only one mustache-wearing Englishman could be smart enough to create this powder, and clever enough to distribute it so discreetly. An Englishman who had once destroyed a vampire long ago in Wales, and would no doubt know that this same vampire was now walking the night again.

"Hey," Olive said suddenly, "where *is* this David dude?"

"I told him to walk home and not talk to anyone or I'd rip his balls off," Fauvette said with a little smile. "He lives in Ellendale; it'll take a while." She looked at Zginski, hoping this would impress him. He had not even noticed.

"My friends," he said at last, "this has become more dangerous than even I anticipated. If the man behind this plot is who I believe it to be, then not only is he capable of destroying us all, he will have anticipated our presence here."

"Colby would have to be dead by now, wouldn't he?" Fauvette said.

"One would assume," Zginski agreed. And on his first day in this world, ensconced in the university library, the final fate of Sir Francis Colby was the first thing Zginski had researched. The sources told him Colby died in his sleep in 1950, at age eighty-five; were he alive now, he would be a staggering 110 years old. Yet if any man could cheat death it was Colby, with his arsenal of arcane tools, spells, and rituals. Perhaps he was merely hanging on to life until he could finish off Zginski once and for all. But that made no *sense*: he'd had Zginski under his power since that day in Wales. Was this an elaborate scheme of torture, then? An old Victorian cat playing with his vampiric mouse?

"So who is this guy?" Leonardo asked.

"A man wiser, cleverer, and more ruthless than you can imagine," Zginski said.

"How do you know?" asked Olive.

"Because, my dear, sixty years ago he destroyed *me*."

CHAPTER 29

EXCEPT FOR THE music pounding through the walls from the show, the room was silent. Finally Leonardo pointed out the obvious. "But you ain't dead. The real kind of dead, I mean. The kind where you don't get up."

"No. At the time, he chose not to eliminate me totally. Believe me, it was not a kindness." He had no specific memories of his time in the void—it was a void, after all—but the sensations of isolation, ennui, and despair still hovered on the edge of his consciousness. "And after more than half a century, he may have changed his mind."

Another moment of silence passed. Someone in the planetarium called out in awe, "I think it's *God!*" followed by applause. At last Mark said, "So . . . let's go find out if it's the same guy. Then we'll know, right?"

They all looked at Zginski. He neither moved nor spoke. In fact, he turned away and walked not toward the auditorium or the passage into the museum itself, but toward the doors to the outside. He stopped with his hand on them.

Another silent moment passed. A long, drawn-out *"Dude"* came through the wall.

"Wait here," Fauvette said. She moved to stand beside Zginski and said quietly, "You're afraid, aren't you?"

He kept his eyes straight ahead. The door showed him an embossed vista of space. He tapped it with his finger. "This is a vacuum. Like the place into which Colby sent me. It is not somewhere I wish to return."

"It may not be him."

"But it may. He defeated me before. A moment or two of circumspection before I face him again seems appropriate."

"He's an old man," she pointed out. "A *really* old man."

"Perhaps," he agreed. "But consider this: human beings rarely live to be older than a century without some sort of extraordinary aid."

She frowned, then understood his meaning. "You think he's become a *vampire*?" she whispered.

He shrugged. "I will not know until I encounter him."

"Was he the kind of guy who'd turn himself into something he hated just to get revenge?"

Again he shrugged. "The answers you seek will not be found in discussion."

"Then like Mark said, we should go find out," she said. "He's a danger to all of us, remember?"

Through clenched teeth he said, "If it is Sir Francis, he is a greater danger than you can conceive." He looked back at the others, who now appeared pathetically fragile to him with their blasé concern and thin bravado. "You would do well to take your friends, flee this city, and resume your scurrying, darkness-seeking lifestyle somewhere far away."

Fauvette was not about to be baited. "You made fun of that, remember?"

He smiled mordantly. "Perhaps that was an error."

She stepped closer. "I won't go."

He looked into her eyes and saw not the silly infatuation he expected, but something deeper and harder to define. He suddenly felt an emotion he had not experienced in a century: embarrassment. If this child could exhibit the courage she'd shown, how could he, Rudolfo Zginski, show fear? He managed a smile.

"You have taught me something, Fauvette," he said. "I thank you." He turned to face the others.

"We going into the lion's den?" Leonardo asked.

"Indeed," Zginski said. "If the man behind the gray powder, and your friend's death, is the man I suspect, he will have many tricks and traps at his disposal. When we encounter him, do not let his elderly appearance catch you off guard; he was nearly fifty when he first defeated me. Be aware of everything around you, and if I give you an order, please follow it without question. Explanations can only be given to survivors."

"But if he kicked your ass once," Olive pointed out, "what makes you think you can outfox him now?"

"There are no guarantees," Zginski agreed. "But this time, I am forewarned. Let us hope that also means I am fore-armed."

The short hallway from the planetarium to the museum was empty, and the doors into the main building had the same AUTHORIZED PERSONNEL ONLY notice. They were also locked, but a simple push popped the latch and forced them open. No alarm sounded. Zginski was not surprised; Colby would not want interlopers like the police interrupting his revenge.

The museum's great central hall, three stories high and the length of the building, stretched before them lit only by security lights carefully arranged so as not to damage the artwork. The walls were covered with paintings, tapestries, and hanging objects, each accompanied by a small informative sign. Entrances into smaller sub-galleries presented dark spaces where someone or something might await its chance to attack.

"Lots of places to hide," Leonardo said softly as they stood in the doorway. "Want me to go check it out first?"

"No," Zginski said firmly. "Separating us, picking us off one by one, would be easiest. We shall stay together."

"I wouldn't just walk into a damn trap," Leonardo protested. "I'm not some retard."

"Then do not mimic the behavior of one," Zginski said flatly. "In a situation where you have the most experience, I will follow your recommendations. In this one, please follow mine."

They entered the hallway. Mark closed the doors behind them and bent the latch back into place.

The huge canvases almost felt like windows through which the painted subjects peered down at them in disdain. Large objects like swords, shields, and various weapons took up the spaces between the artworks. While plain to their vampire eyes, they still seemed dangerous and mysterious in the silence. In fact, except for the thudding of bass from the planetarium behind them, the building seemed deathly quiet.

Zginski led them down the center of the hall. He stood tall and tried to project a calm he most certainly did not feel, although why he cared what they thought was something he'd have to ponder later. Common sense told him to flee, but if he did so, he would spend the rest of his existence looking over his shoulder, wondering where Colby— it *must* be Colby, who else *could* it be?—might again show his face.

He looked up at the portraits lining the walls. Many were in the gray uniform of the Confederacy, the losing side in the American Civil War. The men all had the same gaunt, haunted look, especially one with a slender, aristocratic face and white hair, resplendent in his uniform and identified by his plaque as COLONEL VINCENT DRAKE. Zginski smiled to himself; Drake knew when he posed for this that his side would lose. It was written in his eyes.

"What the hell . . . ?" Leonardo said softly. He stepped away from the group until Olive's hand stopped him.

One of the sub-galleries had been redone as a replica of the first Higgledy Piggledy store, now a national chain of groceries headquartered in Memphis. The exhibit featured shelves stocked with period boxes, freezer displays with fake meat, and all the accoutrements of a small country grocery store, according to the sign. *This was the first Higgledy Piggledy store, opened by Thomas Bosenell in Three Tree, South Carolina, in 1910.*

"It ain't right," Leonardo muttered. "That back door over there should have a 'Colored Only' sign on it." He looked back at them. "I used to come here, to the actual store, to get things for a nice little old white lady who lived near us. First white person I ever met who didn't call me 'nigger.' They made me come to that damn back door every time. No porch over it, either, so if it was raining, I got wet." He snorted. "Seems like it rained a lot back then. Otherwise . . ." He looked around in mild disbelief. "They got it pretty close."

Olive pulled him back to the group. "Don't you be getting deep on me, too." Then she said, "Hey, what's that?"

A door stood slightly open, and a faint light glowed across the main passage's floor. A sign proclaimed CURATORS OFFICES and listed several names, all with degree initials after them. None were Sir Francis Colby or any obvious variation, but Colby would be too smart for that, anyway.

"Trap?" Mark asked quietly.

"We will not know until it springs," Zginski said.

"That sound like the way a rat thinks," Leonardo pointed out.

Zginski pushed the door open all the way. Carpeted stairs descended into the basement. The light came from a single small bulb on the landing halfway down. There was also a sound he couldn't identify, a harsh metallic hiss that came at irregular intervals.

When they reached the bottom, another corridor lined with offices stretched in either direction, running directly beneath the main gallery above. All the doors were closed except one at the far end, the source of the faint light. The hiss continued, louder and sharper.

Zginski suddenly felt cold. He was so seldom aware of temperature that this caught him off guard and he shivered, as if his lifeless blood could be warmed by the activity. Fauvette saw it, and wanted to squeeze his hand reassuringly, but thought better of it.

"Think he's in there?" Mark asked, nodding at the open door.

"Someone sure is," Olive said. "What's that sound?"

"Some kind of breathing machine," Leonardo said. "Maybe the dude so old he need one of those iron lungs."

Zginski led them toward the open door, aware that this might be among his final actions on this earth. Depending on who or what awaited them, he might be experiencing his feet hitting the ground for the last time. Each movement registered in the kind of detail mortals experienced just before impact in a crash.

He stopped at the line where the shaft of light cut across the corridor floor. The hiss was so loud now it had an almost painful edge to it, like fork tines dragged across a plate. Three rapid bursts were followed by silence, and they all remained immobile in the darkness.

Zginski held up his hand for them to stay put, and flattened himself against the wall. As he inched toward the doorjamb the final moments of *Vanishing Point* flashed in his mind: the Polish driver heading toward certain doom, his automobile at top speed as if he could somehow pass through the solid bulldozers if he went fast enough. If Colby did wait inside, if he had lured him here simply to finish him off, he would see no fear in Zginski's eyes, just as none had showed in the Pole's.

He stepped through the door.

The room before him was long, with a low ceiling and two narrow tables. Gooseneck and adjustable lamps were clamped to the edges, ready to shine down on various artifacts being prepared for display. The lights were all dark except at the far end of the room, where a lone figure sat in a small, golden bubble of illumination. Zginski walked toward him, making no effort to hide himself.

The figure was indeed an old man, his back bent and long, wispy white hair falling around his shoulders. He wore a white lab coat, and an array of small metal objects lay scattered on the table before him. He was using compressed air to clean them, the source of that periodic hiss. He did not notice Zginski's approach until Zginski put a hand on his shoulder.

Startled, the old man jumped and whirled, the air nozzle held ready like a weapon. When he saw Zginski his complexion went from pale to almost purple, and then a big grin split his face.

"At last," he said. "At bloody last."

Zginski just stared. The face was withered and distorted by time, but in his mind he had seen it merely days before, and so had no trouble recognizing the man. Knowing his identity explained very little, however.

The two stared at each other. The others carefully crept up behind Zginski and stood silently until, at last, Fauvette said, "Is it Colby?"

Zginski said, "No."

"Who is it, then?" Leonardo asked.

Zginski shook his head in wonder as he answered. *"Signalman Reynolds."*

CHAPTER 30

THE CROWD FILED out of the planetarium in their usual lethargic, vaguely zombielike way. The conversation was sedate and low-key, centered around muted expletives like "wow" and "awesome." They dispersed to their cars, and as engines started across the parking lot, the music of Led Zeppelin's "Living Loving Maid" grew in intensity as the radios, all tuned to Rock 103 FM, blared out the windows into the summer night.

Three young men approached a white Ford LTD. The first to arrive tried the handle on the back door, which was locked. He leaned his back on the fender and looked up at the sky, studying the stars visible through the city haze. "You know, it's just not as cool out here as it is inside," he said.

The driver unlocked his door. "That's a sad thing to say, man. That's the real sky."

The third man, waiting for the passenger door to be unlocked, suddenly tossed his long blond bangs from his eyes and squinted into the dark. "Hey," he said, and pointed. "Ain't that my car?"

The driver followed his gaze. "Sure looks like it. I thought your sister borrowed it and never brought it back."

"She did," he said, his brow knit with confusion. "Did you see her in there?"

Both shook their heads. "Only about four girls in the whole place, and two of 'em left early. That hot little hippie number and the black girl."

"What the fuck," the blond man said, and stalked across the lot toward the other car. When he peered inside, he saw Lee Ann asleep across the front seat. He tried the door, found it locked, and pounded with his palm on the roof. "Hey!"

Lee Ann did not stir. She was in the middle of that same dream, dragging herself up through the dirt toward the air, the light, and something that promised to be wonderful. She did wonder why she'd been buried alive in the first place, but in dream-logic all that mattered was getting to the surface.

He grabbed the door handle again and yanked on it until the whole vehicle rocked. "Lee Ann! Goddammit, Lee Ann, wake up!"

Lee Ann's eyes opened slowly, and she looked momentarily disoriented. She jumped when she realized someone was watching her, then sighed with relief when she recognized him. She sat up and said, "Chris, holy shit, you scared me."

"Open the fucking door, Lee Ann!" he demanded, and slapped the roof for emphasis. "Right now!"

She did and emerged into the night, swatting at the mosquitoes drawn to her. Once again her hair was matted with sweat into a strange configuration. She yawned as her brother said, "What the hell are you doing here?"

"Sleeping," she said, and added petulantly, "is that okay with you?"

"What the fuck are you on?" he said. He turned her arms toward the nearest streetlamp, checking for needle tracks. "Smack? Acid?"

She yanked them away. "No!" she snapped.

He pushed the hair back from her neck. "What's this, then?"

She shoved him back. "It's a heat rash!"

The high from the planetarium had thoroughly faded by this point, and Chris was in full big-brother mode. "Give me the keys, Lee Ann," he said seriously. "Now."

"You're too stoned to drive."

"And you're too . . . too . . . just give me the keys!"

"No." She looked past him, where his two friends waited outside the LTD. They waved uncomfortably, unsure exactly what was going on. "Go on with your friends. I'll bring the car over in the morning."

"*No*, Lee Ann. Give me the keys. Who are you out here waiting for?"

"No one!" she practically screamed. "Now just go away!" Suddenly her heart began to pound, as if emotions not her own were affecting her. She could barely breathe.

"It's my car!" Chris insisted petulantly, falling back into their lifelong rhythms.

A shudder went through her. She turned toward the museum building, and her eyes opened wide in terror. "Oh, God," she whimpered, clasping her hands to her face. "Oh, no, sweet Jesus . . ."

Her distress was so sincere her brother said with concern, "Hey, what's wrong? Lee Ann?"

She pressed the keys into his hand. "Just go, Chris. I love you." Then she ran toward the museum entrance.

Chris stared after her, then shook his head. Lee Ann was always doing weird shit, like skipping awesome concerts to go to work. This shouldn't surprise him. He waved to his friends and climbed into his car, smiling as the motor rumbled to life and the Zeppelin song segued into Yes's "Roundabout."

CHAPTER 31

A GRUDGE AT STAKE:
The Tale of Signalman Reynolds

Prepare for a tale of mystery and magic, of love and death, of the living and the undead. This is my tale.

I will not bore you with my biography, except to say that I was the youngest member of the Aviation Section of the Royal Army Signal Corps when it was established in July of 1914. My family was undistinguished, and my accomplishments whilst in the service of His Majesty were above reproach, but below acclaim. I was one of the faceless many dedicated to King and Country.

When I was still young, and green, I journeyed to the Welsh village of Passelwaithe in the company of the great adventurer and scientist Sir Francis Colby. My fortune and my doom were both made that day.

I knew a little of what brought us to that village. Sir Francis, in his gregarious way, explained that the locals suspected a visiting nobleman of being a vampire, a notion we both considered ludicrous. My job was to test out the latest Larkspur transmitter, whilst in the process establishing contact with the outside world so that the local superstition could not sway justice.

Of the results of this trial, much is known. The infamous Baron Zginski was determined, in fact, to be a vampire, and was dispatched accordingly. Sir Francis received much notoriety and acclaim. I was forgotten.

But my story only began that very night.

As we arrived in Passelwaithe, a veritable swarm of village ladies, young and old, waited outside the tavern where Zginski was to be tried. Among them was a slender, dusky-eyed girl who met my appreciative gaze with one of her own. I was spellbound. If I had been more worldly, and less love-struck, I might have noticed that she, too, wore one of the scarves that seemed to swathe the throats of all the women of Passelwaithe. But alas, I did not.

While the authorities questioned Sir Francis over the next few days, I was left to my own amusements, having been given indefinite leave for this assignment thanks to Sir Francis's reputation with the armed forces. I spent my days ardently pursuing this young lady, Amelia Fulcrum-Jones, and was at last fortunate enough to secure her hand in marriage.

Marriage always brings changes, but this union seemed to alter my very being. On most days I was my normal self; but about once a fortnight, I found myself in the grip of a lethargy that was beyond my ability to shrug off. In those times Amelia would hover about me, cooing and caressing, as I drifted between wakefulness and sleeping. These spells never lasted more than a day or so, and never occurred at a time that threatened my livelihood. It was as if the chronic disease knew precisely when I was best able to indulge its influence.

In the next few years, we watched the world heave

around us as the new terror arose in Germany and threatened the entire planet. I wanted desperately to reenlist, but Amelia would have none of it. I was too old to be of use to anyone but her, she often said playfully, but beneath it I sensed a very real fear. In my naiveté, I assumed it was the fear of my death; but again, I was mistaken.

After Hitler's troops broke their own peace and invaded Poland, I could stand it no longer. I rejoined the Signal Corps and did my part behind the lines to make the world safe again for the monarchy. When V-E Day arrived, I returned home—we had settled near my family in Manchester—intending to re-dedicate myself to beginning the family that had eluded us for so long, despite our best efforts.

Alas, when I returned, I found many things had changed.

A mysterious killer prowled the local factories and townships. Known only as 'The Bleeder,' it was said he attacked his victims in such a way that they bled almost all of the precious fluid from their bodies. In no way did this resemble the predations of the infamous Baron Zginski, who took only enough from each victim to sustain himself, and never to my knowledge killed anyone outright. But the ghastly details of the Bleeder's crimes are not important here, only that the atmosphere among our neighbours was one of constant watchfulness and suspicion. It was commonly thought that the villain had to be a local resident, since he managed to elude detection for so long.

Shortly after I returned home—to find my wife unchanged, and if anything younger and more beautiful than when I left—I was summoned by the local constabulary to assist in their efforts. My skill at communication and my combat experience allowed me to analyse their latest theory: that a gang of some sort was at work, attacking with impunity in locations too far apart to allow any single killer to be responsible. Yet I found nothing to substantiate this, and returned after a weekend of such drudgery to my home, wanting little more than a warm meal and a soft bed. That I returned, in fact, one day earlier than expected proved to be my downfall.

My Amelia was nowhere to be found. I searched the house, the yard, and the forest. I questioned the neighbours, but none save an old German woman, ostracised for her nationality by most of the citizenry, had any conception of what might have occurred. The woman muttered the word '*blutsauger*' and told me to search where all such *blutsaugers* are found: among the dead. I dismissed this as senile rambling.

I returned home, much dismayed, and fell asleep in my great chair. Evening fell, and I was awakened by the soft creak of the opening door. I opened my eyes without moving, and beheld my Amelia, whole and apparently sound. But just as I was about to call her name, I was struck with ghastly horror.

She wore only her nightdress, and from chin to toes was stained with blood. Her hair was a fright, tangled and matted with leaves and twigs. But it was her eyes that bespoke the greatest change. They were the piercing eyes of an animal, a fiend, a monster—eyes that I had seen before, in the moment when Sir Francis unmasked the Baron Zginski's true nature.

I watched her ascend the stairs to the bedroom, and when I heard the door close, I followed. I opened our bedroom door to find her asleep, as naked as when she was born, her body plump and pink and positively gorged with blood. Crimson trickles ran from the corners of her lips, and she seemed to smile.

I acted quickly. Whilst she was unconscious, I lashed her hand and foot to the bed with the stoutest cord I could find. I placed a crucifix upon her neck, and readied a sharp stake for the awful work ahead. Then I waited, breathless with anticipation, for the fluttering of her eyelids that signaled wakefulness.

It came just after dawn. At first she tried to stretch luxuriously and then, finding herself immobilized, struggled frantically. But the sunlight had robbed her of her satanic strength, and when her gaze finally fell upon me it was full of unimaginable pity.

'Oh, my husband, what have you done?' she exclaimed.

'I wonder, rather, what you have done,' I responded. 'You are the infamous Bleeder, are you not? The fiend who has been murdering throughout the region. You are a vampire, as that monstrous Baron Zginski was so long ago.'

'Alas, it is true,' she wept. 'He seduced me in my youth, and when he was destroyed I became so distraught I took my own life, and thus damned myself. I have in fact been dead since shortly after you met me, my husband, but I loved you so much I restrained my nature, taking only what I needed from you as you slept. You were never the wiser, and all would have been well, except you heeded the call of duty. In your absence the hunger grew unbearable, and I became the fiendish hell spawn you see before you.' She managed to control herself. 'Do as you must, my husband. Free me from this curse, and the world from my horror.'

I raised the wooden stake above her breast. 'I will release you from this torment, my precious Amelia. And I will stamp out this curse!' With that, I drove the stake through the heart of the woman I loved.

My life changed dramatically after that. I journeyed

back to Passelwaithe, and found that many of the other victims had similarly tormented their loved ones. With the help of the good Dr. Jermin, I dispatched them as well. None escaped our crusade.

But along with this experience came knowledge, knowledge of the most nefarious sort. I realized that Sir Francis had not, in fact, destroyed the Baron Zginski, but instead had reduced him to immobility so long as the knife remained imbedded in his heart. Should it be removed, the monster would rise again and resume his predation.

At first I approached Sir Francis himself, in the weeks before his death. I offered to purchase the remains, but he rebuked me, and had me arrested when I attempted stealthy entrance to his home. He felt that any being capable of such deception deserved the courtesy, as he put it, of possible revival at some future time when he might be safely awakened, contained, and studied. In this I felt he was being unutterably, unbelievably foolish.

After Sir Francis passed from this world, I kept track of the Zginski coffin, offering many times to buy it for exorbitant amounts. I was always turned away, and often ridiculed. Twice I was imprisoned.

I also began to study. I immersed myself in the legends of the undead, from the Philippine *aswang* to the Greek *vrykolakas*. I sought common denominators that might help me identify the process by which a flesh-and-blood mortal became one of these fiends. Eventually I was able to make certain determinations about the nature of vampires, and this allowed me to create a substance that would destroy the vile beings from within, in the same way opium and other drugs left even the strongest man a helpless, doomed addict.

At last, unable to procure the coffin for myself, I followed it and the rest of Colby's collection to America, to the museum he had endowed in his will. The Red Palace became my new home, and I, employed as a lowly exhibit technician, began my search through its disorganized holdings for the remains of my mortal foe.

I also perfected the substance I called *poudre de la mort vraie* and sought a member of the infernal brotherhood on which to test it. I found one named Toddy, a singularly unintelligent nosferatu who easily became addicted to heavily diluted samples, returning each Saturday for more. At last I entrusted him with an entire bag of the full-strength powder, hoping that, like the poison tracked to its nest by a cockroach, he would carry it back to his brethren.

Eventually I also identified the crate containing Zginski's remains. By then, I was too old to risk opening it myself and facing off against the creature that, although weakened by his imprisonment, would nonetheless still possess his demonic energy. So through forged memoranda and other means, I arranged for it to be opened at the local university. It is unfortunate that it cost the life of the woman in charge, and more unfortunate that others may have suffered since I was unable to be there myself. But if you, Baron Zginski, are reading this, then my trap has been sprung. I have tested my formula, and know that it is effective. A single dose will incapacitate even one as powerful as you, and then you will know you have been defeated. My wife will be avenged, and your scourge will be eliminated from God's creation. The chase of a lifetime, of *my* lifetime, nears its end.

CHAPTER 32

ZGINSKI CLOSED THE folder containing the neatly handwritten confession and placed it on the table. "Concise and well done. And I must say, much better written than Colby's. That certainly explains everything, Signalman Reynolds."

"'Signalman' who?" Fauvette asked. "So that *isn't* Sir Colby?"

"No, as I believe I told you, Sir *Francis* is, apparently, truly dead."

"Alas, it is so," Reynolds agreed.

"Never heard no one really say 'alas,'" Leonardo said softly to Mark.

"Then who is this?" Olive demanded, expressing her confusion with a belligerent head bob.

"An old acquaintance," Zginski said. Now that he knew their pursuer was not Sir Francis, he was ashamed of his own faltering resolve and furious with himself for his cowardice. "The manuscript explains it all."

"That was its purpose," Reynolds said. He placed the spray nozzle in a rack with three others; the compressor beneath the table continued to softly hiss. He carefully adjusted the valves, then stood with apparent great effort. He was pitifully frail, and his clothes hung awkwardly on his bent, gnarled form. He trembled as he tried to straighten his stooped body. "My memory of specific events grows blurry on occasion. This way, you can have no doubt as to who I am and why I must finally, genuinely, kill you."

He peered up at Zginski over his half-glasses. His eyes sparkled with an intelligence unbowed by the passage of time. "I have so looked forward to this moment, Baron Zginski. You can have no idea."

"So this old fart came up with that powder?" Leonardo asked. The suspense had also gotten to him, and like Zginski he now felt foolish. "That means he killed Toddy. Figures the dumb peckerhead would get taken out by someone like this."

Reynolds pulled another pair of glasses, this one with full lenses, from his pocket and replaced the half-spectacles he wore for work. He smiled at Leonardo, revealing irregular yellowed teeth. "You would be Leo. Leonardo, the 'soul brother,' who likes to sit in the rafters. Your friend Toddy told me much about you. He thought you a credit to your people."

"That sounds like him," Leonardo said. "He mean niggers or bloodsuckers?"

Reynolds ignored the question. He looked at the others and pointed a gnarled finger. "Olive, correct? Who is so smart and lovely."

"He thought I was *smart*?" Olive said, eyes wide.

"Well, it *was* Toddy," Mark said.

"And Mark, who thinks he's everyone's big brother. Or should that be *blood* brother?" Reynolds laughed, but it quickly devolved into a wheeze. "And *this* lovely creature would be Fauvette. Toddy thought you the most beautiful thing in the world. He called you his 'shadow goddess.'"

"We shall waste no more time on this," Zginski said. "What is the purpose of this charade?"

Reynolds smiled. "Charade? This is no charade, I assure

you. I have invented a way to rid the world of your kind's pestilence by providing you with an irresistible way of destroying yourselves. And the purpose? Why, I should think it clear. I mean to avenge my wife's untimely demise and prevent others from sharing her fate."

Zginski evaluated his options. Killing the old man was the most expedient resolution, and would certainly take little effort. Yet the man's continued existence seemed a fitter punishment. There was no way this feeble creature could be a threat to him. He would never become addicted to Reynolds's gray powder, the *poudre de la mort vraie*; his elaborate scheme had come to nothing. "We are leaving," he said to the others.

Reynolds's doddering suddenly vanished. With a snarl of contempt he snatched one of the compressed-air sprayers from the rack and shoved the nozzle into Zginski's mouth. A loud emphatic *hiss* followed and a cloud of the gray dust filled the air, most of it forced straight down Zginski's throat. Reynolds fell back against the table, his limited energy spent in that one forceful action.

"No!" Fauvette shouted and pushed Reynolds across the room. He struck the wall between the tables and slid to the floor.

Zginski gagged and clawed at his throat. The powder had been injected down his inert windpipe into both lungs and stomach, and was already doing its damage. A numbness spread within him like a ball being inflated. Worse was the growing emotional turmoil, dredging up every cowardly, base, or demeaning feeling he'd ever experienced. He *was* a walking corpse, feared and unloved, and his diabolical existence was an affront to everything good and beautiful. The memory of all those he had killed, used, or injured rose with lifelike vividness; the women of Passelwaithe swarmed around him, screaming their pain and fury from the hell to which he had condemned them. He *deserved* this dry, desiccating death.

Fauvette and Leonardo grabbed him as he collapsed. Mark yanked all the air nozzles free of their compressor and threw them aside. Olive just stared, hands clapped to her face.

Reynolds laughed as he slowly stood. A trickle of red streaked his white hair, and his eyes gleamed with demented triumph. "He is already dead, *truly* dead. Only living blood can save him, and none of *you* can provide it!"

Leonardo glared at the old man. "*You* full of blood, honky. Don't make me chase you down."

Reynolds pushed up his sleeves to reveal scabbed needle tracks. "My blood is laced with the powder. Drinking from me would only hasten the inevitable. His arrogance has doomed him at last."

He stumbled past Mark and Olive and stared into the vampire's fading, dull eyes. "Your soul will be free, Rudolfo Vladimir Zginski. It is more than you deserve. As to where it ends up, that is between you and the devil."

"Rudy!" a new voice cried.

Lee Ann stood in the doorway. She was disheveled, wide-eyed, and sported cuts on her arms. She dashed into the room, pushed Fauvette aside, and ran her hands over Zginski's stiffening body. "Oh, God, Rudy, what's happened?"

"No!" Reynolds screeched. "No, no, *no!*" He grabbed Lee Ann's shoulders and feebly tried to push her away. "Get out of here! This doesn't concern you!"

Zginski's head lolled back. His eyes were now cloudy and blank.

"It would take all your blood to save him," Reynolds cried desperately to Lee Ann. "You would *die!* You would become one of *them!* Run, while you can!"

Mark pulled Reynolds away. Lee Ann brushed Zginski's hair back from his face. His skin was stained gray from the burst of powder. "Rudy, please, say something, tell me what to do!" Tears ran down her cheeks. "Please, don't leave me, I need you!" Zginski's body grew rigid and immobile. His mouth gaped in a static, silent cry.

Lee Ann looked at Fauvette. In her desperate eyes, Fauvette saw the last thing she expected: real love. "Will my blood save him?" she demanded.

Fauvette shook her head. "I don't know."

Lee Ann whirled to Reynolds. "Will it?"

"Moments to go," Reynolds cackled. "Mere moments. The dose he got was a thousand times what killed Toddy. No one can save him. Look, he's not even struggling. He *wants* this!"

Lee Ann took Fauvette's face in her hands. "Don't let me come back," she said softly.

Fauvette nodded. "I promise."

Then Lee Ann tossed her long hair to one side, exposing Fauvette's bite. She worked her neck against Zginski's mouth until she felt his fangs slice into the flesh over her carotid. She pressed against him, driving the teeth through her skin down to the artery. It burned like a branding iron. Then she gasped as blood burst from her neck into his slack mouth.

For a long moment nothing happened. The only sounds were the labored breathing of the room's two living occupants and the wet trickling of the blood down Zginski's poisoned throat. He showed no reaction or response. Finally Reynolds said, "Too late. I warned you. He is gone to what I truly hope is his just reward."

Lee Ann began to sob.

With a snarl Zginski suddenly wrenched free of Leonardo and Fauvette, seized Lee Ann's head, and drove his fangs deeper into her neck. Tissue and bone crunched together between his jaws. Still growling, he drew the blood in long draughts, oblivious to its source. Like the day he'd awakened in the morgue, he knew only overwhelming physical need, and this was the closest way to satisfy it. The blood dissolved the gray powder he'd ingested, restoring him as his body absorbed it.

Lee Ann cried out but did not struggle. He fed so intensely that she grew pale almost at once. Her eyes opened wide and she stared, not at the ceiling, but at something only she seemed able to see. She reached up with one hand as if to touch something in the air above her. Then her eyes closed. Zginski pulled his red-coated mouth away with a wet, satisfied gasp and let her lifeless body fall to the floor. Her head landed with a loud thud.

The noise broke through his confusion. He blinked and stared at the others like a sleepwalker awakened far from his bed. Then he realized Lee Ann sprawled motionless at his feet.

He looked down, puzzled, and knelt to tentatively touch her. Blood trickled from his mouth and splattered softly on her cheek. He wiped his lips, stared in confusion at his hand, and looked up at the others.

"Are you all right?" Fauvette asked softly.

He nodded, his eyes flickering around the room. "I seem to be somewhat confused, but . . ." Then he spotted Reynolds, fumbling to unlock a side door.

None of the others saw Zginski move. One instant he was on his knees beside Lee Ann, the next he was in front of Reynolds, lifting the old man by the throat with one hand and ripping into his abdomen with the other. He hurled meat and tissue with feral ferocity, his arm cutting wide red arcs through the air. Pieces splattered around the room, and with a roar of fury he hurled the eviscerated body the length of the tables. It landed with a splat.

Again the room was quiet, but this time the silence was total. Everyone remained completely still, and none left standing needed to breathe.

Zginski wiped his bloody hands on a chamois cloth. Then he knelt and picked up Lee Ann's body. Her head fell back with limp finality. Zginski pulled loose a strand of hair stuck to her lips, and his tenderness made Olive start to cry. Leonardo put his arm around her shoulders.

Zginski looked down at Lee Ann's face for a long moment. Then once again he said, "We are leaving."

Fauvette put her hand on his arm. "She didn't want to come back. I promised her."

"She will not come back," he said. "She will . . ."

His face contorted, and for a moment Fauvette feared he was about to scream at her. Then he did scream: a long, loud, torturous wail of pain and fury. The anguish dredged up by the powder had not fully faded, and now it added to his surprisingly intense feelings at the loss of Lee Ann. He raged at the ceiling, at the night sky beyond it, and at the universe that left him without meaning or purpose, just a predator destined for no more than thinning the herd of oblivious mortals. He almost wished to return to the void to which Colby had sentenced him.

The others remained respectfully silent. Olive and Leonardo exchanged a look, while Mark put his hand on Fauvette's shoulder. She covered it with her own.

At last he stopped with a long, drawn-out breath. He turned to them, his resolve restored. "I apologize for that outburst," he said. "The powder's effect was somewhat disorienting. I am, as you say . . . okay now."

"We'll see about that," Olive muttered.

Mark gestured at the destruction. "Should we make some effort to maybe clean this up?" He nudged something wet and bloody with his shoe.

"No," Zginski said firmly. "This place, this whole building, is a place of death, and I no longer wish to be here." He kissed Lee Ann lightly on the lips. "I have things to attend to."

"Ain't like they got our fingerprints and address," Leonardo said to Mark. "And likely nobody'll find him 'til Monday. We'll watch the papers."

Mark nodded. "Yeah. Okay."

They followed Zginski out of the basement. Lee Ann had broken in through a front window, cutting her arms in the process, and they used that to depart. The crowd from the planetarium had dispersed, and Mark's truck was the only vehicle left in the parking lot. They all noticed that Lee Ann's car was missing, but none of them felt the need to mention it.

CHAPTER 33

ZGINSKI AND FAUVETTE remained in the camper with Lee Ann's body. He carefully crossed her ankles and placed her folded hands across her chest. Mark drove with extra care, and frequently glanced in the rearview mirror. He needn't have bothered. Neither Zginski nor Fauvette moved or spoke during the trip back to the warehouse and no blue lights appeared.

Leonardo and Olive rode in the cab with him. Mark was confused, or rather, uncertain. Although he and Fauvette had no spoken commitment, he'd always felt a bond between them, something that implied more in the future. Zginski's presence had altered that, in ways Mark could not comprehend. He desperately wanted time alone with Fauvette to talk about the situation, but she seemed to have eyes only for Zginski. What exactly had they shared, beyond her stories of walking about in the daylight?

"You all right, bro?" Leonardo asked softly. He was exhausted after the night's tension and wanted only to return to his coffin and rest.

Mark nodded. "Better than some."

"Never seen one of us care that much about someone they bleeding. Think it's that powder shit got him all messed up?"

Mark shrugged. "Maybe. He sure didn't seem like the sensitive type before. Even a taste of that stuff can mess you up."

Olive said, "Should we have gotten rid of it, then?"

"Ain't nothing to anyone but us," Leonardo said. "Cops'll think it's just dust. They probably throw it out when they clean up."

"Besides, only the four of us know about it," Mark pointed out.

"Five," Leonardo corrected. "If you count Lord I'm-the-Shit."

"Yeah," Mark said, and chewed his lip thoughtfully. It suddenly struck him that Zginski might, in fact, be around for a long while. The thought did not make him happy.

When they arrived at the warehouse, Zginski carefully placed Lee Ann's body on the loading dock, handling her as if she were a fragile treasure. It was almost as if the powder had changed his very nature, removing the cold arrogance and replacing it with something like compassion. They had seen his rage, though, when he ripped Reynolds apart; the powder had not mellowed *that*.

Zginski turned to Mark. "Will a fire large enough to consume her corpse attract attention?"

"I doubt it," Mark said. "We're pretty far out in the country. As long as it's done before dawn, nobody should notice."

Zginski nodded. In the past, his desire for security would have precluded any such meaningless ceremony; a set of simple mutilations like the ones he used on the doctor who awakened him would have sufficed, and the body could then be disposed of anywhere. But when he looked at Lee Ann, he could not imagine defiling her in such a way. She had saved his life, or rather his existence, at the cost of her own, and specifically asked not to come back. Although his influence over her had no doubt been a factor, the final decision had been made when he was at his weakest, and her will given the most free rein since he'd met her. It had been, he understood, a gesture of love. For *him*.

He could ignore the request, of course. He could be there the next night when she awakened and guide her into this new life. Lee Ann and Fauvette could be his brides, much like the Count's consorts in the Stoker novel, and together they could prowl this nearby river city.

But he could not do that to her. Not against her will, not after what she had done for him. Honor, a concept he normally scorned, demanded otherwise. He looked at her pale, still face and recalled how mobile and alive she had truly been.

"I'll clear some space for you," Mark said. "If we accidentally start a forest fire that burns down the woods around this place, people definitely *will* notice."

Zginski nodded. "Thank you, my friend."

"You're welcome," Mark said reflexively. He started to say more, but instead shook his head and walked away.

Fauvette stood in the dark, uncertain and for some reason fighting panic. The immediate threat was over, and the mystery of Toddy's death was solved. Soon she could tell Leonardo and Olive about the daylight, and lead them all into the sun. Hopefully Zginski would show them other things, like his ability to transform into animals or to vanish altogether.

That was it, she realized. She was panicked, not at the thought Zginski might leave, but that he might *stay*. Because if he did return to his aloof former self, she feared she would beg him for another night like the last one. Toddy's shadow goddess could easily become the mere concubine of this true shadow god.

Zginski constructed Lee Ann's funeral bower from saplings and dead branches. He placed her body on her back, hands clasped over her belly, across the slats. He removed her shoes and her jewelry. Then Zginski lit one end of a stick with Leonardo's lighter and touched it to the summer-dry weeds that provided kindling. In moments the flames spread to the wooden frame and engulfed the body. "You, too, were groovalistic," he murmured as a eulogy.

The fire illuminated the entire back of the warehouse, and sparks rose into the windless sky. The smell of burning flesh filled the night. Olive cried again, and Leonardo stood beside her for comfort. Mark sat on the hood of his truck, while Fauvette stood alone, watching only Zginski.

Zginski stood as close to the flames as he dared. He watched Lee Ann's corpse blacken, then begin to shrivel. When the bower collapsed and fell into the coals, he clenched his fists against a sudden rush of despair. The idea of leaping in with her, of ending his existence by his own hand instead of waiting for someone else like Colby or Reynolds to appear, proved surprisingly powerful. It was what Blacula had done, after all, and the Polish driver. He was unsure if its source was the latent power of the *poudre de la mort vraie*, or something more personal and harder to define.

At last the flames began to die. Lee Ann's body was reduced to ashes. Dawn was a scant hour away, and the eastern sky had already grown visibly lighter. Fauvette at last approached Zginski and stood nearby, waiting to see if he would want to speak.

He looked up at the stars. The trail of smoke was visible against them. "The stars are also suns," he said at last. "Like our own. If sunlight were fatal, starlight should be as well. And the moon reflects the light of the sun; it should also destroy us."

"Never thought about it that way," she said.

He nodded. "We accept the rules as we're given them, because the fear of being wrong is too great. It is ironic that those with no regard for their own lives as mortals will fight so desperately to remain in *this* kind of existence."

"I always wanted to go to the moon," Fauvette said wistfully as she watched the smoke seem to encircle the mostly full orb. "Maybe after what you've showed me, I can. If we ever go back someday."

It took Zginski a moment to register this. "Go back?"

"The Apollo program. I think it ended a couple of years ago, but . . ." She stopped when she saw the look on his face. "You didn't know we'd been to the moon?"

"By 'we,' you mean . . . ?"

"Mankind. 'One small step for man.' You don't know about that?"

He slowly shook his head.

"We sent astronauts to the moon for the first time six years ago. They landed, walked around, planted a flag."

"And they came back alive?"

She nodded, unable to repress a smile. "Yes, they came back. And then we sent more."

"With . . . with technology?"

"I guess. How else would you do it?"

"In my time, black magic would have seemed the only possible way." He shook his head in wonder. "This is almost too much to absorb in one night."

She stepped closer. The fire's dying glow made him especially handsome. "You asked me once to teach you about this time. Things got too busy for many lessons. We need to make up for that."

He smiled. "That will not be necessary. I must return to Europe and attempt to recover my position there. This country, this culture, is too rapid for me."

She had to swallow hard to get the words out. "You're leaving?"

He looked at her tenderly. "Remember, time is an ocean for us, Fauvette, not a river. I may sail away, but the port remains."

"But . . . I don't want you to go."

"Because of last night."

She looked away. "Not entirely."

His voice grew soft and, for the first time since she'd known him, fully kind. "It was not my power so much as your willingness to submit to it. Allow your former paramour Mark to learn your secrets. He will soon be able to provide the same pleasure."

"But he's not you," she said, forcing steadiness into words that wanted to whimper. She recalled the love in Lee Ann's eyes at the moment she decided to sacrifice herself. The girl had been manipulated and used, yet at that instant she had been driven by feelings all her own. Or was Zginski simply such a master, both she and Fauvette truly believed the feelings belonged to them? Was there any way to be sure?

"No," Zginski said. She looked up sharply, unsure if he was responding to her spoken comments or her thoughts.

Leonardo went, "Huh."

Olive said, "What?"

"That's gonna be some trouble." He nodded at Fauvette and Zginski by the fire, then at Mark seated on the hood of his truck.

Olive shrugged. "Maybe not. Fauvette ain't no tease. She decides she wants one of them, she'll tell them both. Nobody going behind nobody's back."

"You think?"

"Honey, we ain't tied up by all the rules. If we want somebody, we say so. She try one for a few years, then the other. Hell, she can have both, long as all three of them are groovy with it."

He looked at her skeptically. "And you never want anybody, do you?"

She shrugged. "Don't know what to tell you. I know what goes where, just ain't got no desire to know what it feels like. Seems kinda . . ." She shivered. "Icky."

He shook his head. "Wish I'd met you 'fore we turned. Had a chance to show you how much fun 'icky' can be."

"Me and you?" Olive said, eyes wide. "That'd be 'icky,' no matter what."

Leonardo laughed.

Mark watched Zginski and Fauvette talk. If he'd concentrated, he could've heard their words, but it seemed rude. It was really none of his business. Then again, if Zginski was going to be around, maybe it was. He seemed like the kind of guy who would have many more unpleasant surprises to reveal.

He hopped from the hood of the truck. "Getting toward daylight," he said. "Might want to be heading indoors."

"Thanks," Fauvette called, then said softly to Zginski, "We should tell them. And *show* them."

"Your knowledge gives you a tremendous advantage," Zginski said. "You might be ill-advised to throw that away."

"These are my friends."

He nodded. "It is your choice." He gestured for her to precede him, and followed her to the warehouse.

Olive was first up the steps to the loading dock, so preoccupied with the night's events that she didn't see Danielle Roseberry waiting in the shadows just inside the door. With a scream of "You *BITCH*!" Danielle knocked Olive backward into the nearest wall. She jammed her left arm against Olive's throat and drove an enormous cardiac hypodermic into her chest. Olive had time to exclaim, "Hey!" before Danielle shoved the plunger and injected several ounces of hydrochloric acid directly into Olive's heart.

Danielle stepped back. Olive clutched at the hypo and

tried to pull it free, but the acid was already dissolving her heart, destroying it as surely as any stake. "Help," she said simply, and bit her lip. Something inside her sizzled and gurgled. Tears filled her eyes. "Please?" she added plaintively.

Leonardo leaped forward and caught her as she fell. The smell of corroding flesh filled the air and her body began to collapse in on itself. All the years that had passed since she became a vampire caught up with her in moments.

"For all you did to me, for all you made me do," Danielle hissed. "For what happened to *my friends.*" She drew her gun and turned to face the others. This wasn't the confrontation she'd hoped for—she'd wanted to catch them in their coffins, inert and helpless, and thoroughly autopsy them while they slept—but she had contingency plans. "Now, you blood-sucking assholes," she snarled, "it's time to pay the check."

CHAPTER 34

"IS SHE DEAD?" Mark gasped. Blood and some sort of foam soaked the front of Olive's tank top.

"I sure hope so," Danielle said triumphantly, proud of her professional insight. Once she'd thought analytically about it, she realized that the heart had to be the central organ in any biological system dependent on fresh blood rather than food for sustenance. It tallied with folklore, too: weren't vampires always dispatched with a stake through the heart? So any method that destroyed a vampire's heart would effectively destroy the vampire, for good.

"Aw, man," Leonardo said plaintively, "you didn't have to kill her." He stroked her hair; clumps of her now-brittle Afro came loose in his fingers.

Danielle's rage surged anew. "After what she put me through? After what she cost me? You bet I did." She looked them over and snapped, "Where is he? That long-haired jackass Rudy."

They looked around. Zginski had disappeared.

Fauvette felt a chill. Either he would save them, or he'd fled and would never return. She could not predict which would happen.

Danielle pointed the gun at Mark. "You. Move away from everyone. You're next."

Mark took a slow step away from Fauvette. He knew the look in this woman's eyes; he remembered it from the mob that killed Praline. There would be no talking her out of this, and he couldn't really blame her. Indirectly, they *had* caused the death of her friends. That didn't mean he'd just stand there and let her shoot him, though.

He reached out with his nosferatic ability. It had no effect: she had smeared herself with a solution made from the gray powder, allowing it to soak into her pores and intimate areas until it permeated her. She also lined her underwear with it for extra protection, which had seemed incredibly silly until this very moment, when it suddenly became brilliant.

"Wait," Fauvette said, moving between Mark and Danielle. She just managed to keep her voice low and even. "Please, let's talk. Just what do you think we are?"

Danielle narrowed her eyes. "I know what you are."

"We're just people, ma'am," she said, going for her best helpless act. "Just like you, no matter what our slightly loony friend told you. You can see he didn't stick around once things got serious. I don't know exactly what happened at the cemetery, but you followed Mark of your own free will, and if things got out of hand later, well, you have to share some of the blame."

"No," Danielle hissed. "I *know* what happened."

"I understand you're upset," Fauvette pressed, not wanting to give Danielle time to think. "You did some grubby things, maybe took some drugs, and your friends also died. I'm very sorry, that *is* a big couple of blows, but to try to blame us, to convince yourself that we're some kind of monsters just to ease your own guilt . . . that's not very sensible, ma'am."

Danielle's resolve crumbled just a bit, but the gun didn't

waver. Could it all really have been drugs? Had the pot been laced with some hallucinogen? "Wait . . . how old are you?"

That caught Fauvette off guard. After a moment's hesitation, she blurted, "Fourteen, ma'am."

"You sound awfully grown-up for fourteen. What music do you like?"

Fauvette drew a blank. She never listened to music except in passing. "Uh—" she said, unable to come up with anything.

"Yeah," Danielle said triumphantly. "A teenager who hangs out on the street and doesn't know the latest music. Right. Now get out of my way, or I start with you."

"For God's sake, you shot some kind of acid into Olive's heart, didn't you?" Fauvette said desperately. "That doesn't prove she was a vampire, that would kill *anybody*."

"It wouldn't kill them *that* way," Danielle said with certainty. "I'm a coroner, bitch, I know a lot about how people die."

"Please . . ." Fauvette started helplessly.

Danielle smiled, stepped to one side, and before Fauvette could again block her, shot Mark in the heart.

Mark grunted at the impact, and it knocked him back a step. But it felt just like any other time he'd been shot, and that brought a rush of relief. He covered the smoking opening with his hands and managed to stand straight.

Danielle narrowed her eyes, and continued to smile. "So much for your bullshit excuses. A normal human being wouldn't be standing there after that."

"Mark?" Fauvette asked warningly.

"It's okay," he said. Then he felt numbness spreading from the injury, burrowing through his body. He recognized it, too: the same sensation the mere taste of the gray powder gave him earlier, but much stronger, wiping out his energy, his ability to move, to think . . .

He fell to his knees, and looked helplessly at Fauvette.

"Ah, hell," he said, disgusted with his own weakness. This was even less dignified than Praline's destruction or Olive's death. He toppled face forward onto the warehouse floor.

"Mark!" Fauvette shrieked. When she raised his head, his eyes had the same glassy look as Zginski's back at the museum. Fauvette glared at Danielle. "You maniac, what did you do?"

She'd dipped a whole box of cartridges in a gelatin solution liberally spiked with what was left of the gray powder Zginski gave her for analysis, but saw no need to explain that. "Doesn't matter. Now it's your turn. Stand up."

"No," Fauvette snarled. "Kill me right here, if you're going to. Next to him." Fate had decided her loyalties, and in these last moments she would honor them.

Danielle grabbed Fauvette by the hair and yanked her to her feet. "I said *move*! You bastards will do what *I* say this time!"

Leonardo said calmly, "Hey, y'all, wait a minute."

Danielle released Fauvette and turned to look at him.

He stood beside Olive's remains, his hands spread in a gesture of supplication. "All right, let's look at this mathematically," he said in what he hoped was the most reasonable tone in the world. "You had two friends get killed 'cause of us, and now you done killed two of ours. Ain't that enough? Ain't we even now?"

Danielle shot him in the heart. The impact knocked him back into the wall, and he slid to the floor. She shrieked, "'Even'? You freak, I'm not doing this for me, I'm doing it so nobody else has to go through that! Do you know what it feels like? Do you have any idea what being one of your . . . your *victims* is like?"

"Yes," Fauvette said quietly. "We all do."

Danielle struck Fauvette hard across the face with the gun. Fauvette snapped her head back up, glaring.

"We were all victims once," Fauvette continued through

clenched teeth, and felt gingerly around the torn, unbleeding skin on her cheek. "That's how we became what we are."

"And what about *your* victims?"

She lowered her eyes. She lacked the energy to continue this, even without the powder. "Hell, maybe you're right. Maybe we should all die. We are what we are." All the elation, all the hope Zginski had brought, disappeared along with him. He'd abandoned them, she realized with certainty. There would be no rescue, no moment when he would charge forward to save them; he was, after all, only interested in himself. How could she have dared to believe the world of daylight would be hers again, that her existence as a demonic killer could coexist with the sun?

"No," Danielle said as she aimed the gun at Fauvette's chest, "what you *were.*"

They both heard a soft, metallic tap and turned toward it. Mark had vanished; a single bullet rested on the floor where his body had sprawled a moment ago.

CHAPTER 35

DANIELLE SPUN IN place. "Where are you?!" she called. "Come out, or I'll blow her damn head off! I mean it!"

Fauvette scooted over to Leonardo, who was barely conscious. "I don't feel anything," he whispered. "My legs don't work, my arms . . ."

Danielle looked around the warehouse. There was no handy place for Mark to hide, and he couldn't have made it all the way to any of the doors . . . could he? She glared at Fauvette. "All right, you slippery bastard," she called to Mark. "You want to hide while your girlfriend dies? Fine."

Mark, now no more than a thin layer of dust hanging in the air, hovered insubstantially in front of Danielle. Transforming into mist had taken all his remaining strength, and he wasn't even sure he could change back. He felt distant, above it all, numb to the reality that this woman was about to kill Fauvette. At one level he wanted to watch, to see if death looked different from this weird perspective.

The bullet had almost completely overwhelmed him when he suddenly recalled the way he'd felt back in his store, when for a moment he believed he actually turned transparent. If Zginski could do it, he should be able to as well.

Fighting the numb apathy, he tried to bring that mind-set back. And then, like some switch being thrown, it worked: he dissolved into a fine cloud of mist. Even his clothes vanished, but because the bullet was coated with the gray powder, it did not, slipping through his misty form and hitting the floor. He rose above them, amazed that everything looked so crystal-clear and peaceful. He moved just by thinking, and drifted slowly in front of Danielle, in position to do . . . what? He couldn't physically act in this state. And now the woman had her gun aimed at Fauvette, who looked helpless and dejected and so very beautiful . . .

Danielle cocked the gun.

With all his strength of will, Mark concentrated on re-constituting himself, dragging his diaphanous form into a single cloud, connecting molecules again to form bones and muscles and skin and hair and clothes. A wave of nausea struck him, and he was conscious of the obscene sense of his own bodily processes as they re-formed and jumped into action all at once . . .

Danielle sighted along the barrel at the spot where Fauvette's cleavage began just above the neckline of her shirt.

Now he felt disoriented, suddenly unsure what was up or down, which way he was falling, if he was falling or just standing still, and the nerve endings fired in an agony of sensation as his feet contacted the floor . . .

Danielle pulled the trigger.

Mark appeared directly in front of Danielle, coagulating out of the dust in the air. The bullet struck him under his left collarbone. He slapped the gun out of her hand, and then grabbed her by the throat. He lifted her and roared his pain and fury. She kicked madly and tore at his face.

Then he snapped her neck. She went limp, eyes wide, and he threw her into the wall.

Mark managed to stay on his feet. The bullet's numbness spread, but it wasn't as intense this time, and he wobbled a bit but didn't fall. Maybe he was developing some sort of immunity to this stuff, or—

"Mark . . ." a small voice said behind him. He turned.

The bullet had passed completely through him and struck its target. The ragged hole between Fauvette's breasts still smoked as she stared down at it. Then she toppled backward, her legs twisted awkwardly under her.

"Fauvette—!" Mark croaked and stumbled over to her. The bullet had pierced her heart, and she stared blankly at the ceiling. But as his face moved over hers, her eyes focused on him.

"That . . . stings . . ." she sighed. But the pain was fading into the numbness she knew so well from the gray powder, and she understood that her death—her second death, her final death—would be painless. She smiled.

Mark plunged his fingers into the hole, trying not to do any additional damage to her heart. He felt past the shivering cardiac flesh to where the bullet had impacted against the tough muscles that expanded the lungs, and pulled the slug free. The top of the nearest auricle was torn and shredded, though, and he felt the blood—thicker than humans, jellylike due to their colder body temperature—oozing out. There was nothing he could do.

With the last of his strength, Leonardo crawled to her. "Hey, Fauvy, looks like we're going on the same trip," he managed.

"It's so . . . peaceful . . ." she sighed.

Mark looked at her helplessly. "Fauvette, damn," he said desperately.

"Just stay with me while I go," she whispered. "So many things I wanted to find out . . ."

"Here," a new voice said. Mark and Leonardo looked up. Zginski dropped Danielle's limp body next to them. "Feed," he said in his most arrogant, commanding tone. "This bitch is not dead yet, and the fresh blood may save you."

Danielle's eyes looked around wildly. She felt nothing from her shattered neck down, and when she tried to speak she seemed to have no air in her lungs. She saw Zginski over her, and his hands turned her head. Something else audibly snapped in her neck, but she didn't feel it. Then he lifted Fauvette and placed her mouth against Danielle's throat. The vague sense of pressure was all she felt as the girl's fangs sank home.

Leonardo took one limp wrist and slid his fangs into her weak, fluttery pulse. Mark did the same with the other wrist. Danielle's head thundered with pain as her blood was quickly and efficiently drained.

Zginski leaned down. "You should have let us vanish

from your lives. You survived the first time you sought us out; you will not survive this."

"I don't care," Danielle croaked wetly. "They're all . . . already gone . . ."

Zginski looked at the others. She was right; there was not enough blood for the three of them to overcome the damage, and Danielle would die within minutes anyway. He thought for a moment, weighing options. Then with a smile of irony, he raised his left wrist to his mouth and bit into his own veins. As the blood began to flow, he pressed the wound to Danielle's lips.

She tried to resist, but lacked even the strength to close her mouth against this invasion. The warm salty liquid trickled over her teeth, oozed around her tongue as she tried to push the vile fluid from her mouth, drained down her throat past the threshold of numbness and into her, *into* her.

Her last conscious thought was of the thunder in her ears as her heart pounded desperately, then went silent.

CHAPTER 36

FAUVETTE OPENED HER eyes. Everything was dark, still, and quiet. Was this true death?

She slowly sat up, and stopped when her head encountered a familiar barrier. She lay back down and, using her hands, carefully pushed aside the lid of her coffin. There was no light outside, but her vampire senses told her everything was as she remembered. If this was the afterlife, it was rather mundane.

She climbed slowly from the box. She wore only her jeans, and on the floor found her tank top, the neckline ragged and burned from the bullet. She immediately felt between her breasts for the hole, but none was there, only smooth cold flesh.

Her last memories were of Mark and Leonardo looking down at her. No, there was more, a vague recollection of feeding on someone, except the blood tasted incredibly different, almost bitterly strong, and it seemed to make her insides itch. But it was more of a sense memory than a true conscious one, and she could recall no details about whose blood it had been.

She pulled on another T-shirt and her flip-flops. Carefully she opened the door and crawled out of the boiler.

The coffins belonging to Leonardo and Toddy were where she remembered them, although Toddy's stood open and Leonardo's was closed. She ran her fingers along the edge of the lid, wondering what she would find if she opened it. Leonardo had been shot, too; was he also good as new? Or was he crumpled to a pile of bones and dusty clothing, like Olive? One simple action and she would know.

She decided to wait. Either way, it seemed the more respectful option.

She went up the stairs. It was night again, or still; either she'd been asleep for minutes, or the whole day. She saw no one in the warehouse proper, so she went into the office where Mark's coffin rested. Its lid was also closed. She rushed to it and was about to open it when a familiar voice said, "Not yet."

She turned. Zginski stood in the office doorway.

"They will join us shortly," he said. "I would like the opportunity to speak privately to you."

She stepped away from the coffin, her fists clenched. Anger and confusion battled for supremacy. "You let that woman . . ." She trailed off, uncertain how to finish. What exactly *had* the raging Dr. Roseberry done to them?

Zginski nodded. "Let us step outside. I will offer no excuses, but will attempt an explanation."

She seriously considered refusing, but ultimately knew she wouldn't. She had to know what had happened.

They crossed the warehouse floor. By the door, Fauvette paused beside what was left of Olive. The rock-dumb but beautiful girl had vanished, replaced by a dusty, sagging cadaver that already bore evidence of rat damage. The hole burned in her chest was big enough for a softball.

"We will deal appropriately with her remains," Zginski said softly, taking her arm and pulling her along.

Outside, Fauvette saw that Lee Ann's funeral pyre was now no more than a blackened patch of bare ground. Low clouds scudded across the stars. The intermittent wind was hot with the promise of the late summer.

Zginski turned to face her, arms crossed. "Your injuries were the most severe, so if you have recovered, I have no doubt your friends will as well."

"Except Olive."

"Yes. I was unable to help her."

"You didn't even try," she hissed, fury rising.

"No," he agreed. "When the good doctor attacked her, I left."

"You *ran*."

He nodded. "As you say. Old habits. I have always considered only myself worthy of my concern."

"Good for you." Her anger rose again, mixing with shame at her own gullibility. "You made us trust you. We helped you."

He shrugged. "Yes. That is a useful skill to develop."

"I'll work on it," she almost spat.

"I will not lie to you. When I saw the confrontation begin, I had every intention of leaving. I believed myself quite willing to sacrifice you and your friends in order to, as the common folk say, 'save my own skin.'"

He looked away, and wind blew his long hair back from his face, as if exposing something previously hidden. "And yet . . . something pulled me back. Do you recall the denouement of the film *Blacula*? He chose destruction rather than being alone, and in a way, I did the same. I was unable to leave you at the mercy of that woman, so I destroyed my former selfishness. I will not descend into maudlin cliché, but I find that I have grown more attached to you than I expected. As I did with the late Lee Ann. I could not save her without violating her wishes. But you . . ."

"How *did* you save us? Leo and I were shot in the heart."

"Unlike your friend Olive, the bullet damaged your heart but did not destroy it. Just as we can heal ourselves if given time, we can aid the healing of others. If we are willing to do so. You had fresh blood, but lacked the strength to fully feed due to your injuries. I mixed my own blood with that of the late Dr. Roseberry, to bolster your healing abilities. Thankfully, it was successful."

"I didn't know we could do that," she said softly.

He nodded, looking down at his shoes. "This ability is not commonly known, and even less frequently used. We tend to be very solitary creatures, so the opportunity seldom arises. When it is used, it binds the injured party and the savior at a very deep level." He sighed as if he could not believe it himself. "We are now bound in such a way. All of us."

"What exactly does that mean?"

He shook his head. "I truly do not know. I have made the acquaintance of only one other vampire who ever used the ability. He refused to speak of it."

"I don't feel any different."

"Nor do I, in any way that can be . . ." He smiled with ironic detachment. "Quantified."

They stood in silence for a long moment. A pair of bats flitted from the warehouse into the sky. Behind her she heard movement as Mark and Leonardo stirred. The wind picked up, blowing a strand of hair into her eyes.

Finally Fauvette said, "So . . . you're staying."

He nodded.

She couldn't hide a smile. "So what happens next?"

He plucked the hair from her eyes and tucked it behind her ear. "We move from the shadows into the light. We join the world. And we feed on it."

CHAPTER 37

DANIELLE ROSEBERRY AWOKE encased in fresh cement, deep in the foundation of a new building. Above her, oblivious crews continued erecting the structure.

Her first sensation was of the confining, obscenely claustrophobic pressure all around her head. The wet concrete had sent tendrils up her nose, into her ears, and past her slack lips into her mouth, where they had solidified. When she tried to work her jaw her skin peeled free from the concrete surrounding it, and her teeth painfully struck the cement protrusion.

Next she realized she could not feel her body past her shattered neck.

And then she felt the *thirst*.

Trapped and paralyzed, unable to call for help, she managed a pathetic, gagged squeak of a scream when she realized she would now discover how long it took a vampire to starve to death.